MY Darling JANE

Strangers in Love Series

Beauty and the Baller
Princess and the Player

Waylon University Series

I Dare You
I Bet You
I Hate You
I Promise You

Stand-Alones

Dear Ava
Fake Fiancée
The Revenge Pact
The Last Guy (with Tia Louise)
The Right Stud (with Tia Louise)
My Darling Bride

MY Darling JANE

ILSA MADDEN-MILLS

Montlake

Published by Montlake, Seattle

www.apub.com

Amazon, the Amazon logo, and Montlake are trademarks of Amazon.com, Inc., or its affiliates.

ISBN-13: 9781662514043 (paperback)
ISBN-13: 9781662514036 (digital)

Cover design by Hang Le
Cover image: © Michelle Lancaster PTY LTD; © Sunflowerr / Shutterstock; © A-Star / Shutterstock

Printed in the United States of America

MY
Darling
JANE

Chapter 1

JANE

There's probably nothing worse than ending a first date with a face full of crotch.

"He didn't!" I say into the phone as the bell over the bookstore door jingles. A pair of teenage lovebirds walks in with their hands intertwined. Inwardly, I smirk. Oh, to be young and naive again.

"You think I'd joke about something like that?" Freida snaps on the other end of the line.

Freida is an acquaintance from my modeling days, but she may never speak to me again after this fiasco.

"I'm sorry," I say.

She tuts and grumbles under her breath. I picture her flipping her wavy brown hair over her shoulder inside her apartment on the Upper East Side. She's probably wearing her signature coral lipstick. "We had a lovely time, and he was a gentleman," she says, "up until we were saying goodbye. Before I got out of the car, I gave him a kiss, nothing crazy. Then he pushed my head toward his pants! How does he go from a clumsy good night kiss to fellatio?"

I cringe. "Did he say anything?"

"'Suck it.' He didn't even say 'please.'"

"No," I say, anger spiking.

This isn't just about bad dates; it's about respect, something Stefano Marks clearly lacks.

"Yeah. Apparently, according to him, I owed him because he spent all that money on the sign-up fee for Cupid's Arrow. Pig."

A long exhale comes from my chest. "If I'd known he was like that, I never would have let him become a member. He was vetted, I assure you. I'm so sorry."

"He probably lied through his perfect teeth."

Positioned behind the counter of the bookstore, I track the pair of teenagers as they meander down the aisle toward the self-help section. My bet's on them making a beeline for the Kama Sutra.

They disappear from my view, and I focus back on Freida.

"Let me check his account." I don't have my laptop near me, so I reach under the counter and grab my folder of paper copies of the membership forms. I keep it handy whether I'm at home or here at the store. Technically, I'm working as a manager today, but Emmy, my older sister who owns the store with her husband, has given me a pass to work on my business here. I'm even using the office to vet clients.

I find his file. Stefano Marks. Thirty-two. Attorney at a top firm. Recommendations from three references? Check. No criminal record and a good credit score. Check. The photograph I have of him is hand-some with a great smile.

On paper, this man is golden. There's nothing in here that says creep.

Not only that, but the match was also perfect. Besides the inter-views with me personally, the algorithm gave them a 90 percent chance of success. They both liked sushi. Both were career oriented and inter-ested in travel and cooking. They even had a similar five-year plan— they wanted to move to the country and open a bed-and-breakfast or a general store of some type. I couldn't have imagined a better couple if I tried.

But something went wrong.

I draw an X over Stefano's face and crumple the page in my hand, noting my list of eligible men is growing thin. "Everything checked out with him, but obviously he isn't the kind of client I want. He'll be removed from the database. I'm really sorry, Freida. If there is anything—"

"I trusted you to do better than this," she says, cutting me off. "I asked for someone wealthy, someone with similar goals, and you did deliver that, but he's a total prick. Whatever. It's fine."

It's not fine. My lips tighten. If my business is ever going to take off, I need client satisfaction. Word of mouth is key.

"I can find someone else for you," I offer quickly as I page through my thin list of eligible men. Gil Davis. "Here's one. He's a doctor—"

"Forget it. I think I'll take another chance on Tinder."

Otherwise known as the ninth circle of hell.

I scramble for what to say. "Again, I'm deeply sorry, and if you decide to try again, just—"

"Yeah, Jane. No thanks. Maybe give up on the matchmaking gig. I'll see you."

Freida hangs up, leaving me reeling as I slump over the counter. My fist beats on the counter as I cry out in frustration. It's been three months since I started my venture, and my bottom line is still in the red. I invested twenty grand, and the idea of it all going down the drain makes me want to weep.

I'm so deep in thought that I almost don't hear the slurp.

I glance down the self-help aisle and witness a full-blown teenage make-out session. The boy is attacking her face like a lion devouring prey, while casually holding the Kama Sutra in his other hand. I have to applaud him for his multitasking abilities. Not that I would know, seeing as my own sexual experience has been on hiatus since my daughter was conceived.

My vagina might as well be a ghost town out West with tumbleweeds and cobwebs.

Or I've grown a new hymen. Who knows.

3

I move in their direction, inhaling the comforting smell of coffee as I walk. My favorite scent in the store is the woody aroma of the shelves. It's like I'm in a forest right in the middle of Manhattan.

The Darling Bookstore is a historic three-story building near Central Park, with a marble rotunda entrance and a gorgeously carved staircase that spirals up to the other floors. It's a special place. I grew up running around the shelves, reading in the hidey-holes, and eating in the kitchen. My gran used to work here, and now my sister and her husband own it.

But it's the customers I adore the most. Some are quirky, some are charming, and some are downright wacko.

But when it comes to two teens, their intentions are less of a mystery.

"Guys. Break it up," I call out to them. "That book isn't just about s-e-x, you know. It's about living a balanced life. It's about being happy."

They separate, and the young man, maybe seventeen or eighteen, gapes at me in surprise. The hardcover book drops to the floor, and I wince. It's a pricey book.

What must it feel like to be so in love that you don't even notice other people?

I cross my arms. "Do you even know the author? The importance of the book?"

"Um . . . sorry? Who are you?" He shakes his head as his gaze darts around the store, looking for an escape, but I've blocked the aisle.

I smile thinly. "I'm the manager. The author is Vātsyāyana. The book is actually an ancient Hindu text written in the third century during the golden age. He was a philosopher, I suppose, and his book is really about the science of love. It's not just a sexual-position manual that you can come in and try out when you're bored."

"Okay, fine, whatever, we're leaving," the young girl says as she edges away from me, grabbing her boyfriend's hand.

I follow them down the aisle on their heels. "It discusses how to live a good life. True, he did focus on the sexual aspect, which must have been revolutionary at the time, but he wanted people to embrace our desires and be in harmony with other responsibilities." We reach the rotunda. "You may go now. Unless you want to buy the book? It's fifty-two dollars."

"What? No way," the boy mutters as they fast walk to the exit.

"I didn't think so. Bye," I say cheerily as they vanish.

I head back to the shelves and bend down to scoop up the book. My fingers trace over the cover. As I flip through the pages, my eyes widen at the Queen of Heaven sex position. The woman's legs are squished up to her chest as the man enters her. Cocking my head, I study the couple, noting that while it does look difficult, it also looks kinda hot. With a sigh, I remind myself that my matchmaking business is my priority now, not my depressing sex life. Maybe someday I'll give it another shot, but for now, I'll stick to playing cupid for others.

Still. This position is interesting, the way she has her body. I tilt my head, studying the book as I lean against the shelf and raise one of my legs—

"If only you had a man to practice those moves with," a voice says from the stacks.

I yelp in surprise as I snap the book closed and glance through an opening in the shelves, where Babs smirks at me with a knowing look. With her sleek red bob and green pantsuit, she's a tiny tornado of fashion and sass. There's twenty-five years between us, but she's become my bestie since my sister, Emmy, got married.

Shoving the book in the space to block her out, I mutter a "No, thank you," and mosey back to the register like she didn't just catch me being weird in the stacks.

Yes, I am pathetic. Yes, I've only felt the intimacy of a vibrator in the past five years.

I feel her gaze (and her) following me as I flounce away, but I can't resist turning back to give her a pretend withering look.

She comes up to the counter holding a stack of books that could topple her five-foot-two frame. "I heard you on the phone. Was that another satisfied Cupid's Arrow customer?"

"Far from it. Freida said that her date wanted a blow job." I take a sip of my latte.

She nods as if she understands. "Not everyone will be good for the business, man or woman, but you've spent hours interviewing people. You're really trying, Jane. Those other apps don't care what happens to their clients."

I go through my files and show her the heavy stack, probably seventy-five pages. "These are all the eligible single women in the database." Most of them are acquaintances I met while modeling. The majority of them haven't paid the full fee to be part of the service. To jump-start my client list, I gave a "friend" discount to them.

Then I whip out the other stack.

"And these are the single men. I have twenty. I'm doing something wrong. Maybe I need more online ads or another marketing campaign."

She wrinkles her nose. "We should go to a man convention. When's the next boat-and-RV show in New York? I bet we'd find some nice guys there."

"Sure," I say, then sigh. The irony of being a matchmaker doesn't escape me. I'm trying to build a career on love, a concept I've never truly experienced.

But the magic I witnessed between Emmy and her husband, Graham, did spark an idea.

Cupid's Arrow wasn't born from a fairy-tale fantasy, nor was it based on an encounter I had with someone who made my heart skip a beat.

Please. I'm not a romantic.

I'm merely focused on using the *idea* of love. Starting my business was strategic, a decision to capitalize on a universal emotion.

To me, love is simply a tool, a powerful force that can be harnessed and used to make my business a success. I want to build an empire from the ground up, something different from the usual dating apps like Tinder.

What I had with Tomas, Londyn's sperm donor, wasn't real. I was barely twenty and a virgin, and I knew nothing about relationships.

I imagined him to be soulful and deep and mysterious.

He was none of those.

I shove the memories away and organize the Cupid's Arrow business cards. I smile at the logo, a bright-red heart with a golden arrow piercing through it. I want to be a success. So much. At twenty-five, I don't have a college degree and I don't have time to get one. The truth is, I'm not sure I could sit still long enough to do the studying it would take.

Emmy is the one with the college degree, but I'm just a former model who was pushed out of the business when I had a baby. Not that I wanted to go back into modeling. I was done with it after Londyn was born. It wasn't stable enough to support us.

"Once word gets out about your business, people will line up," Babs says as she grabs a warm orange-cranberry scone off a tray before an employee puts them in the bakery case.

"You're only saying that because you snagged an awesome guy," I say. She and Ray are one of my success stories. I've even got a sweet picture of them holding hands on my website.

"He's now a master of all the positions in the Kama Sutra." A giggle comes from her. "Of course, I taught him everything he knows. Splitting the Bamboo, now that one is my fave. It's where—"

"Nope. I don't need to know."

She bats her lash extensions. "Yes, you do. I encourage you to buy that book and take it home. Ray's favorite position is the Lotus Blossom. You do it like this." She drags a chair over and points at the seat. "He sits there, and I get in his lap . . ." She sits on the chair backward and lets her head fall as she juts her hips back and forth and makes sex noises.

I shake my head at her. "Stop before someone sees you. You need help."

She smiles sweetly as she stands up. "No, dear, you do. Find a teachable man like Ray. There's nothing better than a man who will listen."

"True," I say.

Despite his accounting job in the financial district, he always takes time to bring Babs lunch on days when she's too swamped to get it herself. He never fails to come with a smile, a kiss, and her favorite chicken curry. And the best part? He became a Cupid's Arrow client through one of my business cards. He came into the bookstore one day, and I dropped one in his bag when he checked out.

Babs watches me as I fiddle with a pen, twirling it between my fingers.

"Are you getting one of your ideas?"

I fidget, dropping the pen and tapping my fingernail against my latte with increasing intensity. "We could make a book club exclusively for men. Select thrillers and nonfiction books that cater to their interests."

She gets a glazed look on her face. "A bookstore full of men. Yassss."

I perk up. "And we could partner with a local brewery or whiskey distillery and offer top-notch spirits. That will definitely draw quite the crowd." The image of our bookstore bustling with men discussing their favorite novels, sipping on fine whiskeys, flashes before my eyes.

"Then we'd be stuck with a store full of drunk men," she says, frowning. "That's no fun."

My shoulders slump. "True. It might have some kinks, but . . ." I sigh. "Anyway, I'll need to run it past Emmy." She and her husband are currently on an extended vacation in the Greek Isles with their baby, Hazel.

I glance down at the paper files, my mind going back to the conversation with Freida. "This is the third bad date I've set up this month. Can today get any worse?"

Babs snorts. "Now you're just asking for karma to bitch-slap you."

I grab my phone to check my messages. I confirm that I have no texts. I open my email, saying a prayer under my breath for good news.

Instead, I see Tomas Vincent.

And that's when I realize Babs is right.

Things can get worse.

You'd think I wouldn't have any heart left for him to crush, but the ache blooming in my chest says otherwise.

My finger hovers over the open icon, anxiety trickling down my spine as I stare at the unopened email. After almost five years of raising Londyn on my own, his name flashing on my screen feels like a ghost from the past, jolting me back to a time I've worked hard to move beyond.

A rush of questions floods my mind. Does he want to see Londyn? My heart clenches at the thought. He's never seen her, never wanted to. And now, out of the blue, he emails.

I take a deep breath. I can't forbid him from seeing her, not legally. He's her father, after all. But the fear of what this means for Londyn grips me. I can't bear the thought of her facing the disappointment I've felt. The idea of him promising to be there for her and then vanishing.

I close my eyes, gathering my courage. Londyn is my world, and I've been both mother and father to her. She's happy and loved, and she's never known the absence of her father.

I open the email, heart hammering as I brace for words that might shatter the equilibrium of our lives. But no, it's not what I feared, nor anything I could have imagined.

It's an invitation.

A save-the-date wedding invitation.

To someone named Savannah Wood.

The screen blurs as I stare at it, mouth agape, emotions swirling. Mr. You-Can't-Tie-Me-Down, the man who fled at the mention of fatherhood, is getting hitched in the armpit of the world, New Jersey. The irony is a bitter pill, lodging itself in my throat.

My legs wobble, and instinctively I reach out, grabbing the edge of the counter for support.

Why would he invite me?

Is this some twisted way of reaching out, or did he just want to hurt me?

"What is it?" Babs's voice cuts through my thoughts. She's by my side in an instant, her concern evident as she grabs the phone from my hand. Her eyes widen as she reads, and she gasps in disbelief. "The asshole is getting married. And he invited you? Why?"

I shake my head, hollow laughter bubbling up. "I have no idea," I manage to say.

After every milestone he's missed with Londyn, he surfaces with an invitation to witness his commitment to someone else. It feels like a joke, a mocking reminder of what he couldn't give us.

I quickly bring up a news article about Tomas's TV show, *Dr. Romantic*, and sure enough Savannah Wood is the real name of one of the actresses on the show, where Tomas plays a brooding doctor with a troubled past. She's one of the doctors on the show.

My throat tightens. I've never watched it.

I can't bring myself to see him be successful, and maybe that makes me a terrible person.

Babs puts an arm around me. "He shouldn't have sent that, and I'm sorry for it, but you're better off without him." She glares at the invitation. "And honestly? Email invites are so tacky. Doesn't he have money now?"

I swallow the lump in my throat as Babs goes on a tirade about how society is losing all sense of etiquette, but I'm barely listening. The memory of the time I told him I was pregnant plays in my head like a movie. That day inside our favorite café in Chelsea, I was wearing a turquoise floral dress, the one he liked because it brought out the green of my eyes. I'd ordered us both coffees and croissants and waited, my mind grappling with the pregnancy test I'd taken two days before.

I recall the rhythmic hiss of the espresso machine, the clink of cups inside the café.

I was terrified. I was a little thrilled. We'd only been together for six months.

He sat down across from me, buzzing about a minor character part he'd gotten on a show. I listened, trying to find the perfect moment, and with my dress crumpled in clenched fists under the table, I told him.

His eyes, the ones I thought were soulful, turned icy.

"My career is on the rise. I want nothing to do with a kid, Jane."

For the thousandth time, I'm left wondering how someone I loved so fiercely could treat me with such disregard.

You never really know someone's heart until something difficult appears.

You figure out who sticks around and who runs.

He ran.

Five years ago, his rejection devastated me, leaving me to question if I was even lovable, if anyone would ever want me. To him, Londyn and I were burdens too heavy to bear.

She's not a burden. She's a gift, my strength in life.

I force my eyes to move over the words of the invitation again. It's in four months. The date stares back at me, bold and mocking.

"Well, good news," Babs says after a few minutes, checking the clock. "It's almost time to close. I'll lock up, and you go home early. Grab a couple of smoothies for you and Londyn on the way. Then tuck her into bed and sink into a bubble bath. That'll make you feel better."

That's usually the recipe to put a smile on my face. But I can't today.

I reach for my heart-shaped purse, the one Emmy gifted to me after I shared my fledgling idea for the matchmaking company. The thought of disappointing her tightens a knot in my stomach. She devoted her life to raising me and has never wavered in her belief that I could be more, do more.

I need to believe in myself.

I clutch the purse and feel a surge of determination.

I can't let fear dictate my future—or memories of Tomas.

I need to make this dream a reality.

I pile my business cards in my hand. I still have an hour and a half before I pick up Londyn from her preschool. "There's a bar two blocks down that opened a few months back. I talked to the owner last week, and she said I can pass out cards there."

I've already hit up Marcelle's—the martini place across the street—and a few other places close to the bookstore. I might as well try the new place.

"There have to be some normal guys there. Right?" My voice is hopeful.

"Are you going to wear that outfit?"

She means the toga I have hanging in my office. A wry laugh comes from me. "Yep. It always gets questions."

She pouts. "It's so weird, dear."

"But it works."

She's still talking about how gaudy it is as I head to my office at the back of the store on the first level. I shut the door and lean against it. The truth is, I needed to get away from Babs so she wouldn't ask any more prying questions about Tomas. I haven't told my family all the details about what happened. Mostly, I didn't want my sister and brother hunting him down and forcing him to be in Londyn's life. I don't even want his money—not that he had much back then.

I swap my usual slacks, blouse, and heels for a long white toga, adorned with glittery pink and red hearts. I attach the fluttery white wings with a sigh.

Slinging a small bow and quiver of little wooden arrows over my shoulder, I try to channel some confidence. My long honey-blond hair, usually left to fall around my shoulders, is now twisted into a neat, no-nonsense bun. Bright-red lipstick adds a splash of color, and a swipe of mascara attempts to mask the paleness of my face.

I practice a smile.

Look out, men, here comes cupid.

I wave goodbye to Babs and head out the door and down the street. My cupid getup earns a few curious glances, but this is New York and strange is the norm.

Pushing open the door to Carson's bar, I step inside. The room buzzes with energy, its walls covered with flat-screen TVs broadcasting sports events. Neon signs and sports memorabilia decorate the space. It's not upscale by any stretch, but it's got a laid-back vibe.

I take a moment to scan the room, just another patron.

I can't help but inwardly groan at the scene.

The women are cute. The men, on the other hand . . .

There's a fellow at the bar who's rummaging through the peanuts with the fervor of Indiana Jones on an archaeological dig. Another guy, in a biker vest, nonchalantly cleans his nails with a toothpick. And then there's Mr. Jukebox, who throws me a wink. His toupee seems to have a life of its own.

Welcome to the dating pool, Jane.

You're going to need more than arrows to navigate this one.

Steel nerves and a bright smile in place, I remind myself that there might be someone worthwhile. With a shrug that's more for my benefit than anyone else's, I make my way to the bar.

That's when Indiana Jones Peanut Hunter, mid-dig, looks up. Our eyes meet, and a sheepish grin replaces his intense focus as if he realizes how funny he must look. Or maybe he thinks I look funny.

He does a somewhat comical sweep of peanut debris off his hands before offering one to me. "Sorry. I missed lunch today," he says. "I'm Mitch." He seems to be in his thirties, his brown hair styled off his face with a friendly smile revealing a dimple. His hazel eyes meet mine with a respectful look, seemingly unfazed by my toga's bare-shoulder reveal. Dressed in blue slacks and a dress shirt, he has a certain put-togetherness, and my eyes flick to his hand—no wedding ring. Score one for Jane.

Finding a diamond in the rough like Mitch might just be the sign I need that Cupid's Arrow is on the right track.

I return the handshake. "Jane," I say briskly as I take the stool next to him and prop my chin up with my palm. I give him a blinding smile as I pop a peanut in my mouth. "So, Mitch, I'm a matchmaker. As you can see, I'm playing cupid tonight. Are you looking for someone special in your life?"

Chapter 2
JASPER

I burst through the double doors of the neighborhood bar. A sea of faces turns toward me, some recognizing me, others reacting to the fury etched on my face.

I'm usually the life of any party, but not today. Today, my mood is as dark as my expression must be. I'm on a mission.

"Macy! Lacy!" My voice booms across the room, slicing through the buzz of conversations and the strains of an Aerosmith classic playing in the background. The chatter dies down, eyes on me, but I'm focused on one mission only.

There, huddled in the back corner, are the culprits, my nieces, or as I like to call them, Thing One and Thing Two. Their shiny blond ponytails, so like their mother's, are a dead giveaway. They're just seventeen, but with a knack for wreaking havoc that rivals a category-five hurricane.

I march toward them, my stride purposeful, parting the crowd. Whispers trail in my wake.

"Hey, isn't that Jasper Jannich?" I hear someone say.

Another voice pipes up. "Wonder who pissed him off."

Normally, I'd bask in the attention and say hello. The energy of a sports bar crowd is my fuel. But tonight, my focus is on those brats. They're so engrossed in whatever mischief they're cooking up they don't even notice me bearing down on them.

I'm about to lay down the law.

At least it's not as bad as I imagined. When I went into their bedroom in my apartment to check on them and found the room empty, I half expected to come in and find them dancing on the bar. Doing shots. Flirting with people old enough to have given them life.

Instead, they're gathered around a pinball machine, giggling as Lacy shoots the ball. They're not drinking as far as I can see, and they're wearing modest shorts and shirts.

I smirk at their faces, illuminated by the flickering lights of the machine. The pinball machine itself is a *Guardians of the Galaxy* one, its glossy surface a riot of colors as the silver ball ricochets off bumpers and slides through tunnels.

Macy, who is more extroverted, glances over at me as if she expected me to show up. She waves excitedly. "Lacy is killing it on this game."

I cross my arms. "Hey! Here's the funny thing . . . this doesn't look like your bedroom."

Macy shrugs. "It's not. You evidently decided to take a nap during the movie, and we didn't want to wake you up. We left you a note on the fridge, so you can't be mad at us. And this game is so fun. You have another quarter?"

They stare at me, waiting for me to blow my lid. That's what they want me to do. They've been trying my patience for two weeks, and I never imagined how hard it would be just to keep track of them. How on earth does my sister Rayna do it?

"But you suck at it," I tell them. I've never been able to stay mad at them for long. "Stand aside. You need to be quick with your fingers. Let the master work."

They exchange a surprised look and then let me through. "So you're not going to tell Mom we snuck out?" Macy asks.

I'm used to keeping things from Rayna. I grew up doing it. Probably the reason she was reluctant to drop her kids off with me while she went on a girls' trip through Europe. She gave me a laundry list of shit she didn't want them doing, as if she just knew they'd try it.

And they have. The difference is, I'm not the mom. I'm the fun uncle.

I fish a quarter from my pocket and feed it into the machine. "Nah. Watch."

Shooting the ball, I work the buttons expertly, racking up the points. They shriek and clap around me in their excitement, which just keeps me going. I probably should be raising hell and getting them home, since they're underage, but they're not drinking. This is just good, harmless fun.

But we are in a bar. Ugh. I'm a terrible parental figure.

Which is why I'm never having kids.

A fact I've been reminded of lately by these two walking advertisements for birth control.

They drank all my OJ. They leave their dirty dishes everywhere. They yell at me for getting in the way of their TikTok dances. Not to mention they leave clothes and feminine products scattered around my apartment.

I should know how it is. I grew up with four older sisters.

But here's one thing I know: sharing a locker room with the New York Pythons is like a day at the beach compared to sharing a house with females.

My sister owes me big time.

Soon, other people gather around, watching me tear up the machine, cheering me on.

But then I time it wrong and the ball slips past the flippers, officially ending my run. I check the score: 477,435,000.

My nieces applaud and grab my arms as they jump up and down. "You got the high score!" they say in unison. It's weird how they say things at the same time, in the same tone.

I give them a thumbs-up. "Okay. Let's get you h—"

"Aw, come on, Jasper. Can't we just play a little longer?" Macy says.

They are adorable, and their pouts are going to break a lot of hearts one day. I'm putty in their hands. I fish another few quarters out of my jeans and hand the coins to them. "Just until this is gone. Okay?"

They jump up and grab it and set to work. I point to the bar, not that they're paying attention to me.

"I'm going to get a . . ." I trail off. It doesn't matter. I've lost them to the machine.

I sidle up to the bar. "Hey, Lee," I say to the bartender, checking to see what they have on tap. I don't know why I do. This place has become my local watering hole this summer, and their offerings never change.

"Give me a Guinness."

He pours me the draft and slides it over to me. That's when I look up and see her at the other side of the bar. My eyebrows shoot up in surprise.

You can't miss her.

She's taller than most of the men around her.

And gorgeous with those wide-set green eyes that tilt up at the corners.

She's got lush lips and a sprinkle of freckles over her nose and upper cheeks.

She's that perfect mix of girl next door and dead sexy.

Too bad she's repulsive to me.

There she is. Jane Darling, dressed in some god-awful toga.

I smirk at the bow and arrow strapped to her back. Does she think it's Halloween? It's like she's lost a bet.

I've known Jane for a while, our paths crossing thanks to her sister being married to my buddy Graham for the past few years. She's always had this air of disapproval about her whenever I'm around, like I'm some kind of sports cliché, a meathead football player. And sure, I can play that part, but there's more to me than touchdowns and tabloids.

Her eyes scan the crowd, and I can't help but watch her. There's something about her that intrigues me, despite my aversion.

Maybe it's the challenge of a woman who doesn't like me.

She's talking to some motorcycle dude now, his studded leather jacket and tattoos a stark contrast to her angelic getup. I can't hear their conversation, but by the way she's tilting her head and listening intently, she's in full cupid mode. I stifle a laugh.

Part of me wants to march over there and ruffle her feathers (angel wings) a bit. It's always fun to get a rise out of her.

"Why's that girl dressed like she's about to shoot arrows?" I ask the bartender, nodding subtly in her direction.

He laughs. "Matchmaking gig. Trying to drum up business. She came in and talked to the owner last week."

I take a sip of my beer, the cool liquid sliding down my throat. Jane, the grump, playing cupid? The world's full of surprises.

I recall a conversation with Graham where he mentioned she was starting her own business. I guess this must be it.

I take another swig of my beer, my mind drifting back to the last time I crossed paths with Jane. It was at Graham's apartment. He'd invited me down for a birthday party for his wife, Emmy. It was a big group of people, mostly Emmy's friends, Graham's family, and a couple of players from the team. Jane, ever snippy with me, had gotten a little tipsy and sloshed her red wine all over me.

Was it on purpose? Perhaps.

Graham offered me a dry dress shirt, and I changed into it in the bathroom. I'd just gotten it buttoned up when a girl I'd been seeing called me on the phone. Sure, I heard Jane knocking on the door, saying she had to go to the bathroom, and asking why I was so slow, but she knew Graham's place had several bathrooms. I ignored her, chuckling at the way she grumbled through the door. Then the minx picked the lock with a hairpin and walked right in. She gave me a scathing glance, grabbed my phone, and told the girl I was a jerk. She marched past me, hiked up her little dress, and peed right in front of me. I gaped at her as she sashayed away.

Throughout the evening, she kept making these snide remarks under her breath, just loud enough for me to catch. "Typical jock," she'd mutter as I chatted with some of the guys, or "Bet he can't even spell 'commitment.'"

It was barbed—classic Jane.

Then there was the time she slapped me a few years ago after I'd kissed her out of the blue. That memory always brings a smug smile to my face. Best slap ever.

She finishes her conversation with Mr. Motorcycle and turns away, her toga swishing dramatically. I find myself considering going over there and talking to her. Not as the football star, but just as a guy who can't handle it when someone doesn't like him.

I take another swig of my beer as she moves on to another fellow at the bar.

A few minutes pass, and I can tell he's clearly into her. What red-blooded guy wouldn't be? But from the vibe she's giving off, the feeling isn't mutual. She keeps looking around, like she's waiting for a knight to come along.

That ain't me. But if the situation calls for it, I can pretend.

Chugging the rest of my beer, I decide to dust off my armor.

I look back at my nieces, who are fully absorbed in the game.

Then I slip off the stool and head for the shrew.

Chapter 3
JANE

I knew the moment I walked in that it was slim pickings at Carson's, but Mitch was nice and seemed mildly interested in Cupid's Arrow, but after him, it went downhill fast.

William, the motorcycle guy who was in town on vacation, declined my card. He said he was happily married, which I appreciated.

Now, I'm trapped in a conversation with Bryan, a real estate agent with a groomed goatee.

I initially thought there was a hint of charm there. I was wrong.

For the past torturous five minutes, it's been all about his gym regimen. Bi's, tri's, chest, and now, the grand finale, his abs. "Want to see 'em?" he asks, and I'm mentally drafting an SOS message.

My finger is practically glued to the business card I gave him, inching it back millimeter by millimeter. But as he looks up, I freeze. "No, that's—"

Too late. He lifts his shirt. "Washboard. Not a six-pack. An eight-pack. See that?"

All I see is a forest of dark, wiry hair masquerading as abs. "Want to touch 'em?" he offers, with what I assume is his idea of a seductive grin.

"No." I finally reclaim my card and scoot off the stool. "Okay, well, it was great to meet you but—"

His hand grips my wrist. "Where're you going? I thought you wanted me to have that card, baby. With your number." His eyes have that glazed look of drunken interest, and I mentally kick myself for not making my professional intentions clearer.

I remove his hand from my arm. "Like I said. Nice meeting you, but I've got to go—"

"Without me?" He stands, and I can't help but notice he's significantly shorter than me. Most guys are, and it usually works as a natural deterrent. But not with Bryan. Unfazed, he slings an arm around my shoulders, trying to reel me in.

Just great. Trapped by a pint-size real estate agent.

Before I can push him off, a deep voice behind me says, "Let the lady go."

A man puts his big hands on Bryan's shoulders.

I turn and look up.

This new guy is like the statue of David. Big, beautiful, broad perfection.

Standing tall with a commanding presence, he has blond hair that falls in waves to his shoulders and frames his face, accentuating a sun-kissed complexion that speaks of days in the fresh air.

He's the kind of man that turns heads.

Whatever. It's only Jasper. I stick my tongue out at him.

Bryan lets go of me, but I'm too annoyed at the sight of the star quarterback to be relieved.

"Uh, sure," Bryan says, blinking. "I'm, uh, Bryan. I'm a huge fan of yours."

"Hey, Bryan, would you mind giving us a moment?" Jasper's voice is smooth. "Jane and I go way back, we're good friends, and I'd like to catch up with her."

Good friends? That's a stretch.

Bryan stumbles back to his stool with awe and disappointment on his face. "Oh, uh, sure, man. Great to see you. Too bad about the playoffs this year. Maybe this season will be better."

Jasper's eyes narrow at him. "It will be."

I wince. Everyone knows we lost in the playoffs because Jasper threw three interceptions at the Seattle game.

Jasper seems to gather himself, then turns to me, flashing his infuriating grin that says, "I'm everybody's favorite." His gaze drifts over me, pausing on the wings strapped to my back. "Hello, angel. Did you fall from heaven just for me tonight?"

"Ugh," I mutter. "Lucky me. It's Jasper to the rescue."

He does a mock head bow. "At your service. You okay?"

I want to keep up my usual icy front, but frustratingly, part of me is relieved he's here. It's nice to see a familiar face.

"I'm fine. I didn't need your help, though. I could have handled him."

He raises an eyebrow. "Is that so?"

"I can take care of myself," I retort, thinking of all the years I've managed just fine, especially with Londyn.

He holds up his hands, stepping back. "Okay, okay. Sorry," he says. "It just looked like he had his hands on you and you weren't into it."

Remorse hits. He was trying to help, and I'm snapping at him. "No, it's fine. I'm sorry. Thanks for noticing."

He drags a stool over and plops down next to me. His blue eyes skate over my toga as a small chuckle comes from him. "I guess you're mixing business with pleasure tonight?"

I rub my temple. "Not much pleasure, to be honest. I'm not even drinking, but maybe I should have had at least one. My head is starting to hurt."

"Ah. I see." The bartender drops off a beer for him, and he takes a sip, the strong muscles of his throat moving as he swallows. "They say the best cure for a headache is good company."

"Then I should probably find some, shouldn't I?"

He smiles, never missing a beat. "You're in luck. I happen to come with excellent references."

"Do those references include modesty? Because it seems like you forgot to pack that."

"Modesty doesn't win football games. But I can tone it down for you. Say, over dinner?"

I scoff. Boy! He's really on a roll. "I prefer my meals without a side of ego. Thanks, though."

"Ah, come on, Jane. Admit it, you love our banter. We make sparks fly. We light up the sky, angel."

I smirk. "No, we don't."

"Lie detected. So, how's the world of matchmaking treating you? Found any soulmates lately?"

A long breath leaves my lips as I think about my lack of success today. "Oh, you know, just the usual, turning hopeless romantics into slightly more hopeful romantics."

He shrugs, showcasing his broad shoulders, currently encased in a Pythons shirt. "Sounds like a noble cause. You ever consider matching yourself, or are you just the puppet master?"

I lean in conspiratorially. "I prefer 'mastermind.' And I don't mix work with personal disasters."

"'Disasters'? I get the subtext. You think I'm a disaster. Wow. You're such a grump. I prefer to call them 'adventures.'" He waves his hand through the air in the shape of a rainbow.

"Well, in that case," I murmur, thinking of Tomas, "my life would be bestseller material."

"I'd buy a copy. But only if I get a mention in the acknowledgments. As the best night you ever had."

I snort. "You'd be in the footnotes, Jasper. Tiny, tiny print. Like your penis."

A low whistle comes from him as his eyes capture mine, holding the stare for several moments. He's always been big on eye contact, and it makes me squirm. "Ouch, again with the sting. Here I am, pouring my heart out, and you're being mean."

"Hmm, I must have missed the part where you poured your heart out."

"It's subtle, angel. You need to read between the lines."

"Don't call me 'angel,' and I'm a pro at reading fine print. Comes with the matchmaking territory."

"In that case, how about you read my intentions? They involve us having dinner."

"Oh, Jasper. It's not going to work. Your charm bounces off me like rubber."

"I might just surprise you. I can bounce really well."

"You already surprise me, Jasper. Every time you speak."

He tosses his head back and laughs, the sound drawing attention from the patrons. "Damn. You're tough. I guess this means I should leave you alone and let you work the crowd."

He makes to get off the stool, and I touch his arm. A sizzle of heat dances down my skin, but I push it away almost absently, a learned reaction I've acquired over the years when it comes to the opposite sex.

"Wait," I say, an idea striking me. I grab one of my business cards from the bar. "Actually, I'm promoting my business, so you might as well have one too."

He reads the card, his lips moving slightly.

I've always found mouthing (while reading) annoying. I wait for this habit to make him less attractive.

But no such luck. His nose is strong and chiseled, with a slight bump at the bridge, while his cheekbones are high, casting shadows across his strong jawline. And his blue eyes are the color of a summer sky, with creases in the corners that show he laughs a lot. The best part? I've always loved his lashes, long and thick and extra curly.

Not that I'd ever tell him that.

"Funny that someone as prickly as you wants to play matchmaker," he says.

"I'm only prickly with certain people," I shoot back.

He brushes a lock of hair from his forehead, boyish charm in full swing. "I'd be a great client. I'm single."

"Looking for love?" I ask, skepticism clear in my tone.

"Always. Or a good time."

Typical Jasper.

Everything's a joke to him.

But . . .

When I first started the business, I did consider asking Graham, a former professional football player, to help bring in some high-profile clients. In the end I didn't because I didn't want to involve my family, not when my sister had already done so much for me.

I want to do this on my own. I don't want to be a burden to anyone again. Ever.

But this is different. Here we are in the same bar, and Jasper is offering. It would be great to have a professional athlete on my roster. His fans would see he's a member, and maybe he'd bring in people. Like more men. He has a huge fan base.

Just as I'm considering the potential of adding him—if he's serious—a girl in black leather shorts and a red V-neck shirt sashays over to him. "Oh my god, Jasper Jannich is here! I'm so glad I came tonight! You are so hot, even better in person."

He grins sheepishly. "Ah, thank you."

She eases in closer to him, putting herself between us. I don't think she even glanced at me. "Can I have your autograph? And a photo? Please."

He obliges, all charm, as she showers him with compliments and flirts. I watch as her hand feels up the muscles of his arm.

Annoyance rises inside me, at the idea that she thinks she can just touch him and it's okay. I wait for him to push her off, but he doesn't.

I feel my resolve crumbling.

Jasper *is* a player. He dates models and actresses.

Wait. Didn't Graham tell me that Jasper was a member at a private sex club? A place called Decadence, where the membership fee is super expensive. Yes, he did.

When his fan finally moves away, he opens his wallet to stick my business card in. I start to grab it away, but he holds tight. "What are you doing?"

"Forget what I said, Jasper. Your application is denied."

"What? I haven't even—"

"Denied," I repeat. Though I'm a little confused why someone like him, a star football player with a multimillion-dollar contract, needs help. I bet he's already screwed most of the female population in New York and plans to go through my entire list of female clients like a pack of Kleenex.

I make a play for the card again, but he closes it up in his wallet and then shoves it in his back pocket before I can grab it. "I'm going to apply anyway. See what happens."

"Don't waste your time," I grumble. "I have sole discretion over who I admit into my database."

He leans into me, and I start at how close our faces are. His gaze traces the lines of my face. My heart races. I smell his cologne, something woodsy and rich. "You have the most adorable scowl right now," he murmurs.

Scowl?

Oh, he hasn't seen anything yet.

I give him the most anger-filled glare I can muster.

He rears back and chuckles, breaking the intensity. "Hey! There's the girl I remember—and you run a dating service? That's messed up."

I'm preparing to give him the double-middle-finger salute as two blond girls that have to be underage bound up to him.

"Jasper!" one bubbles, wrapping her arm possessively around him.

I blink rapidly.

"Ready to go home?" she asks him.

Holy . . . he came with them? Like, they're on a date? I can't believe I was actually considering him for my dating service. Am I out of my mind?

The other girl leans her head on his shoulder and gazes up at him adoringly. "Can we stop at the convenience store and get some ice cream? Please?"

He boops her on the nose. "Sure thing, darlin'."

I'm still reeling as he turns to leave with them. He glances over at me. "So you can expect my application—"

"I'll delete your application the second it comes in," I fire back.

He simply shrugs, as if to say, "We'll see about that," and walks out, bookended by his jailbait.

Chapter 4
JASPER

As we approach the Wickham apartments, their grandeur hits me anew, with their fancy cornices and wrought iron balconies. The windows face either the street or Central Park, with no bad view from either side. Remembering my early, dirt-poor years before the Jannich family took me in sharpens my appreciation for how far I've come.

The girls chatter excitedly as we walk through the lobby, their eyes wide as always as they take in the marble floors and art deco lighting. The doorman, Herman, tips his hat to us as he opens the doors. "Evening, Mr. Jannich," he says warmly. "Hello, girls."

"Evening, Herman," I reply, ushering Macy and Lacy toward the elevator. They're still buzzing from their ice cream high as the elevator glides up. I'm not in the penthouse—that territory belongs to Tuck, a former player who's traded the field for family life.

But my place? It's expansive, the result of merging two apartments into one sprawling space a few years ago. It's got more room than I know what to do with, a luxury not lost on me.

Once the twins are inside my apartment, the living room becomes their playground. After they've played several rounds on my gaming console, I decide it's time to play the responsible uncle.

"All right, bedtime," I say, and their protests start immediately.

"But can't we just stay up—"

I point firmly toward their room. "If you want to stay up, do it there. And no more sneaking off. I don't trust you two roaming around the city. This isn't Utah. It's a metropolitan area with millions of people."

Macy grumbles, "Feels like prison."

"And we want to make cookies," Lacy adds, trying to push her luck, with Macy echoing her.

No. The last thing I need is another kitchen disaster. They made tacos for me last week, and while I appreciated the effort—I ate three—they tasted terrible. Come to find out, Lacy had put sugar and cinnamon in with the taco seasoning. On purpose? Maybe. Regardless, they dirtied every dish in the kitchen. It took me two hours to get it straight. "Bed. Now."

They huff in unison and skitter off down the hall, socks sliding on the hardwood.

I head to the bathroom but catch their glances in the mirror's reflection. I know that look well. It's the precursor to chaos.

Sure enough when I lift the toilet lid in my bathroom, there's their handiwork: plastic wrap, stretched tight. Amateur hour. I chuckle, peeling it off and crumpling it into a ball. Rookie stuff.

Stepping back into the hallway, I find them lurking, barely containing giggles. "Thanks for the gift, girls," I say, feigning seriousness. Then, in a sudden move, I lob the crumpled ball at them. "It's covered in pee!"

Their shrieks fill the apartment as they dodge the ball, scampering into their bedroom and slamming the door, laughter echoing behind them.

Shaking my head, I go to the fridge and grab a Guinness, my mind turning to Jane.

Her scowl. It's the stuff of horror movies. But I kind of like it too. I fish the card out of my wallet and read it over.

Cupid's Arrow

A personalized approach to finding the love of
your life

Jane Darling

www.CupidsArrow.com/register

It sounds entirely too glass-half-full for the girl who was just sitting
at the bar with me.

I grab my phone and navigate to the website. Among photographs
of some happy couple walking on the beach, feeding each other cake,
giggling like they're on crack, I find the application.

It starts so easy: Name?

Hmm, I take a swig of beer. She didn't want me to apply.

But I've always lived for the challenge.

I type in: JJ

She'll never guess.

I fill in the vitals with a fake address and phone number, recalling
that she does have my cell number. For the email address, I use the one
that's reserved for spam mail. Then it gets down to the nitty-gritty.

Please tell us about yourself.

Well, there's not much to tell.

I live for football.

And sex, I add just to irk her.

She'll like that. I'm sure of it. I chuckle.

What are you looking for in a mate?

I think for a second. Oh, I've got a great idea. Let's really make her
blow her top.

Find me a goddess, and I'll be her devout worshiper.
She's gotta be tall cause I'm not into doing yoga
moves just to kiss. Family-wise? Think Kennedys'

class mashed with Kardashians' flair, but no kids of her own. Her attention needs to be on me.

She needs a brain that can jump from quantum physics to why Batman beats Superman, all before breakfast. Her laugh? A symphony of angels, none of that snort-laughing business.

Football is her religion. She should dream in touchdowns and speak in stats.

Culinary skills? Mandatory. I want a chocolate soufflé so good it brings tears to my eyes. Tidiness and massage skills? Big pluses. Waking up beautiful would save a lot of time. And at night, serenade me with sweet Disney songs, post-great sex, of course.

Hair color? True blonde. I'm talking genuine, roots-to-ends. First date might involve a subtle, uh, color verification.

That's my dream girl.

I howl with laughter, practically crying as I reread it. She's going to love me.

Then it asks me a series of questions about myself.

The first one: What are your passions?

I don't even think. I just type one word: Sex.

It isn't true, but let's be honest, I'm doing this to piss her off.

Next question: What is your hidden talent?

Well, that's easy—and true. I type: Sex.

What would be your perfect date?

I think it goes without saying. Sex.

What's your favorite breakfast look like? Pussy.

What's the number one thing on your bucket list? Sex.

This is fun.

What's the best compliment you ever received? I'm awesome at sex.

Have your friends ever tried to set you up with someone? How did it go? Sex.

What was the best birthday present you've ever gotten? Sex.

What is your best pickup line? Sex?

How do you like to bond with your family?

I stop. Shit. She got me. I leave that one blank. My family is pretty awesome, adoptive parents and my four older sisters, and I can't bring them into this sex thing.

The wind taken out of my sails, I scroll through the rest of it and hit Submit. Then I forward the reference page to ten of my football buddies and Graham, my reasoning being that at least three of them will fill it out for me.

With a satisfied smile, I prop my legs up on the coffee table.

I'll probably never hear back from her.

Which is too bad. I can only imagine what she'd look like in bed, underneath me.

Ah, hell no.

That's no way to think about Jane.

I shove that thought away.

But I did sort of ask her out, and she blew me off. Whatever. I didn't mean it.

Moving on, I put my phone away and plop in front of the TV to watch ESPN and see if they're talking about next season's chances, but all they want to discuss is the horrible Seattle game that ruined our chances at the playoffs.

I end up picking up my phone again and googling Jane.

I find a lot of modeling photos of her in designer clothes where she's clearly younger, and her scowl is more of a pout. My body stills as I focus on those pillowy lips of hers. Damn, she is beautiful.

Then I'm picturing her on her knees in front of me—

I shut it down.

Hearing my name, I look up at the television. One of the announcers says, "You think it's going to be heartbreak for the Pythons again, or is Jannich going to lead them to victory this time?"

I mutter under my breath, ire rising. True, I'm thirty-one, but I've still got some good years in me.

I check my email, anxious to see if Jane has seen my application and sent me a scathing reply.

Instead, I have a text from an unfamiliar number.

(212) 555-2789: Is this JJ?

I grin. This is promising. It's not her cell number, which I already have, but a new number, one I guess she uses for the business.

Me: Why yes, it is. Is my application already in review? I'm so eager for love.

(212) 555-2789: Sorry, "Jasper Jannich." I told you you'd be denied.

So it is her. Ha. I've chipped the ice princess's shield. After all, if she really wanted nothing to do with me, she could've sent that rejection email. But she texted me.

Me: Come on, I just want some love.

Jane: No, you want sex. And I'm not going to subject any of my clients to that.

Me: Why? They'll probably thank you.

Jane: No. My clients don't want a meaningless hook-up. They can go to Tinder for that. They want their forever. That's what I'm trying to provide.

I think for a moment.

Me: I'm open to that.

Jane: Sure you are.

There's no doubt Graham's been talking about my past. Yes, I'm a member of a private sex club in New York, but I haven't been in ages. Obviously, she's been paying close attention. But I'm not antirelationship. Far from it. I've had some good relationships, but for some reason, they never stick for long. When I was first drafted, it was because all I wanted to do was focus on my career. Then later after I got superstar status, it seemed like most of the women just wanted a celebrity to hang around. I'm not sure they really knew who the real Jasper was.

Me: I am. If the right woman came along . . . I'm down.

I'm not certain that is true, but I push the thought away.

Jane: I saw those girls with you tonight. They looked young.

Me: Because they're my nieces. I'm babysitting them while my sister goes on vacation.

I hold the phone, waiting an entire minute before she replies.

Jane: Still. Why didn't you say something at the bar or introduce me?

Me: I thought you'd know that I don't date teenagers. I didn't think of introducing you because I only wanted to get them home.

Jane: Whatever. It's still your fault.

Me: Only you would put the blame on me for YOU making a wrong assumption.

Jane: Let's move on. According to your profile, you want a football-loving woman with a carpet that matches the drapes. Don't you think that's too much to ask? And we can't forget, the "right woman" has to have a one-track-mind for sex.

Me: If they have it with me, that will be all they want.

Jane: I don't have anyone in my database to match with you.

Me: Okay, fine, she doesn't have to be able to cook. Or sing. Or talk about physics. But the sex part is nonnegotiable. I like a woman who is lusty. I like it when she grabs my ass or my dick and makes me her boy-toy.

The three dots, indicating she's replying, dance for a long time. I think I've stricken her speechless. Finally, her reply comes through.

Jane: Sorry, I'll keep your application on file. I don't have a match.

She's trying so hard to be professional. I bet her face is red and she's got steam coming out of her ears. I scrub my stubble with my hand. Hmm, the truth is, I don't want a match. Not with anyone in her database, anyway.

Me: What about you? I stare at the words I've just typed and groan aloud. Why the hell did I say that?

Jane: What?

Me: Are you seeing someone? In for a penny, in for a pound.

Jane: No. I'm not interested.

Me: Why not?

Jane: For many reasons, the least of which being that I don't care about sex quite as much as you do.

I'm just typing in Because you haven't had it with me when another response comes through:

Jane: And it's not just because I haven't had it with you.

I whistle. Huh. I love a girl who has my number. As I'm deleting and trying to think of something witty to reply with, she responds again.

Jane: I'm really, truly, 100% NOT INTERESTED.

Me: And yet you're messaging me, late at night, when you could've just declined me by email.

Jane: Good night.

Shit. She's really not going to change her mind.
Fuck it. I throw the phone down. Her loss.
But then I think back to earlier in the night, about how I was hyped up with people watching me beat some idiot pinball game. That's how far I've sunk. I haven't been out in weeks, because the guys on the team

are all busy with their families, girlfriends, et cetera. They've all gotten whipped by their ladies. The suckers.

I need something to fill my lonely days.

How long has it been since I've gotten laid?

I grab the phone back and type something desperate.

Me: I'm not joking.

Jane: Yes, you are.

Me: No, I'm serious. I'm sick of playing around.

I'm sure somewhere, she's laughing her ass off at that.

She responds a moment later.

Jane: Fine.

I pump my fist.

Me: So you'll go out with me?

Jane: No. Stop playing with me. I know you're just trying to irk me when you say stuff like that. But I'll set you up with one of the girls from my database. It won't be a perfect match to your profile as I think some vibrators would have trouble meeting your expectations, but . . . just pay the sign-up fee. We also need to set up a time for you to come in for an interview with me.

Me: For what? You know me.

Jane: It's just standard.

Me: So we'll have to talk, one on one.

Jane: Yes.

All right. Fine.

I navigate to the website, credit card in hand, and prepare to enter in my digits. When I get to the fee screen, I chuckle. A $2,000 sign-up fee. Pretty steep. But it's supported by a money-back guarantee if you aren't happy after three matches.

After I complete the transaction, I send her another text.

Me: Paid. Just let me know the time and the place.

Jane: I will. But Jasper, understand one thing. If you hurt her . . .
I will hurt you.

Chapter 5

JANE

Earlier in the evening . . .

I glance around the apartment and pause to take in the place Londyn and I now call home. The two-bedroom apartment we share with my brother, Andrew, a brief walk from the bookstore, is a world away from the spacious apartment where we all once lived with Emmy. She's living at Wickham now with Graham. After much debate, the three of us siblings sold the place where we grew up and divided the money between us. It's what I used to start my business.

The living room flows into a tiny kitchen. Our dining area is simple, just a bay window with a round table, enough for the three of us.

Down the hall, Londyn's wicker daybed, draped with soft pink netting, is tucked into a corner of the biggest bedroom, one we share. Her stuffed animals and favorite books are neatly arranged on shelves, while her drawings decorate the walls.

My bed is opposite hers, a rustic metal frame, joined by a night-stand that holds a lamp and a stack of my current reads. Between our beds, a cute braided rug adds warmth to the hardwood floor.

Londyn takes off her shoes in a flash, then makes a run for her toys in the living room while I change into gray joggers and a baggy black T-shirt. Off goes the strapless bra, not that I really need one with my A cup. I adjust the toga and its accessories on a hanger and place it inside an antique bureau, one of the pieces of furniture that belonged to my gran. My lashes flutter as I glare at the toga. It's truly hideous. Whatever. I'll try again tomorrow.

I crank up the Cranberries' music and set the table for dinner. Londyn requested pancakes and eggs, and I have everything in the cabinets and fridge. I'm just ladling the first scoop of batter over a hot skillet when Andrew bursts through the door. "Jane! Your best brother is home!"

"My only brother," I call back.

"Hey, little genius!" he says as he sweeps inside the living room with a wide grin, scooping Londyn into his arms. He ruffles her flyaway blond hair as she giggles and wraps her tiny arms around his neck.

My brother, a year younger than me, is all charm. At 6 feet, he stands a quarter inch shy of my model-like height—a detail I love to remind him of. His hair, a cascade of dark strands, falls over his eyes.

"Dinner's ready!" I say, placing the food on the table. We gather around, ready to dig in.

Andrew, armed with his fork, is about to attack his stack of pancakes when Londyn, seated in her booster chair, beams at him. "Uncle Andrew, guess what!" she says, her small hands barely containing her enthusiasm. "I go potty ten times at preschool! Ten!"

Suppressing a laugh, I watch as she proudly holds up ten fingers.

Andrew halts, eyes widening. "Whoa. That's some serious business, Captain Pisser!"

I shoot him a look. "Let's not teach her 'pisser.'"

Londyn, missing the memo, echoes, "I'm a good pisser! My teacher loves me!"

Andrew grins. "A potty hero! The best little pisser in Manhattan."

"I also drawed a house," Londyn adds, chomping on her egg.

"Oh? Do tell," I say.

"It's big, with a purple door, and a slide from the window to a yard with toys."

Andrew chuckles. "Do I get my own room?"

Londyn nods seriously. "In the kitchen. For sandmaches."

I can't help but snort. Andrew's culinary skills are limited to sandwich artistry, which is why he only cooks twice a week. "The master chef at work," I tease.

Londyn's hands dance as she describes her dream house. "There's flowers, butterflies, and a big tree for climbing!"

Andrew winks at her. "And two potties, right, Captain Pisser?"

"Two," she confirms.

"We have two potties here," I remind her.

"But no slide," Andrew points out.

Londyn looks at me, serious. "Yeah, Mommy, no slide."

"Hmm," Andrew says, "we're on the tenth floor, so a slide isn't feasible, but it would still be awesome."

She squirms, her attention distracted. "Okay. I gotta pee now!"

I offer help, but she's fiercely independent. "I do it myself!"

"Call if you need me," I remind her.

"I won't!" she shouts back, scampering toward the bathroom.

"Don't forget to wash your hands, Captain Pisser," Andrew tells her as she disappears.

Being quiet so she won't hear me, I stand in the hallway, my ear tuned to the sounds coming from the bathroom, ready to leap into action. As I wait, the stress and anxiety of my day ebb away, replaced by gratitude. I close my eyes briefly, sending a silent prayer of thanks for these tiny moments. The way her eyes light up when she talks about her day fills the spaces in my heart that worry and doubt usually occupy.

As I hear the sound of the toilet flushing and Londyn's little feet padding on the floor, I dart back to the kitchen table.

Postdinner cleanup is in full swing with Andrew on dish duty and me attacking the counters. I've just finished regaling him with my Carson's-bar escapade, conveniently omitting the Jasper cameo.

Andrew shakes his head, chuckling. "Seriously, if you need more guys, I'm your man."

"You don't quite fit the business model." He's still in college and works part time.

He hums, then, "All right, instead of dressing up like a moron, try activities, like Rolling Romance Night. Speed dating on roller skates. Genius, yeah?"

I raise an eyebrow. "So they literally roll into love?"

He gives me a fist bump. "And if they fall? Perfect metaphor."

I shake my head. "You, raised by women, have turned into the king of cheese."

He grins, unabashed. "Women love it, sis. Cheese is my middle name. Okay, next idea: Puppy Love Night at the bookstore. Bring your pet and find your human match."

I put away a plate. "That's . . . actually not the worst."

"Told you I'm a genius." He dodges as I hip check him. "Want more?"

"Hit me," I say, leaning against the counter.

He tilts his head, thinking. "Love in the Dark. Blindfolded convos. Pure personality connection, no looks."

I roll my eyes as I put the skillet back in the drawer. "Okay, that's enough to think on. I need to go check on Londyn."

"Wait a second. There's actually something else I wanted . . ." He frowns, chewing on his lip.

"What?"

He opens his mouth as a hesitant expression flashes over his face. "Uh . . ."

Londyn comes in and wants him to play with her, and the moment is lost.

Later, she tugs at my hand, signaling it's story time. I settle beside her on the bed, opening *Goodnight Moon*. As I read, her eyes grow heavy, her breathing slows. When she's asleep, I close the door, the soft click barely audible.

Andrew's pacing in the hallway immediately sets off alarms in my head. His face appears troubled.

"What's up?" I ask, unease brewing inside.

He halts, facing me with a seriousness that's rare for him. "I gotta tell you something. I wanted to earlier, but thought I'd wait until Londyn was asleep."

I give a nod, a silent go-ahead.

He inhales sharply. "I'm moving out. Found this co-op near campus with a couple of guys. It's practical for school and all."

A knot forms in my gut. "Oh," I say, my voice flat. "When?"

"In a few weeks. Don't worry, I'll still pay for next month's rent."

That's sweet of him, but it isn't about the rent. It's about no more of his easy laughter and wacky sandwiches. First Gran died, then Emmy left, and now it's his turn. And before that it was Tomas. And before anyone, it was my mother. She left me when I was a toddler for Emmy and Gran to raise. Everyone leaves, eventually.

I muster a smile. "That's . . . that's great, Andrew."

His face shows excitement, but I see the guilt there too. "I'm sorry, really. I know you depend on me for a lot, and I can still do things for you and Londyn. We'll get together, and I'll see you at the bookstore when I have a shift."

I nod. "Sure." It's not just the thought of his absence that stings—it's the echo of past abandonment. Tomas's shadow follows me no matter what.

And now, watching Andrew, I can't shake the feeling of déjà vu.

Is my reliance on him pushing him away?

The thought that I might be a burden to Andrew, too, makes me cringe. He assured me his departure is just a change in living arrangements, but I'm scared I'm too much.

We are too much.

"Yeah. I totally get it. We'll be fine. Your sandwiches suck anyway. We'll get takeout on those nights."

He smirks. "You always eat every bite. Even when I put spinach in with the turkey club." He pauses. "I'm not abandoning you, sis. I know what it feels like, too, you know. Mom left us both, but I'll only be a few blocks away."

I dip my head. He was always good at reading my thoughts. "I know, I do, really. You aren't Mom or Tomas. You're my brother that I adore. You're an adult, and of course you want to be closer to school and hang out with your buddies. Ass." I pretend to glare at him and cross my arms.

"Ah, there she is." He grins and picks me up off the ground for a quick hug.

He heads off to shower, leaving me in the hallway, the silence enveloping me.

The apartment feels emptier already. Tears prick my eyes, but I shove them away.

Chapter 6
JANE

In the bathroom mirror, my reflection stares back—dark circles, hair with split ends, and a worried expression. I'm twenty-five, but the weight of the world makes me older.

"Listen up, Jane," I say sharply to the mirror. "It's not the end of the world if he moves out."

I recall the time I had to throw a man out of the bookstore for indecent exposure during a book club. Didn't flinch. Didn't hesitate. Even when his floppy bits got close to my leg.

Once I even waved an axe at a man who threatened my sister.

"Raised by strong women," I say. "Modern, unbreakable. You've weathered storms."

I think of Londyn. "Teaching her to be fierce, independent. Just like you. You've got this. For Londyn. For yourself. For every strong woman who's paved the way."

I am capable.

I am resilient.

After my pep talk, I sink into the claw-foot tub in my bathroom with a glass of wine and my worn copy of *Jane Eyre*, ready to get lost.

The second I do, though, my phone buzzes. I make the mistake of looking at it.

Jasper: Nice threat. Unnecessary, really. I'm the perfect gentleman.

Whatever. I flip my business phone to silent and rest it on the table that stretches across the tub. I really hope I'm not going to subject one of my clients to the worst night of their life.

Hmm.

I'll think about it later. Right now, it's time to read. Settling deeper into the bubbles, I open my book, eager for a quiet moment. But before I can start, Londyn pushes open the bathroom door and appears.

"Hi, sweetie. I thought you were sleeping."

"I forgot something," she says, her voice tinged with sleepiness. Her lower lip pouts just a bit.

"What did you forget?"

"Robbie asked me who my daddy is, and I didn't know," she says, her words simple.

Robbie is a little boy at school that she plays with. My stomach clenches. That question. The email from Tomas earlier today seems to have unwittingly opened the door.

I smile reassuringly as I get out of the bath, wrapping a towel around me as I dry off. "Well, you do have a daddy, but he lives in a place called California. He and Mommy aren't together, and he knew Mommy would take the best care of you."

It's not like I can say that he never wanted her at all. I want to protect her innocence for as long as I can.

Londyn blinks. "Why he not pick me from school? Other daddies do."

Gathering my thoughts, I slip on my robe and cinch it. I sigh, kneeling down to her level. "He lives too far away. But Uncle Andrew and I are always there to pick you up, right?"

"Is California on the moon?"

"No, it's on Earth. I'll show you on the map tomorrow."

"Okay." She seems satisfied for now.

"Do you want another bedtime story once I'm all done?"

She watches me brush my teeth. I make a funny face at her, then spit in the sink dramatically. She giggles. "Yeah. The one about the alligator."

"You got it."

After another story and getting her asleep, I curl up on my bed and decide to check my phone one more time before I put it on the charger for the night, which winds up being a mistake. I have three more messages from Jasper.

Jasper: No response to that? Something tells me you don't believe me.

Jasper: Hello?

Jasper: You there?

Jesus, he is so needy. I have to go back and reread our convo, my hands tightening on my cell. Ugh. Part of me is glad that I wasn't hanging on his every word like most women must do.

Rightfully so. Even if he is a macho-football-player cliché, he's quite the panty dropper. Not that that matters. As far as I can see, every woman on my list would want a date from him. They'd be thrilled to have a date with a gorgeous football star.

But after the novelty wore off? It'd all fall apart.

Oh, who am I kidding? He'd never let it get that far. Women probably have an expiration date of exactly five minutes after he ejaculates.

How can I possibly subject any one of my clients to that? They want their forever. That's what they signed up for.

But then my phone buzzes with a notification from my wireless company: Your bill for May is overdue.

That's weird. I'm sure I paid it.

I navigate to my bank account and quickly find the reason. My checking account balance is negative twelve dollars.

"Ack. How is that possible? I just transferred money last week."

I open up my savings account. It used to be pretty flush when I was modeling, but that was before I got pregnant. But gradually, the money's disappeared, and now it's at crisis level. I have less than $500 in there. And I'll have to save extra money for rent for the apartment once Andrew is gone. Plus, I've been trying to sock money away for Londyn's college fund. At this rate, I'll have enough for her to attend when she's eighty.

I clench my teeth so hard my jaw hurts.

I start to tap my fingernails on the night table, thinking.

Then I remember.

I go to the email and see the notification. JJ has paid you $2,000.

I check my business account, and sure enough, there it is, with all its pretty little zeros. Whew. I do have money.

Actually . . . I don't. One condition of that fee is that I find him a date.

Hmm.

I glance at a discarded pile of profiles in the corner, then bolt over and snatch them up. Maybe . . .

Flipping through them, friends and acquaintances all, I hit a roadblock. None of them deserve Jasper's circus.

Who could handle him?

Maybe someone tough.

A woman who's unimpressed by glitz because she's got her own glitter.

A put-you-in-your-place kind of woman.

That's when it clicks. Abigail Carey.

She's new to my list, a Yale lawyer turned skin-care mogul. Wealthy, driven, independent. When we met, she was straight-up intimidating, saying, "I don't need a man. I need an equal."

I remember squirming, admitting I had no matches yet. But now, it's like fate. I make a mental note to enter Jasper into the database and see if she pops up.

I stare at her photo. She's blond (I'm not sure it's real), with razor-sharp eyes that dare anyone to try anything. Jasper's antics won't faze her.

If they match, she'll either fuck his brains out or tear him apart like a tigress with a piece of meat.

I can't help but grin.

I fall back on the bed and quietly giggle up at the ceiling fan.

Chapter 7
JASPER

The June sun blasts down on my Escalade as I crawl off the interstate into a classic New York traffic jam. A delivery truck's hogging the road, and a couple of drivers are locked in a horn-blaring standoff. Typical city gridlock.

In my rearview mirror, Mr. Prius is flipping me off like I'm the one causing this mess. Right, buddy, because I control traffic.

I crank up the radio to escape the chaos. It's the *Dog and Jerry Show* on air, a sports-talk duo.

"The Pythons snagging Dalton Talley in the draft? That's a game changer," Dog says.

Jerry's quick to counter. "Kid's a walking red flag. Two colleges in four years? Flake alert."

Dog laughs. "Hey, the guy's just shopping for the right fit. Besides, after Jasper's disaster in Seattle, Dalton Talley might just be our new golden boy."

Ah, the Seattle game. My favorite nightmare.

Then Dog's voice perks up. "Breaking news: Jasper's thrown another interception in practice!"

Jerry cackles like it's the best joke he's heard all year. "Jasper's so bad, Seattle threw a parade in his honor!"

"He's so old, he farts dust!" Dog says.

Jerry chimes in. "He's so old he remembers when a touchdown dance was a polite handshake—"

I snap the radio off and go back to the symphony of horns. Still better than those clowns rehashing the same jokes every year.

The Tundra ahead eases up, and I'm finally moving. Pulling into the training-facility lot, I spy a Porsche squatting in my spot. **QB**, the sign reads, clear as day.

"What the hell?" I say to the silver car parked in my spot.

To be fair, there are three front spots, all labeled "QB," but everyone knows I park in the first one. I pull into the second, beside the Porsche, and think about bumping it with my door, but don't. It's a nice ride, and I have a pretty good idea of who owns it. Dalton Talley.

Stepping out of my Escalade, I grab my gym bag just as a deep voice booms from behind, "Yo, bro, why do you glory boys get prime parking, while us linemen are exiled to dumpster-ville?"

I turn to see Simo Tualea, our team's behemoth of a lineman. "Because your blocking is shoddy, big man," I shoot back, clasping his hand and forearm in our customary post-touchdown handshake.

He grins. "How was the break, QB1?"

"QB1? With Talley around? I'm thinking kicker might be a safer bet," I joke, only half kidding.

"Nah, you're the face of this team. Fans would riot if they benched you. Hey, speaking of, got some helmets in my truck. Mind signing them? Birthday gifts for family."

"Drop them with marketing. I'll sort it out."

"Think you can get Talley to sign too? A bit of the old and new?"

I raise an eyebrow. "Seriously?"

"Love you, man, but yeah. Can you?"

I sigh heavily. "Sure. When I meet the kid, I'll make it priority one," I say, my tone full of sarcasm.

Simo holds the weight room door for me, and I continue. "Let me know when the whole line's around. Got new bracelets for everyone." I show him the latest one on my wrist. I had it handmade in three shades of leather with a unity charm in the center.

"Nice. Better than last year's. Lost mine in the snow during the Cleveland game." He gives me a backslap and heads off to the leg machines, where several guys are.

Reaching my locker, I notice the one next to mine, freshly labeled **DALTON TALLEY**, already filled with street clothes. A note from Coach Duval sticks on my locker: "See me."

Quickly changing into shorts and a tank, I then make my way to his office. He's in a conference room with Dalton. My eyes study the new recruit. Tall, lean, and fresh faced, he's the picture of youthful ambition. I push down a wave of envy and step in.

"You wanted to see me, Pete?" I tighten my shoulders, ready for whatever's coming.

Pete stands and smiles and shakes my hand, but Dalton is too engrossed in the film to acknowledge me. Typical rookie arrogance.

I clear my throat, trying to grab Dalton's attention, but he remains fixated on the screen. Coach Duval shoots him a brief glance, then turns his focus back to me.

Pete says, "I've got Dalton in today. Have you two met?"

I shake my head. "Nope."

Dalton gives me a head nod without standing. "What's up?"

"Not much," I murmur, annoyance rising.

Pete clears his throat. "We're planning some film sessions, something to jump-start Dalton on how we run plays. How about Tuesday and Thursday mornings until camp? Can you meet with him?"

Dalton, without missing a beat, interjects, "Monday and Thursday afternoons."

I shoot a glance at the rookie, then back at Pete. "Thursday afternoon's a no-go for me. Got my nutritionist appointment."

Dalton deigns to look at me again, sizing me up. "Whatever, man."

Pete tries again. "Okay, how about Wednesday and Friday mornings? Work for you, Jasper?"

"I can make it," Dalton cuts in and smirks, throwing a challenging look my way.

Pete seems ready to wrap up. "Great, let's start with the Seattle—"

"No," I say, cutting him off. The last thing I want is to relive that game.

Pete's taken aback. I'm usually easy going—hell, I'm the team mascot, practically—but not with a new quarterback who can't even get up to shake my hand. "What works for you, then?"

"Our regular QB meetings on Wednesdays. That's it. I'm here to train, not babysit. Dalton can watch tape with you. Might pick up some manners."

Dalton shrugs and returns his focus to the screen. "Fine. Don't need him anyway."

Pete pulls me aside, a frown creasing his forehead as he talks in hushed tones. "I thought you'd help mentor him. No need to feel threatened, Jasper. You're still our guy."

Am I, though?

I watch Dalton taking notes on a laptop as he watches the film. Mixed emotions churn inside me. He's the fresh face, the new talent, and while I know I'm secure in my role as the quarterback, his arrival stirs fear within me—a fear that isn't really about football at all.

I've always prided myself on being the leader, the one the team looks up to, but I can't help but wonder, What if I'm not enough anymore? It's not that I doubt my skills on the field; it's the fear of losing my place in this makeshift family we've become as a team.

I stand firm. "I'm here to play, not to coach. I've got my own game to focus on." I pivot toward the door.

Dalton's quick with a comeback. "Sure, man. I'll learn loads here watching your tape, like what not to do."

I spin around. "Just for the record, I'm a three-time Super Bowl quarterback. Also, you parked in my spot. Don't do that shit."

Pete jumps in. "Enough. Dalton, back to the film. Jasper, go on to training. No need for you here today."

Yeah, that sounds better.

Dalton grunts, sinking back into his seat.

Shaking my head, I stride out, leaving the door ajar, Coach's voice trailing after me. "We'll sort this out."

Postworkout, I change in peace, Dalton's locker thankfully empty. But outside, my relief fades. He's lounging against my Escalade, clutching a paper.

"What's the deal with you?" I ask, dropping my bag, braced for round two.

He hesitates, then offers the paper. "Found this on my windshield. It's not meant for me, so I guess it's yours."

I snatch it, scanning the words. My hands clench around it.

Dear Jasper,

I can barely write these words. My hands are trembling with fear and suppressed love. It's been a lifetime since I held you in my arms, a lifetime filled with regret and silent whispers of your name.

Seeing you from afar, witnessing your life unfold, fills me with both pride and an indescribable ache. I've carried the weight of our separation every day, the memory of your tiny fingers slipping from my grasp haunting me. My heart lives in the shadow of the choice I made. It was the hardest decision of my life, but seeing the incredible person you've become, I cling to the belief that it was the right one for you.

You have every reason to hate me, to throw away this letter and curse the day I walked out of your life. I understand, more than you can imagine. The pain I've caused you is my life's greatest sorrow. But if there's a shred of forgiveness or curiosity in your heart, know this, you were loved every single day of your absence. Loved fiercely by a mother who never stopped thinking about you, worrying about you, loving you.

I'm leaving you my number, not with the expectation of a call, but with the hope of one. Perhaps to hear your voice, to say the words I've rehearsed in my mind a thousand times, or just to listen to whatever you need to say to me, even if it's anger.

You don't have to forgive me. You don't even have to understand. Just know that I am here, bearing the weight of my choices, and loving you.

Mom (445-555-5790)

I reread it, then glance around the parking lot searching for her. My throat feels tight, and my chest rises as I take deep breaths.

Is this for real? Did she actually come here?

Dalton cuts into my thoughts. "If I'd known it was for you, I wouldn't—"

I cut him off. "Don't play nice right now. You missed your shot, rookie."

He steps back. "I legit thought it was for me. My bad."

I'm silent, my mind racing. The last thing I want to do is get emotional in front of Dalton.

He crosses his arms. "We all got family drama. My own's a mess. When'd you last talk to her?"

I haven't seen her since I was five years old.

"None of your business," I say as I open my door and get inside.

He is still standing behind his car, staring as I drive through the parking lot.

As I idle at the highway on-ramp, the note in the passenger side is like a grenade.

State champion, college standout, pro footballer, and not a peep from her. Now, suddenly, a note. A number. It feels like a mockery of all my achievements.

Growing up, even with the best adoptive parents, there was this empty space she left. I had everything a kid could want, except answers.

Why did she leave?

Would she ever come back, even just to explain?

I remember my tenth birthday vividly. My adoptive parents, Paulina and Elijah Jannich, outdid themselves with a party and a brand-new skateboard. They rented the skate park, and it was epic. But that night, I lay in bed, tears streaming down my face because she wasn't there. Part of me, the innocent part, had hoped just because it was my birthday and it had been five years since she left, she'd appear.

I remember the ache in my chest, the feeling of abandonment so acute it was almost tangible. I told myself she was dead. It was easier to grieve than to hope. I swore I'd never waste another thought on whether she was still out there.

For years, I kept that promise.

No, she doesn't get to come back now. Not after leaving a kid to wonder, to hope. To me, she remains what I decided long ago, a part of my past that I buried deep down.

I grab the paper, crumpling it up, and toss it into the back seat. She's still dead to me.

Chapter 8

JASPER

A week later I'm piled up on the couch watching ESPN. The twins are seeing *Hamilton* with one of my sister's friends who has kids about the same age. I've already checked the Find My Friends app to see where they are, and it shows them there. At least their phones are in the right place. They invited me to tag along, but musicals aren't my thing. I'd be snoring five minutes in.

My phone dings. I glance and see a notification.

Cupid's Arrow: Don't forget Abigail C will meet you at The Urban Elixir at 7:30. From your location please allow 43 minutes to arrive at your destination with normal traffic.

Dammit. I completely forgot about the date, and for a brief moment, I toy with the idea of bailing, but I can't do that to Jane.

I spring into action. It's showtime.

Twenty-nine minutes later, I make it to the front door of Wickham. Jane said Abigail is a businesswoman, so I went with a navy blue pin-striped Armani suit, white shirt, and no tie. It's the same outfit I wore into the stadium two years ago for the Super Bowl.

The doorman greets me with a smile. "Looking sharp tonight, Mr. Jannich. Cab?"

"Thanks, Herman. Headed to the Urban Elixir. It's in the financial district."

"Yes, sir. Nice place, I hear," Herman says as he stands out in front of the building and flags down a cab for me. "Should I tell the girls you'll be late tonight?"

"I appreciate it, but I'll text them." They are actually staying the night with the mom and her kids. I get into the waiting car.

Forty minutes later the cab pulls up to an alley between two monstrous glass buildings. The financial district is crawling with people at noon, but this time of night, it's empty.

As I step into the bar, the sounds of a piano intertwined with the notes of a saxophone greet me. The burly bouncer at the entrance gives me a knowing nod, recognizing me. Despite the building's modern concrete-and-glass exterior, the interior walls have rustic exposed brick.

The bar itself is a focal point, showing top-shelf whiskeys and scotches, the bottles gleaming under the lighting. I inhale the scent of peat and wood, my mouth watering. I do love a good whiskey.

Surrounding the stage, high-backed round booths line the walls, creating an intimate place. Two women clad in flapper dresses stand near the bar with bright smiles on their faces. One has dark-brown hair, while the other is a redhead.

"Welcome to the Urban Elixir," says the brunette. "But shh, it's a speakeasy. Don't tell the cops. Do you have a reservation?"

Cute. "Yes, Abigail made it," I reply.

The brunette nods knowingly. "Ah yes, Ms. Carey is expecting a guest."

Suddenly, the redhead's eyes widen in recognition. "Wait, are you Jasper from the Pythons?" she asks excitedly. "Can I get a selfie?"

Before I can even respond, she's extending her phone toward me. As we pose, both girls master the art of the selfie pout, angling their faces to catch the light. The flash pops, unexpectedly bright in the bar, drawing curious glances from other patrons. The bartender, sporting a waxed and styled mustache, shoots us a look of mild irritation.

She inspects the photo, wrinkling her nose. "I wasn't quite ready. Let's take one more," she insists, pushing the phone back into my hands.

I'm conscious of the time and the eyes on us. "I really need to get going—my date's waiting. And, well, the flash is kind of harsh for the vibe here." I offer them an apologetic smile and a polite nod, keen to find Abigail.

I'm led to a secluded circular booth in the back corner.

My gaze lands on my date as she stares at her phone. She's striking, dressed in a tailored gray jacket and skirt that accentuate her figure. The white blouse she's wearing is snug, revealing a hint of cleavage. Her blond hair is blunt and cut to her chin in a sleek style that frames an oval face. She looks around my age.

"Abigail?"

She gets up to shake my hand with a firm grasp. "Jasper. You're taller than I expected."

"I aim to exceed expectations," I say wryly, letting her slide back into the booth first.

She gives me a once-over as I settle in, and when she finally smiles, it's a flash of pearly whites. "Hi."

"Hi," I murmur.

She's very pretty.

Nice choice, Jane. She's no substitute for you, but I'm curious to see where this goes.

"Thank you for arriving on time. I appreciate punctuality," she says, leaning back in the seat. "I've already ordered for us. Our drinks will be here soon."

"Actually, I was thinking of trying a whiskey—"

"Not yet. I got us martinis," she says gently, cutting in. "They're made with gin from their own copper-pot still, Prohibition style. It's exceptional and not to be missed."

Martinis are not usually my thing, but hey, why not? I smile broadly. "Martini it is, then. When in Rome, or in a Prohibition-style bar."

"Good." She smiles. "I thought we would start our date discussing each other. Obviously, we were both able to research each other to get any information available. I know you were a successful quarterback with the Pythons—"

"I'm still a successful quarterback. I've got several years left in me. Retirement is far away." Despite Dalton Talley showing up.

"Right. And the playboy image, the string of girlfriends. That's accurate, right?" Her brow arches.

"Well, there's more to it than that, but I'm assuming you've read the online tabloids."

She nods. "No problem. I get it. People will write anything to get attention in the media. I assume you're up to speed on my achievements, *Forbes* ranking, and philanthropy. All true. But the Berrysoft scandal? I was only advising the board. I'm totally innocent. My lawyers and I are clear on that."

"Ah." I have no clue what Berrysoft was.

"With that out of the way, let's dive into the more interesting stuff."

Our martinis arrive, and I take a sip, wincing at the taste. It's more terrible than I expected.

I nod. "Uh, yeah, did my homework too. Impressive stuff, really."

"Oh? What did you find out?"

"Uh, well . . . the money you've made. My research showed you to be very impressive." I read the profile Jane sent but did zero research on my own. I thought that's what the date was for.

She shifts gears. "So what are you looking for in a partner?"

This woman gets down to business quick.

Where's the flirty banter, the lingering gazes?

I toy with the napkin under my glass and decide to just put it all out there. "Someone who wants to be with me because of who I am inside. Somebody authentic. What about you?"

Abigail speaks with the precision of a tough lawyer, each word measured. "In any relationship, it's about partnership, a balanced exchange of benefits. As long as both parties gain proportionately, the relationship flourishes. But the moment there's an imbalance, where one person feels they're giving more than they're receiving, it's bound to break down."

She pauses, gauging my reaction.

A "balanced exchange of benefits"? Huh.

"Sure," I say, filling the empty air.

"True loyalty," she continues, "is contingent on this balance. It's unrealistic to expect devotion without considering future mutual benefits. The partner I seek must be an intellectual equal, someone who matches, if not exceeds, my ambition and achievements."

"Got it," I add, trying not to zone out.

"I'm not looking for a caretaker, nor do I intend to be one. I need someone who can independently thrive, especially during times when my career demands my full attention. And, of course, I'm prepared to offer them the same independence."

I gaze into my drink, her words echoing, but my thoughts drift to my bio mother. Was that her reasoning? A pursuit of "her balance" that didn't include me? Did she expect me to thrive without her? Have a better life?

I shake my head, trying to dispel the thoughts. I'm here to escape, not cut into that wound.

"What if your partner becomes sick? Or needs more emotional support?" I ask. My adoptive mom lost most of her vision in her fifties due to a genetic disease, and my dad was her rock. He learned braille. He had the house modified to prevent accidents. He learned all the new technology that helps with vision issues. He became her eyes, describing every person and setting.

It hasn't slowed Mom down one bit, but it's because he's been there.

"I don't plan on being sick. I have yearly exams, physical and mental."

I smirk. "But life is about surprises. You don't know what's around the corner. Sure, some are bad, like illness, but some are good, like finding a twenty in an old coat."

She shrugs it off. "If I discovered lost money, it would make me angry at the opportunity loss, and if I became ill, I'd want to be alone. I have the means to support myself. I'd hire doctors and nurses to live with me."

"I see. Interesting."

She smiles. "When Jane called me about our match, I was excited. Your success is important to me. You're clearly accomplished."

"Thank you," I reply.

"You're obviously attractive," she adds.

"My mom says people have layers like an onion. Hopefully we're all more than just our outward appearances."

She nods. "Easy for you to say. You're one of the hottest guys I've had drinks with."

"Ah."

"Moving on, you're dedicated to your sport, with little time for anything else. Like me with my career. We match in that regard. Agree?"

My mind shifts, struggling to stay present. I've started watching the guy who's playing the saxophone. "I want to be needed. To miss and be missed. Maybe I'm a true romantic at heart."

She frowns. "I'm not."

I chuckle. "Oops."

The conversation bounces back and forth. She lays out her cards: no kids, ever. Separate finances, always. Each person footing their own bills. She loves the city and hates nature. Her worst nightmare is to go camping. She prefers high-end experiences, art, and food. She is goal oriented and loves a schedule with every minute planned. She has her own personal Pilates instructor and chef. It's a clear, no-nonsense blueprint of herself.

I counter her points. I talk about spoiling my family with gifts and going on big family vacations. I detest ballet and musicals. I do love a schedule, but I'm spontaneous. I try to eat healthy, but in the summer it's beer and whatever I can find that's delicious—then I work it off. I don't mind footing the bill, but I'm not opposed to a woman paying her own way.

Then the waiter swings by our table and asks if we're having dinner.

I'm down to eat, and I tell her I'm hungry, but she's not, so I order a whiskey, quickly, before she can order another martini.

"How long is your penis?"

I nearly spit out my drink. "Wow, that's direct."

"I'd rather be up front now than find out later we're not compatible. Experience has taught me looks can be deceiving. You're tall, athletic, but that doesn't always mean, well, you know."

Part of me is bemused by her up-front attitude, but the other side is feeling awkward as hell.

"It's not just about length, of course," she says with an elegant shrug. "The ratio of length to girth matters."

I match her straightforwardness. "How about you?"

She replies coolly. "I've never had complaints. I do what it takes to keep my men from getting bored."

"Ever been in love? Found your soulmate?"

Her smirk is cynical. "That's a fairy tale. Sure, there might be a few men I can tolerate. But just one for forever? Hardly. In fact, I'm not opposed to having an open relationship. We'd need to have a contract for it and agree to get regularly checked for diseases."

I decide to address her earlier question. "Well," I say, "size isn't everything. It's about how you use what you have. Let's just say I have a monster truck and know how to drive it."

Her lips curl into a slow smile. "Now we're getting somewhere," she purrs.

I lean in closer, our faces mere inches apart. "Tell me, what is it that you truly desire?"

She drains the last of her drink. "My office is nearby with an apartment for late nights. Want to come over and find out?" She runs a finger down my hand. "I like you, Jasper, but let's be real, we're like oil and water. Still, I wouldn't mind a little fun. Wanna bang a billionaire?"

I am a billionaire.

Have I ever fucked one?

I don't think so.

She's undeniably attractive, and I like how focused she is on what she wants. I admire the intensity. I'm the same when it comes to football.

Her eyes hold mine. I'm intrigued by her refusal to conform to conventional notions of love and relationships. There's an authenticity about her. I could fuck her. And we'd probably hook up a few more times, then call it quits. Been there and done that. It feels good at the time, but then it's empty.

"Gonna pass, Abigail."

Her eyebrows rise. "Really? Now, that's unexpected."

I need more than physical attraction. I like softness, a little vulnerability in a woman. "Should I apologize?"

"No, of course not." She snaps her fingers at a passing waiter, then smiles at me. "I'm paying the bill, then I'd like you to escort me to a cab. Perhaps you'll change your mind on the way out."

Chapter 9

JANE

The cat clock on the wall in the living room strikes ten as I take a sip of my wine. I'm on my second glass. Dressed in my faded unicorn pajama shorts and a tank top, I'm settled in for the night when I'm startled by a knock at the door. With Andrew out with his buddies and Londyn asleep, I approach the door cautiously.

Looking through the peephole, I can't help but grunt. There stands Jasper, cloaked in a suit so fine I want to stroke it. His broad shoulders are perfectly framed by the cut, and his hair is pulled up into a man bun.

He presses the bell again, his voice muffled but insistent through the door. "Jane, I know you're there. I texted Andrew, and he said you're here. Open up."

Ugh. I dash to the bathroom and pull my hair up into a ponytail, swipe gloss on my lips, and run back to the hallway. I swing the door open and fix him with a stern look. "What in the world are you doing here so late?"

He breezes past me without an invitation, a hint of whiskey lingering in his wake. He stops for a moment and takes the place in with a sweeping glance, then heads straight to the kitchen as I follow. "Nice place. We need to talk. Abigail was a no-go."

My thoughts leap to the most obvious scenario. "Let me guess, she turned you down?"

Bending down with his back to me, he rummages through my fridge. "Oh, she did not turn me down. She wanted the sex. She wanted it so bad. She wanted to know how big I was. My penis."

And there it is.

I cross my arms, irritation rising. "So, you jumped into bed with her. Typical."

He retrieves last night's spaghetti and turns to face me, expression earnest. "She wanted to fuck me, but we were not a match."

He takes his jacket off and slings it over a chair, then grabs a plate from the cupboard, his movements fluid and practiced. He pops the lid off the container and dumps the spaghetti onto the plate.

My arms remain crossed, but my curiosity is piqued.

He pauses, putting the spaghetti into the microwave. "Once she figured out I wasn't what she wanted, she didn't even want to have dinner. She just wanted me. In her vagina. Apparently, she keeps an apartment near her office." The microwave hums to life, and he leans against the counter, facing me.

His eyes meet mine. "It's not flattering being seen as just a way to get off, you know?"

I smirk. "Welcome to the club, Jasper. Women have been dealing with that for ages."

The microwave beeps, and he takes out the steaming plate. "I wouldn't understand how it is for women, but it goes both ways, let me assure you." He trails off, forking a mouthful of spaghetti. "She made me drink a martini. I hate those. And I was so dang . . ." He stops to chew.

"Hungry? So you came to eat my leftovers?"

He nods, his mouth full. "I came to give you a hard time for picking her. The spaghetti is a bonus." Carrying a heaping plate of spaghetti, he tosses me a charming grin as he strides toward the living room. I trail behind him, irritation brewing.

He moves some pillows round, then plops down on the couch, making himself at home. "I felt like I was in a boardroom when I was talking to her, and get this, if we were together and I got sick, she'd dump me."

I can see that with Abigail. "Everyone has different needs from a partner," I remind him. "We aren't all cookie cutters of each other."

"I get it. We're all unique and have different needs in a relationship. It's just her way is not my way."

I nod. Got it.

"Your spaghetti's not half bad," he comments, twirling a forkful and taking a big bite. "I didn't see any garlic bread. You got any?"

"Not your personal chef, Jasper."

"Please? Pretty please? I'll give you a back massage if you have bread."

"No thanks," I say as I huff at him and march back to the kitchen. I pull the leftover french bread out of the cupboard and microwave it and bring it back to him.

His eyes glow as he stares at it, then takes a giant bite and moans. "Oh, Jesus, angel. I think I love you. I'd definitely have sex with you just for this bread alone."

I thump him on the forehead.

"Ouch. What was that for?" he mumbles as he chews.

"For intruding and eating my food. For offering sex. I'm not attracted to you. My world does not revolve around you. I'm not on call for your personal venting."

"You have my two grand."

"Let me write you a check, and let's call this quits. Get off my couch and get out."

"Ahhhh, wait a minute," he says as he holds up a hand. "I'm sorry for barging in. I just needed to talk, okay? And I am your most famous client . . ." He grins, continuing, "And most difficult, it seems. But hey, you're getting a sneak peek into the glamorous life."

I roll my eyes. "Don't tell me you're one of those being-famous-is-so-hard types."

"Not at all. But you don't meet a guy like me every day. I had two girls at the place we went to asking me for pics with them. Fine, it's fine, I get it all the time, but admit it, I'm good for your business."

"But are you worth the headache?"

He winks at me. "I'm growing on you."

"Like a fungus."

"Hey, some fungi are essential," he retorts, tucking the last piece of bread into his mouth.

I sit down opposite him and poke him in the shoulder. "So, Mr. Fungus, what's your next move in the dating game? I suggest we have that one-on-one interview." He winces. "I really shouldn't have let you go on the date with Abigail without it. It's my fault."

"Nah, it's fine. Just find me someone less corporate and more real."

I raise an eyebrow. "Real? Like someone who doesn't live in the spotlight?"

He nods. "Exactly. Someone who understands life isn't just touchdowns and red carpets. Someone who gets that sometimes, you just want to chill on a couch, eat spaghetti, and have a normal conversation." Jasper grins, setting the empty plate down. "Ordinary can be extraordinary. You of all people should know that."

My eyes narrow. "So I'm ordinary."

A teasing look grows on his face. "Never, angel. Never. Especially in that cupid getup. You looked good enough to eat."

We lock eyes for a moment, something unspoken buzzing in the air. Tingles break out over my skin, and I will them to go away. I break the gaze, crossing my arms. "Well, time for you to leave. I have ordinary things to do, like clean up your mess."

"Ah, wait, now, I can't just eat and leave. Let's chat. I need some Jane therapy. Let's do the interview now."

"It's late, Jasper. I told you to come by the bookstore."

He gestures to the TV, where my K-drama flickers. "You're up watching television, the night's still young. Plus, the twins are sleeping over at a friend's house, and honestly, I don't feel like heading back to an empty apartment." He frowns. "I'm bored out of my mind. I wish the season would start already."

"Boredom's a frequent visitor, huh?"

He nods, wiping his mouth with a napkin. "All my friends are cozied up with their partners. Tuck and Francesca and Graham and Emmy. Most of the guys on the offense are married. I feel strange in my singlehood. It's just, I'm just . . ."

"Lonely?"

He sighs as his shoulders slump. "Yeah. I guess. I grew up with four amazing sisters, then I was the popular guy in high school and college. On the field, I'm surrounded by teammates and fans. Off the field, it's like this silence. Sure, I have fans who want to talk to me, but something is just missing." He pauses. "Wow. You are like therapy. I didn't realize I even felt that way."

"Loneliness doesn't discriminate based on popularity. It just means you're human," I say softly. "Is what you're missing a relationship with a woman?" I reach out and touch his shoulder, and his eyes follow my hand. He looks back at me, and I quickly move it back. I forget how easy he is to touch because he's so open.

I clear my throat. "Perhaps it's about finding yourself first."

"Do you read tarot cards too? I love those."

I glare at him. "I have tarot cards that Babs gave me for my birthday, but they're just for fun. I'm a good people reader. It comes from watching people in the store. I was born this way, like Gran and Emmy, and it helps me be a good matchmaker." I pause. "If I may offer some advice . . ."

He nods. "Uh-huh."

"If your close friends are married, make a new friend, someone unexpected. Like a surprise."

"I literally just said the same thing to Abigail. Well, I told her that surprises can be good." He cocks his head as he studies me. "Still, name a surprise that's worked out well for you."

"Londyn."

His expression softens. "Okay, fine. That's one."

"How about Emmy and Graham? She surprised him when she stole his car," I say as I laugh.

He chuckles. "True. If everything were predictable, it would be pretty boring."

I nod. "Exactly. Sometimes it's the unexpected moments that lead us to where we're meant to be. It's about being open. You never know what opportunities might come your way. Just think of them as life's little plot twists."

"Oops."

"What?"

"I might have missed out on a potential friend. There's a rookie quarterback on the team, but he's such a prick." He grunts. "He took my parking spot last week."

I can't help but laugh at his peevishness. "Sounds like a great start."

"Yeah, right. Dalton Talley. The guy's a legend in his own mind. He comes in and acts like I'm the old guy. I'm not."

"Maybe he's just trying to find his footing," I suggest. "Being a rookie isn't easy, especially with big expectations. Wasn't he the first pick in the draft? That is serious pressure, plus he's got *you* to contend with. Your fans think you are perfect. Your teammates love you. It's a tough act to follow."

He seems to muse on that. "Maybe. But he's really pushing my buttons by being rude as fuck."

"Sometimes," I say, "the people who push our buttons the most can end up being the ones we need. They challenge us."

He looks at me, his expression softening. "Is that what you're doing? Pushing my buttons?"

A breathless feeling takes hold of my chest. I try to catch my breath. "Am I succeeding?"

His gaze locks with mine, and tension rises in the air. "You might be, angel."

"See? You're already getting better at making new friends." I nudge him playfully, trying to push the electricity between us away. "Maybe give him a chance. Who knows? You might find some common ground."

He nods, changing gears. "You have those tarot cards lying around?"

I nod my head at the media center. "Over there. Why?"

"I know how to read them."

I scoff. "Please."

Ignoring me, he gets up and opens the bottom cabinets of the media center, moving things out of his way to find the cards. I shake my head in disbelief. It's as if he owns the place.

"Found them!" He jumps to his feet in an athletic move that widens my eyes. "I'm going to do you. Read you, that is. Not the other thing."

I watch as he flits around the room, rummaging through another set of drawers in the bureau in the foyer, where he pulls out a couple of scented candles. He asks me for a lighter, and I dig one out from the kitchen. With a flourish, he lights them and sets them on the coffee table. A satisfied sigh comes from his chest as he dims the lights in the living room. "Now, let's sit on the floor around the coffee table."

Jeez. Okay. We're really doing this.

I plop down some pillows for me, then hand him a few, but he waves them away as he sits cross-legged facing me.

He shuffles the cards with ease. "I studied folklore in college, and tarot was in one of my classes. My youngest sister, Rayna, loves to do readings."

"Where do they come from?"

He lays the deck down between us. "They originated from a game similar to bridge for the rich. In the eighteenth century they began to be associated with the mystical and the occult."

"Like devil worshippers?"

He pauses for a moment, the corners of his mouth twitching as if he's fighting back a grin. "No. There'll be no summoning the devil with me."

"Good. I don't think my lease allows for demons."

He pokes me in the arm. "We're just going to have some insight about you tonight."

I narrow my gaze at him. "You sound awfully delighted to be in charge of this."

He leans in over the table and puts his face close to mine. "I'm stoked, angel. Absolutely vibrating with excitement."

I shiver at the tingle of awareness that zings between us. I push it away as I clear my throat. "All right. Show me what these magic cards can do."

"They aren't going to tell you exact things. It's more like a mirror, where you see things in your life in a new light."

"So it won't tell me why I keep killing the houseplants at the bookstore?" I sigh. "I even gave them names and personalities and talk to them, but it doesn't help."

"You're such a weirdo."

I smile. "A little."

He shuffles the cards with a seriousness that makes me want to giggle. He goes on, explaining some of the nuances of tarot.

"Upright cards emphasize primary messages, while reversed cards mean internal challenges." He places a card upright, then flips it to show its reversed position. "But context is key. The question you ask, the spread, and even the reader play a part in the message."

"So I have to trust that you know what you're doing."

"Hmm." He smirks. "Don't trust me?"

I'm cool, it's just, I'm rather bemused by how much he's into this. We started out with me giving him advice, and now it's switched.

"Think of a question or area of your life you want help with," he says, and I nod, closing my eyes and pretending like I'm pondering the secrets of the universe when I'm really thinking about how great his cologne smells.

I think of the perfect question to ask the cards. "Okay, got it," I say, popping one eye open to peek at him. He fans the cards out with a flourish.

"Pick three," he instructs.

I choose my cards, trying to feel the energy or whatever I'm supposed to be sensing.

Jasper reveals my choices, the Star, the Ten of Cups, and the Lovers. He waggles his eyebrows at the last one.

"This one, the Star, is a sign of hope, of believing in a better tomorrow," he says. "Perhaps good things are coming your way. It could be related to your business—if that's what you asked for. Do you want to tell me what you asked? You don't have to, but it might help." He tries to say it lightly, but I can tell that he really wants to know.

"I didn't ask about the business."

"Oh? About Tomas then?"

Nope. And there's no way in hell I'll admit what I actually asked for. Love.

Will I have it in my life someday? Will I ever find the match for *me*? I brush him off. "What's the reverse side of the Star mean?"

"It means you might get hit by a train."

I glare at him, and he smiles. "But you didn't get the shadow side. It's all good for you."

Then he gets to the Ten of Cups, talking about emotional fulfillment as he waves it in front of me. "It's about families, a very positive card. It means you'll have more fulfilment in that area of your life. You're getting really lucky tonight."

Oh. I stare at the art, a rainbow arching over a joyful family. The scene is so serene, so perfect. My mom, who chose a life without me, flashes in my mind. And then there's Tomas, who walked away the moment I mentioned pregnancy.

The card feels like a distant dream.

I trace the edge of the card, my finger pausing on the picture of the children dancing.

But I have Londyn.

And our life *is* beautiful. And I'm ready for more of that.

"Hey," he says. "You got lost in thought there. You all right? Wanna talk?"

I shake my head. "What about you? Would you like to get this card?"

He considers it, then nods. "Of course. I'm dealing with my own shit right now. My bio mom contacted me recently and wants to talk to me. She left me when I was five."

I glance at him in surprise. "I never knew you were adopted."

A sigh comes from him. "It's a long story, one I don't really want to get into right now."

I nod. I get it. Meeting his biological mom is something he's still grappling with. "All right, do the last one."

"The Lovers," he murmurs dramatically.

I study the card he holds. Two figures stand in a garden, like Adam and Eve, with an angel above them.

A half smile plays on my lips. "Does this mean I'm about to find romance? Because my last date was a millennium ago and honestly, I prefer my electric blanket to men."

He pouts. "That's a shame, angel."

"I'm doing just fine on my own."

"Yes, of course you are, but maybe the card isn't just about romantic love. It suggests a decision to be made, one that reflects your true self."

A decision?

"Like if I want Indian food or Mexican?"

He grunts as he gives me a pretend withering look. "You aren't taking any of this seriously."

I glance down at the Star, the Ten of Cups, and the Lovers. "According to this, I'm headed for hope, domestic bliss, and maybe love? Sounds like a fairy tale."

He shoots me a knowing look, one eyebrow raised. "It can happen."

I shrug, trying to appear nonchalant, but the reading has brought up feelings I usually keep at bay. Part of me, the side that's hidden behind practicality and skepticism, yearns for the cards to be right.

I pick up the Star. Hope feels like a luxury when every day is a battle to keep my business going and take care of Londyn.

Then there's the Ten of Cups. My family is in a state of flux. Emmy is out of the country, and my brother is moving out. Londyn is the light of my life, but Tomas's abandonment looms over us both. How can I believe in a card that promises familial bliss when my family is hurting?

But staring at the card, I want desperately to believe it's true, that good things are coming.

But it's the Lovers card that hits hardest. Love? That's something for other people. I've built walls around my heart so high, I'm not sure anyone could scale them. And yet, as I stare at the card, the figures intertwined under the eye of an angel, longing slices through me.

For connection, for someone to really see me and choose me in spite of it.

I shake my head, trying to dispel the thoughts. "You make it all sound so simple."

He leans back, his gaze soft. "Maybe it is, maybe it isn't. But isn't it nice to think about what could be?"

And as much as I want to forget the reading, I can't deny the warmth spreading through me at the thought. Maybe it's the ambiance, or maybe it's the way Jasper's looking at me, but for the first time in a long time, I allow myself to hope.

To dream about a future where the impossible seems just a little bit more possible.

"This was fun, watching you get hyped up about it." I smile as I stand. "But now, I think it's time we did your interview. Let me grab my laptop from the bedroom. And I'll change."

He glances at my shorts, his gaze lingering on my legs. His words are soft. "You look perfect."

Ignoring the appreciative look in his eyes, I leave, and moments later, laptop in hand, I resettle in my chair. "I've got your initial survey, but something tells me it's overdone. You seemed to have sex on the brain."

He returns from the kitchen, having rinsed his plate. A grin curls his lips. "Imagining your reaction while typing that nonsense was the highlight of my day." He pauses, patting his flat stomach. "Man, I wish you had more spaghetti."

"You're still hungry?" I ask in disbelief.

"Missed dinner, and that spaghetti was a teaser. How about I order something? Pizza? Chinese? Indian?"

I throw my hands up, exasperated. "Go ahead, Jasper. Order whatever you want. Make my place your home."

"Your wish is my command." He picks up his phone to order pizza from the place around the corner, a gloating smile playing on his lips.

I clear my throat. "Okay, let's start. Tell me about the date. What kind of girl were you hoping to meet tonight?"

He sprawls back on the couch and looks up at the ceiling. "Just someone who gets me, who understands that I'm sincere. It's not an act. I genuinely like people. Abigail seems like a nice person, but she wasn't much fun."

She really isn't. "She has other assets."

"Which aren't for me."

"Noted. Anything else?" I ask.

He muses for a moment. "She should have a sense of humor, definitely. And be able to put up with my schedule."

"A sense of humor to tolerate your ego, you mean?"

"Ha ha." He cups his chin as he stares at me, making me feel unsettled. "She should love football, of course."

I type rapidly. "Got it. You aren't asking for much, of course."

He points at me. "You love to give me a hard time, but underneath you do like me."

I let out a breath, trying to keep my focus on the computer screen. Jasper is a whirlwind I'm not sure I'm ready to handle. I'm not unaware of the heat I feel around him. It's downright heady when he walks into a room and puts those blue eyes on me. But this isn't about me. I'm in no place to be interested in someone. "All right, let's keep going. Anything else?"

He leans back and stares at me for several moments, his gaze caressing my face and lingering on my lips. He breaks the silence, his voice serious.

"Do you think you can really find me a girl?"

A tingle dances down my spine, of how much I really do want him to find a little piece of happiness. I nod.

He takes a deep breath. "I need someone who gets my humor, yes. But it's more than that. I need someone who can laugh with me and at the world. Life's too short for anything else.

"I want someone independent. Someone who has her own ambitions. I admire strength. Emotional resilience. The kind of strength that's been tested."

I glance up from my typing. "Because you've been tested?"

He nods, his brow furrowing. "I went through some crazy stuff as a kid. My bio mom and I ended up in this cult in Northern California. I'm pretty sure it was involved in drugs and the cartel. We stayed in cabins with other families and worked the marijuana fields. After she left, I didn't speak for three months."

I don't type those words. They're too personal.

A long exhale comes from him, and he rolls his neck as if shaking off the memories.

"Anyway, forget all that. What I need is someone who believes in the 'us' concept. Someone who fights for us even when things get tough. I want someone who's open to adventure. I won't always be a football player. Someday I want to be a dad, a really good one. I want to give my kids the beginning I never had. Family is important to me."

I blink in surprise. "You said in your first profile that you didn't want kids."

His eyes travel to the hallway, near where Londyn is asleep. "I want a big house out in the middle of nowhere, maybe somewhere in Vermont or Maine, with a ton of kids." He smiles. "You know, I wasn't looking forward to all your prying, but this is a lot of fun."

I raise an eyebrow. "You thought it would be torture?"

"Nah, angel. I enjoy our back-and-forth. We're a lively pair."

"I have been known to hold my own."

"You have no idea how many times I sit and think of comebacks to say to you." He laughs as he says it, the corners of his eyes crinkling. "If you weren't so repulsive, we'd be a great match."

"Repulsive? You jerk!" I toss a pillow at him, which he easily dodges. "If I thought you were attractive, *which I don't*, I might give you the time of day. Besides, I'm not looking for a relationship. Love is dead to me."

"Because you have a kid?"

I shrug. I mean, yeah, that's part of it. Why would I bring someone into Londyn's life that may not stick around? It's too hard to explain to Londyn when people disappear from our lives. I want to shield her from as much pain as I can. But the other part of me doesn't want to be hurt again. I don't trust love, not when people just walk away and break your heart.

"How can you say love is dead when you're a matchmaker?" He pops an eyebrow at me.

"It's just not part of my plan at the moment. I'm doing this business because I see a need—in others. I've seen how much Emmy and Graham adore each other. I love how he loves her."

"But it's not you."

I nod.

"You make me sad, angel."

My cell rings, and I glance at it, noticing it's a number I don't recognize. Probably spam. It's been happening all day, and I consider answering it but don't. If it were my business phone, I'd pick it up. I focus back on Jasper.

He stands up and rolls his neck. "You got any beer?"

He doesn't wait for my answer as he heads to the kitchen and grabs a beer from the fridge, then picks up the wine bottle on the coffee table and fills up my glass. He hands it to me. "Come on, let's make a toast."

"To what?"

He thinks on that, eyes tracing my features, lingering longer than they should. "On finding the right girl."

I raise an eyebrow. "Sometimes you have the right person but it's the wrong time."

He smirks, lifting his beer. "Ah, but that's where you come in. I'm counting on you to choose the perfect one at the right time. Though, I have to say, my standards are pretty high."

I take a sip, the wine crisp. "Well, I hope your standards include someone who doesn't mind you barging into their house in the middle of the night."

He laughs, a genuine sound that fills the small space. "Stop acting like you're eighty. It's only eleven at night, and I make excellent company. My food theft is a quirk that people adore. It means I like their food. I'm a very good friend to have. All right, your turn. What are we toasting to for you?"

I think for a moment. "To the success of Cupid's Arrow. May it thrive and not suffer from clients who think they're God's gift to women."

"Ouch," he says as he feigns hurt, placing a hand over his heart. "I'll have you know I'm very humble. It's just one of my many, many great qualities."

"Sure, and I'm the Queen of England," I say, sipping my wine again.

"Your Majesty," Jasper says as he bows mockingly, "I'm merely a humble subject in your regal presence." His smile is infectious, but I don't let it affect me.

"Keep dreaming. It's going to take more than charm to find your match."

His eyes lower to half-mast. "Challenge accepted. But remember, sometimes what we're searching for is right in front of us."

The words hang between us, an implication there I push away.

I mentally slap myself away from the gravitational force that is Jasper. Come on, Jane, resist! You're stronger than the cliché of falling for the hot quarterback. This isn't high school, and you're definitely not the cheerleader.

But oh, how the universe loves irony. Here I am, trying to act all business, while part of me is doing heart cartwheels every time he smiles.

Focus! You've dealt with worse.

Remember that time you accidentally dyed your hair green before your senior year? If you can handle that, you can handle a little (okay, a lot of) quarterback charm.

Don't let the way his shoulders stretch inside his white shirt get to you. They're just . . . strategically placed muscles. Yeah, muscles that probably have their own fan club and IG handle.

I take a deep breath to fortify my resolve. Jane Darling, you are a strong, independent businesswoman who doesn't need to fall into the plot of a rom-com. Especially not one with Jasper as the leading man.

I mentally erect a barrier around myself, a no-quarterback zone. You've got this. Just think of him as a very tall, very handsome . . . broccoli. Nutritious but not particularly exciting.

"May we both find what we're looking for," I say.

"To finding what we're looking for," he echoes as he holds my gaze.

We clink glasses again just as the doorbell rings.

"Must be the pizza," he calls as he rises and goes to the door.

He pauses to look through the peephole. "Wait. It's some guy without a pie," he says. "Do you have someone coming over?"

Before I can say, "Let me see who it is," Jasper swings open the door.

As my eyes adjust to the light, I am struck by the figure standing before me.

Tomas.

My heart races, and my palms sweat at the sight of him. Dressed in crisp white linen and tailored slacks, he looks like he just walked off a beach.

We first met at a photo shoot. I was there to do a lipstick layout, and he was just the hot guy in the background. Afterward, he followed me out of the studio and onto the street and begged for my number. I'd been working as a model since I was fifteen. I was such an innocent. I'd barely dated. I'd never made a lot of friends. Most of my time was spent with my gran and Emmy and Andrew.

I wasn't interested in love. But he was full of life. And so dreamy.

He's tall and lean, his physique more like a runner's than a football player's. His dark hair is styled carefully, and his face has matured, his jawline more rugged—not surprising since he's five years older than me.

"Wait. Are you Jasper, the quarterback?" he stammers as he drops my gaze and glances at the football player.

Jasper nods. "And you are?"

Tomas's eyes shift between Jasper and me, surprise flickering on his face. "I'm Tomas. I'm here to see Jane." His eyes drift over my face, lingering. His face softens. "Hi. It's been a while."

Just "hi"? The sheer ridiculousness of him being at my door makes anger rise to the surface like a volcano. I can't even speak.

He shifts his feet. "I tried calling a few times today, but no one ever answered. I went to your old address, but someone else lives there, so I got your new one from an old friend. I'm back in town for a bit."

Jasper subtly positions himself beside me and casually drapes an arm around my shoulders. "It's late to be coming over."

Tomas's eyes flicker to Jasper's arm around my shoulders. "Yeah, I know. I didn't realize how late it was until I got here. I'm still on LA time, I guess. I just . . . I wanted to talk to Jane."

Jasper's grip on my shoulder tightens, his protective instinct kicking in. "She's a little busy," Jasper replies. "With me."

Tomas's gaze shifts between us again. "I didn't mean to interrupt anything. I'm sorry. I'm flying back to LA tomorrow, and I really wanted to touch base."

"I'm surprised to see you. It's been five years," I finally say as I smile bitterly. I lean into Jasper. An instinct, maybe. Or perhaps I just needed someone to keep me from falling down.

He nods, guilt written all over his face. "I just wanted to clear the air, I guess."

Clear the air? I frown at him. "About what?"

"Savannah—that's my fiancée—we sent out save-the-date invitations, and some emails were accidentally included, so . . ." He trails off awkwardly.

"Oh, I understand. Ex-girlfriends or baby mamas weren't supposed to be on the guest list," I say.

Tomas's face reddens. "I'm sure you didn't want to come anyway."

"No, I definitely don't," I reply coldly. "But congratulations. I never thought you'd commit to anyone."

"Right," he mumbles sheepishly.

"You could have just texted me, Tomas. That would have avoided this whole awkward situation," I say, unable to hide the edge in my voice.

He runs a hand through his hair in frustration, but it falls back perfectly in place. "I know, but I'd like to catch up soon. I'll be back and forth from LA to New York this summer since I'm on hiatus, and I'd like to see you when I'm here. Regardless of the accidental invitation, I've been wanting to talk to you."

I stiffen, and Jasper must feel it because he slides a hand under my hair at the nape of my neck. "You're okay, angel," he says in my ear before turning to face Tomas.

The realization hits me that Tomas is the one who has been calling me repeatedly. My throat tightens at the thought of what he might want to speak to me about.

Does he want to see Londyn? My heart aches at the thought.

"We have nothing left to discuss, Tomas," I say firmly, my hands clenching at my sides in an attempt to contain my emotions.

A flash of determination crosses his face. "We do. Please. Just let me say what I need to. I'll text you the next time I'm in town."

"Do whatever you want. You always have," I say as I slam the door shut, my chest rising and falling rapidly as I try to process everything that just happened.

Jasper's hand strokes the back of my neck. "Is he . . . ," he begins hesitantly, then continues, "Londyn's dad?"

"The one who left us."

He turns me to face him and tilts my chin up. Blue eyes stare into mine for a long time. "And he's getting married? Shit. You wanna talk about it, angel?"

My lips tremble at his show of gentleness. "I want another glass of wine."

He nods, then kisses me on the forehead, a friend-to-friend gesture. "Done. You go sit, and I'll open a new bottle."

I stumble toward the living room, my mind still reeling. The weight of the revelation settles heavily on my chest, memories flooding back like a wave crashing against the shore. It has been years since I last saw him, but the wounds are as fresh as if they never healed.

As I sink into the comfy couch, the fabric slightly sticking to my clammy skin, I catch a glimpse of Londyn's picture on the mantelpiece. The dimples in her cheeks taunt me, a reminder of the trait she shares with Tomas.

Jasper returns with a freshly opened bottle of wine, his eyes filled with concern as he hands me a glass. The aroma fills my senses, and I take a long sip.

He settles beside me on the couch and wraps his arm around my shoulder. I lean into his warmth, relaxing in the steady rhythm of his breath.

For a while, we sit in silence, the only sound filling the room being the distant hum of New York traffic. Jasper's hand finds mine, and he intertwines our fingers.

I glance down, momentarily taken aback, but then I relax. It's Jasper. He would hold anyone's hand who'd just had her ex show up at her door.

"Thank you," I murmur, not quite meeting his eyes. "Tomas was everything to me once. Young love, you know?" I set my glass on the coffee table. "I thought it would last forever, and he made me feel like the center of his world."

"Your first boyfriend?"

I nod. "I'd never dated. I was too focused on making money for the family. Gran was sick, and Emmy was going to school and working and taking care of us. Andrew was just a kid." I glance at him. "You know how we grew up, right?"

He nods. "Graham mentioned that your mom was a victim of domestic abuse and she shot and killed your dad when you were a toddler."

My throat tightens. "Then she left. Just up and moved away and told Gran to raise us. Emmy became my mom as best she could."

"Why do you think Tomas showed up here?"

I shake my head. "No clue. When I told him I was pregnant, he panicked. Said he wasn't ready. He left for LA a few months later, and that was it. He chose his dreams over us."

"He never tried to reach out or see her?" Jasper's voice is soft.

"Never. I sent him a photo of her after she was born, but he never replied. And now, suddenly he wants to talk? Why? What does he want after all this time?"

"Jesus, what an asshole, but listen, you don't have to figure it out tonight. But whatever it is, you're not alone. You've got Emmy and Graham and Andrew. You have good people to depend on."

His words crack the dam I've built around my emotions. "I really miss my sister. I know she has Graham and a new baby, but she's been part of my life for so long." A tear slips down my cheek, and Jasper's thumb brushes it away gently.

"Ah, angel."

"Sorry. Ignore the tears. I'm just scared of what he might want."

Jasper's grip on my hand tightens. "Whatever he wants, I'll make sure you don't get hurt."

How does he do that? How does he manage to say exactly what I need to hear?

I sink into his body, the warmth of his hand enveloping mine like a promise. It's strange, this feeling of safety he conjures. For so long, I've been the one to fend off the world, a lone warrior protecting Londyn and myself. And now, here's Jasper, offering his strength as if it's the most natural thing in the world.

It's okay to be vulnerable. It's okay to lean on someone else for a change.

The fear of what Tomas's return could mean for Londyn sends a shiver down my spine. The thought of losing her, of facing a battle I never wanted, is terrifying.

And yet, with Jasper's hand in mine . . .

I take a deep breath. "You're right," I say, my voice steadier. "I won't let him, but legally, he has a right to her."

"Focus on the now," Jasper says, and I gaze at him.

"What do you mean?"

"It's something my adoptive dad used to say whenever I got confused, which was a lot growing up. He always told me that my family had my back. Always. Things might get scary, we might have ups and downs, but we had each other. You have that too. And me. I'm your friend," he says gently. "Plus you have your Wilbur-the-pig stuffed animal. Want me to go get him for you?"

I shake my head, wondering how he knew that, and I guess it's one of those things Graham must have mentioned. I smile. *Charlotte's Web* was my favorite book growing up, and whenever I felt sad or scared,

I always held Wilbur. "It's in my room, and Londyn is asleep, so you don't—"

"I'll be quiet," he says. "I'm known for my stealth." He rises from the couch, a small grin on his face, and disappears into the hallway.

Moments later, he returns, holding Wilbur in his outstretched hand like a cherished treasure. His eyes meet mine as he gently places the worn-out stuffed animal in my lap, its soft fabric bringing back memories of simpler times.

I run my fingers over the faded fur. "Thank you," I whisper, my voice filled with gratitude. "I'm glad you were here."

"Come here." He pulls me close to him, and I lean my head on his shoulder. He twirls a piece of my hair around his fingers. Warmth spreads, maybe from his closeness, or the wine, but I don't really care because I just want to forget that Tomas showed up at my door, that I'm still single and lonely, while he is getting married.

I tilt my head up at Jasper, and he smiles. "You okay?"

I shake my head. "I'm repulsive, but would you kiss me? I haven't had a real one in about five years."

He looks startled. "Okay, the repulsive thing was a joke, and five years? What the fuck?"

"Scared you won't be worth it?"

His eyes search my face. "Not in the least, angel. Are you sure? I mean, I'm me and you're you. We don't really like each other. Right?"

I feel a blush rising up in my cheeks.

Did I really just ask Jasper for a kiss?

Who am I?

"True, but I have to start somewhere. At the bottom feels right."

He laughs, studying my face. "There she is. My favorite. Jane with the scowl. Let's see if I can make it disappear."

"Wha—"

Before I can finish, he leans in and takes my mouth.

Oh, why are my palms sweating?

Can lips sweat too? Is that a thing?

He cups my face with both hands and stares down at me.

Our breaths mingle as we share the same pocket of air. He leans in, his eyes locked onto mine, and the world around us fades. His lips meet mine in a slow, oh-so-gentle kiss, like the unfolding of flowers. The warmth of his mouth envelops me, sending waves of sensation through my body. And as our lips reluctantly part, I yearn for more.

My brain, usually an endless stream of to-do lists, goes blissfully blank. All I can think is, Wow, why did I wait five years?

He strokes my cheek, then leans in again, this one deeper, and I'm fully here for it, leaning into his chest as my hands wrap around his neck. The world narrows down to his lips on mine, and the realization that I've been missing out for a damn long time.

"Good enough?" he asks huskily as he gazes down at me.

"Terrible. Hated the whole thing."

"Angel, you're making my heart flutter, being mean. I kind of like it, so stop it."

I touch the curve of his bottom lip, grazing my thumb over the lush lines. "Sorry?"

He chuckles, the sound rumbling in his chest as he comes closer. This time, the kiss is filled with a hunger, a desire that ignites fire inside me.

We pull away, both of us breathing heavily. I can see a flicker of uncertainty in Jasper's eyes. "I didn't mean to rush into things. You're feeling vulnerable. I can't take advantage of that."

I tug his face to mine. "I want you to."

His eyes widen in surprise, searching my face for any signs of doubt or hesitation. But all he finds is desire. He leans in again, his lips claiming mine with a renewed intensity, as if he's been waiting for this moment.

I work the buttons on his dress shirt. One by one, they give way under my trembling fingers, revealing the expanse of his bare chest. My hands trace the contours of his defined muscles, feeling the warmth of his skin beneath my touch. He groans into the kiss, his hands sliding down to the small of my back, pulling me closer against him.

His chest ripples with muscles and strength. It's broad and defined, his pecs bulging with each movement. Veins run along his arms, showcasing his dedication to his training.

My head dips as I taste his neck. I move down, my tongue flicking against his nipple, inhaling the heady smell of his cologne. I watch how his chest rises and falls with each breath. A hot man in his prime is right in front of me.

His touch is gentle, his hands leaving trails of heat along my skin as they wander down my back and come to rest on my hips.

We kiss, oh god, we kiss and kiss. It's everything I've missed. Everything.

It might stop at any moment, and I don't want it to. The thought makes me desperate. I run my fingers through his hair, tugging on his bun, making him groan.

He slips his hand under my tank top and cups my breast. His fingers circle around my sensitive skin until finally he tugs on my nipple. My head falls back as a jolt of heat goes straight to my core.

His lips find my neck, his breath warm against my skin. His hand moves down, sliding over my waist and coming to rest on the edge of my sleep shorts. He grips them tightly, pulling me toward him.

He eases me up until I'm sitting on top of him on the couch, straddling him.

"Maybe we should slow down," he says as he holds my face, his eyes searching mine.

"No." I grind on him. His head falls back on the couch, blue eyes dilated and blown.

"I know what you need, angel." He eases me onto the couch, pushing me against the back of it as he lies down next to me. "Just hang on."

He kisses me as his hand slips under my shorts and toys with the waistband of my panties.

As his fingers trace the edge of the fabric, my breath quickens. Desire blooms deeper.

Jasper's hands are everywhere, tracing the curves of my body, exploring every inch of me as if he's committing it all to memory.

"You're so beautiful," he murmurs, his breath hot against my skin.

I close my eyes and let myself be lost in the moment.

A finger glides inside my panties.

I arch my back, moaning softly into his mouth as his finger slides in and out of me. The sensation is so overwhelming.

"Do you like that?"

"Yes," I say, "I love it."

His finger moves faster, his thumb rolling my clit in small, circular motions. The sensations build, spiraling into a vortex of pleasure that seems to consume me.

Just as I think I can't take any more, he adds another finger. He toys with my nub, playing with it with the pad of his hand as he fingers me. My back arches off the couch.

"I'm going to come, but I don't want to," I tell him, with my face in his throat, and he eases up, removing his hand to cup my ass and knead it. I mewl out my disappointment, and he chuckles in my ear.

"You can't make up your mind. Want me to do it again?"

"Yes."

He slides his hand back between my legs, and I feel his fingers graze my wetness. He brushes my clit and begins to stroke it. The man has magic fingers. He's got me. I am lost.

His eyes watch my face as my breaths become more ragged. His fingers don't stop moving.

"I want to taste you," he says softly, his lips brushing against mine. He bites down on my bottom lip, and I moan as I close my eyes and nod.

He moves down my body, his fingers dancing over my stomach and past my waistband. He pulls my sleep shorts down just enough to reveal my pussy.

He blows over my wetness, his breath sending shivers down my spine. The anticipation of his mouth on me is almost too much to handle. He licks gently along the length of my skin, tasting me.

My hips buck upward, seeking more of his attention. He chuckles softly, then dances his tongue over me. I gasp, my hands tangling in his hair as I try to hold on.

He circles my clit in maddening strokes. I feel myself getting closer and closer. He moves faster, one hand digging into my thighs to hold me down.

It's only been less than a minute and I . . .

"I'm going to come," I say, my voice shaking with the intensity of the pleasure building.

He smiles against my skin, then licks me again, his fingers delving deep inside me. I cry out as fireworks detonate. My hips convulse, my core spasming as the sensations explode inside my body.

As I float back down to earth, his lips press against my inner thigh, his warm breath fanning over my skin. I reach down and touch his hair, pulling him up to kiss him, tasting myself on his lips.

"Thank you," I murmur.

"You're welcome."

A blush rises up my cheeks.

He smirks. "Feeling shy now? Too late, angel. I saw everything. All the parts. And the carpet matches the drapes."

I groan in embarrassment, and he just laughs. We're lying face to face, and it's more male contact than I'm used to. Gah. What do I do next? Should we lie here and chitchat? Should I say something about the weather?

He must be a mind reader. He grabs a pillow and positions it for me to rest my head on. "Relax. It's okay. Nothing bad happened. We just played around."

I know that, but still.

I swallow. "Um, thank you?"

His touch is gentle as he moves my hair out of my face. "I'm here to help."

I frown. "No, I mean, it wasn't like that. I didn't, I mean, I wanted . . ." My words trail off. "I don't want to be your pity project. I don't want you to feel used either."

"Hey, let it go. We kissed. I wanted it. You wanted it. Let it go. Just be in the moment."

"You wanted to kiss me?"

"Just go back to being 'mean Jane.'" He pokes me in the arm.

Oh, wait a minute, is he feeling shy too?

I clear my throat. "What are we going to do now? Just watch TV or something? More tarot cards?"

"TV."

"Okay," I say finally, a small smile tugging at the corners of my lips.

The doorbell rings, and we both look at each other. He laughs. "I forgot about the pizza. I'll get it." He rises up and stretches, and I can't help but watch him move through my apartment like it's his house. There's something about him, shirtless and in dress pants, that's utterly captivating. The way his muscles shift under his skin with each step, the relaxed confidence in his stride—it's a sight that etches itself into my memory. A mental snapshot I know I'll revisit more times than I care to admit.

But even as my heart races and my mind replays him kissing me, touching me, a sobering thought pushes its way through.

It's not just about the professional boundaries I've crossed. It's about the complexities he brings. He's a famous football player, a public figure, and I'm, well, just Jane. I'm not exactly a football-loving woman who adores him.

He returns with the pizza, napkins, and two bottles of water.

I chew on my lips. This moment between us was just a moment. Part of me wishes things could be different, but I have more than just my own heart to protect. I have Londyn.

I glance at him, his profile lit by the glow of the lamp. There's a part of me that wants to lean over, close the gap, and feel his lips against mine again. But there's another voice in my head that reminds me of my responsibilities.

"Jasper," I say, my voice unsure, "this, um, what happened, I shouldn't have . . ."

He gives me a wry look. "I knew you'd say that. It took you longer than I expected actually. Okay, whatever. Let's find something good to watch," he says, sprawling on the couch next to me and flipping through channels. "How about something with real bite? Like a vampire movie?"

I groan. "Really?"

He chuckles. "They're folklore. I dig the tragic vibe. Vampires have style. Romania is a cool place. It's on my bucket list to go there."

"Are you a *Twilight* fan too?"

He pretends to be offended as he flips through the channels. "What about *Interview with a Vampire*? A classic."

I scoff, nudging him with my foot. "Your taste in movies sucks. See what I did there?"

He grins. "Fine, if not vampires, then what?"

"Anything." I just want him to watch the television instead of looking at me because all I'm thinking about is how he had me at his mercy.

He laughs, settling on a Formula One reality show. "All right, you win since your spaghetti was a masterpiece. But next time, it's my choice."

Next time?

Butterflies take off in my stomach, and I squash them down. "Deal."

See? Everything seems fine. We're fine. Totally. Absolutely. We are back to normal.

Okay, Jane, act normal. Because nothing says "just friends" like making out with New York's most eligible quarterback, then casually chowing down on pizza like two buddies.

Yep, this is totally how all platonic friends spend their Saturdays, isn't it? Next, we'll be braiding each other's hair and talking about our feelings. Oh, wait I already spilled my guts about Tomas.

I steal a glance at Jasper, who seems engrossed in the race. Or at least, he's doing a better job of pretending everything's normal than I am.

How can he just sit there, all calm and collected?

"Good show," I say, desperately trying to find something, anything, to talk about that doesn't involve the first man-sponsored orgasm I've had in ages.

"Yep," Jasper replies, not taking his focus off the screen. Ah, yes, the sound of two people tiptoeing around the elephant in the room.

I focus on my pizza, but even that feels weird now. Like, is there a certain way to eat pizza postorgasm? Should I be dainty? Take smaller bites?

The silence stretches on, filled with the revving of engines from the TV and my increasingly ridiculous thoughts. I chance another look at Jasper. He's relaxed, at ease, the complete opposite of my internal meltdown. How does he do it? Did he take a class on post-finger-banging composure?

Jasper turns to me, his smile making my chest tighten. "Good race, huh?"

"Yeah, the way those cars just . . . raced," I say, nodding sagely. Because clearly, I'm now an expert on all things that involve speed and not getting caught up in feelings.

Later, when he leaves and I follow him to the door, I lean against the wall and watch him button his shirt back up, then put on his jacket. With a small wave, he tells me bye, and then he's gone. The apartment is silent. So silent.

And just when I think worries about Tomas will intrude and keep me up, when I crawl into bed, it's Jasper I'm thinking about.

I close my eyes, trying to push away the thoughts. But every time I try to escape, his image resurfaces, his touch still lingering on my lips. I knew this would happen, that allowing myself to be vulnerable would only complicate things further.

Yet, part of me yearns for the forbidden.

As I lie there, tangled in a mess of sheets and emotions, memories of us kissing flood back. The way his hands felt against my skin, the intensity in his eyes. Ugh.

My mind drifts to Londyn. She deserves a stable life without complications.

And Jasper? He's one big headache just waiting to happen.

Chapter 10

JASPER

I stride into a diner near the training facility, but I'm not here for the usual postpractice bite. I'm here to confront a ghost.

Anxiety spikes as I scan the room, and my throat prickles with emotion when I finally see her at a booth next to the window. My biological mother, the woman who left me over pancakes at a truck stop. I recall how good they tasted, the syrup and butter mixed together. I recall the terror of realizing she'd left me there alone. I didn't speak for three months afterward. At first, my social worker assumed I was mute from birth. It took weeks of therapy to get me to start talking. My silence came from a place of deep pain. I'd watched her talking to a man outside the truck stop, then watched as she got inside his truck. I'd watched her drive away from me.

I try to relax, rolling my neck back and forth.

Initially I resisted texting her.

But I haven't been sleeping well. My mind is fuzzy.

Memories of her hit me in odd moments—when I lift weights, when I watch TV, when I take a shower.

What if there's more to her story?

What if understanding her reasons gives me a peace I hadn't realized I needed?

It's answers. I need to hear her say the words of why she abandoned me. Closure, maybe. A way to quiet the curiosity since I found that note.

After all, her blood runs through my veins. She has made me who I am today, whether it's indirectly or not. She's left blanks in my life, and I need to fill them in.

I have to know why.

I take a deep breath, grounding myself, before making my way toward her booth. Her eyes meet mine as I approach, and I glimpse the flicker of recognition in her gaze. A trace of remorse brushes across her face, but it quickly fades into nervousness.

She looks at me intently, maybe looking for traces of the little kid she left behind all those years ago.

"Sunflower?" I ask as I approach.

She blinks up at me, her eyes the same clear blue as mine. "Jasper," she says with a hint of a smile. "Hi. I go by Rae-Anne now."

I sit across from her. All my rehearsed words vanish.

She's pretty, with faded auburn hair and a face that looks fuller than the one I remember. She's wearing jeans and a flowy shirt. My gaze falls to the silver band on her finger. Not Dad's ring. He died when I was a baby. Who is she now?

"Thanks for meeting me," she says quietly. "It's hard to approach a star athlete. I hope me leaving the note was okay."

It really wasn't. She had to somehow drive past the guard at the front of the lot. Maybe she slipped in while he was doing something else. It makes me wonder how desperate she is. I nod. "It's been a while."

She fiddles with a napkin. "I saw you play a game once in high school. I drove all the way to Utah from Kansas. That's where I ended up for a few years."

My hands clench. She came to a game.

"Why not come up to me? Why stay gone all this time?"

She looks down at the table. "I lost my nerve. I didn't deserve to be around you after what happened. Call me 'mom.' Please. If you want. Sorry. Maybe that's too much."

I grit my teeth. "Yeah, my mom's Paulina. Elijah's my dad. Nothing you do can spoil that."

She shreds the napkin. "Of course. I don't want to. I'm here now. Ask me anything."

"Fine, why'd you leave me?"

She nods, clearly expecting the question. "I didn't leave you. I escaped. I made sure you escaped too. It wasn't safe for us there. It was planned actually. It was the only way to get you away from Harry and his people."

"You mean the cult?" Harry was their leader, a bearded man who wore a robe like a monk.

She nods, eyes downcast. "I planned to return for you. Do you remember the compound?"

The images rush back, of barbed wire fences, dead-eyed followers, and extensive greenhouses. I remember we grew pot and we'd load it onto trucks every week. Who knows what else he was doing inside some of those buildings. There were probably other drugs too. Harry preached about living off the land and getting away from material things, when in the end, he was reaping major profits.

I remember her, too, the way she held my hand when we'd walk through the redwood trees of Northern California, the silly songs she'd sing. I pack that memory away.

She reaches out, her hands shaking. I stick mine under the table.

"I understand if you don't trust me," she says. "But, please, just hear me out."

I pull my hands out from under the table and meet her gaze. "I recall Harry was your boyfriend, right? He was always around us." I didn't like him, and he pretty much ignored me. I can't recall a single time he ever said my name. He just called me "you."

She takes a deep breath, seeming to gather her thoughts before speaking. "Harry wasn't who he claimed to be. He manipulated us all. The compound was nothing but a cover. The local police were already investigating him, but I escaped with you."

"I see." So she left before the hammer fell down on Harry.

"I'm sorry," she says as a tear falls down her cheek. "Leaving you was my biggest regret."

Her words float in the charged air. I study her face for lies, but all I see is sadness. Her shoulders tremble as she sobs, and I find myself handing her napkins, a reflex.

"I never meant to leave you," she says. "I was terrified. For me, for you. I took you to that truck stop, praying I'd find help. I called the cops before I left and told them where you were. Then I hitched a ride to Kansas to some friends."

"Why not take me?"

She swallows hard. "I thought I could escape, clear my head, then come back."

"But you didn't."

It takes her a few moments to reply, as if she doesn't really want to tell me. "I fell in love," she admits, her voice barely audible. "I met someone, and things changed."

I can't help the bitter laugh that escapes.

She nods, guilt on her face. "Please, I'm sorry for not coming back. I have another family now, Jasper—a husband and a son. We live in Philly."

Her confession hits me like a gut punch. Abandoned for a new life, a new family.

"Happy ending for you, then."

The diner feels smaller, the air thicker. Her pain, her excuses, they don't change a thing. They don't fill the hurt she left inside me.

As the waitress approaches, I avert my gaze from Rae-Anne. We each order coffee, silence stretching between us. My adoptive parents filled in some blanks when I was older, and I scoured the internet as a teen. Harry and his group got busted for drug trafficking about a year after I was found.

The coffee lands on our table, and I'm just sitting there, watching Rae-Anne mechanically open a sugar packet.

I shake my head. "You could've reached out. I even wondered if you were dead."

"The cops were after me for other stuff. It was safer for you, not being with me." Her voice is low. "I'm different now. I go to PTA meetings and work as a receptionist where my husband works, at a construction company."

"So why did you write the note?" I ask.

Her smile is faint. "I feel like I earned the chance to see you now."

I swallow, wishing I could get up and leave.

I don't agree with her.

I'm not sure I believe her.

She could have come back for me.

The pain of her leaving is still raw, but there's a tiny part of me, the kid in me, who really wants to find something in her that makes the pain vanish.

I take a deep breath, willing myself to stay composed.

"There's not another reason you wanted to see me?" I ask.

She hesitates, her eyes tracing the tablecloth as if searching for the right words. "I know I can't undo the past or the hurt I've caused," she says softly. "But I spent years reflecting on my choices and how they affected you. I'd like us to get to know each other."

I tap my finger on the table. I'm not an idiot. It's been all over the news about my new contract with the Pythons. This could be about money.

"I realized that I've been running away from meeting you," she says. "I thought leaving was the answer then, but maybe it was a mistake. I was only twenty-five."

I inhale a sharp breath as a realization dawns.

She left me at the same age as Jane is now.

The difference between them is unbelievable. Jane, who is good and kind and devoted to Londyn, and then there's Rae-Anne, who dumped me and went off to start a new family.

The diner door swings open, and Dalton steps in, heading straight to the counter for a to-go order. Desperate for an escape, I seize the moment. "Talley! Hey! Over here, man."

He looks up, sees me, and frowns. Yeah, our relationship is still on thin ice. We've had a couple of meetings where we watched tape with Pete.

Juggling his takeout, he approaches, his expression irritated. I don't give him a chance to speak.

"Where were you?" I blurt, feigning frustration. "We were supposed to go over game tapes. You bailed. What gives?"

He starts to respond. "Hang on a damn—"

I cut him off. "Forget it. Let's just go. You've got your food. No breaks for us, right? This is the grind."

I stand up quickly, signaling the waitress. I point to our table, miming, "Check please."

Rae-Anne's voice trembles. "Jasper, when can we meet again? I have so much more to tell you."

I avoid her eyes, my gut twisting. "I've got your number. We'll talk later," I say.

She looks like she wants to argue, but I'm already moving. I hand the waitress a fifty. "This covers everything. Keep the change," I say in a mumble.

As Dalton and I step out of the diner, he nudges me, his frustration palpable. "What's with the act back there? You've been icing me out, and suddenly we're pals in public?"

Maybe. But he was the jerk first.

"It's complicated." I sigh, not ready to dive into the heart of it.

His gaze drifts past me, landing on Rae-Anne's profile by the window. "Her? Your mom?"

"Bio mother," I correct. "Look, let's not do this here. Carson's?" I suggest, a tentative olive branch.

"Didn't think I was your kind of company."

I manage a half smile. "Maybe we both need a change of scenery."

Reluctantly, he agrees. "All right, I'll follow you."

At Carson's, the bar's dim light and the murmur of conversations offer a semblance of normalcy. I push away the conversation with Rae-Anne as we settle onto our barstools.

"What went down at the diner?" he asks, his curiosity not quite casual.

I give him the CliffsNotes—my mom, my real parents, the silence of years. He listens, his expression neutral, giving me the space to just talk.

I swirl my beer, the weight of Rae-Anne heavy in my gut. "No clue what she's after. Money, redemption, a kidney. It's all a guess."

"Sucks, man."

I pause. "And about the day we met. We're in this season together. Time to act like it. Let's start fresh. What do you think?"

He winces. "Yeah, about that. I've been a bit of a jerk. Pete's been pushing hard, and well, my ex chose that day to walk. I'm from a small town in Texas, and now I'm living in a big city. I don't know anyone." He stares down at his beer. "I'm not exactly a people person. It sort of feels like everyone is watching and judging me to make sure I live up to the hype, you know?"

I study the lines of his face. Man, he's just a kid. He's barely twenty-two. "It's a big change, I get it, but you'll find your footing, both on the team and in the city. I'm always around if you need an ear. Work together, yeah?"

"Deal," he says, a lopsided grin breaking through. "And just so you know, I'm not after your spot. Not this season, anyway."

We laugh, our glasses meeting.

Later, we move to the pinball machine, and he's found some of his cockiness. "Show me what you've got, old man."

He's surprisingly good, but not quite good enough. "Looks like I got played," he says after I take my turn and blow his score away.

"Double or nothing, rookie?"

"You're on," he shoots back with a grin.

It's been over a week since the Jane Orgasm. That's what I've dubbed it in my head, because it's too monumental to be just another night. It feels like forever since I've seen her, but she's been in contact with me over texting for another match. Maybe it feels like it's been so long because so much has happened. I met my bio mom and connected with Dalton.

Then, last night, with encouragement from Jane, I met up for a date with my second match.

It sucked.

Now here I am, hood up, sprinting through a downpour after my training session. Destination: the Darling Bookstore.

I push through, and the door chimes as I step in. Water trails from my soaked hoodie, dripping from my nose to my gray shorts.

I glance upward, admiring the high ceiling and fancy molding. My eyes are drawn to the staircase in the center, its wood steps polished. Past the stairs, the café buzzes with quiet activity.

The tranquility makes me want to let out a yell, just for the fun of breaking the silence.

"Jasper is in the house," I say under my breath as I wipe rain from my eyes.

"Can I help you?" calls a voice, and I squint and spot Babs, grinning like she's in on a joke. I've always liked her vibe.

"Hey, Babs," I say with a wave. "Jane around?"

She gives a subtle glance to the side. Then, from behind an aisle, a walking fortress of books emerges, unmistakably Jane by the long legs. As she peeks around her load, it starts to topple and I lunge forward, catching a couple of novels before they hit the ground. The rest tumble down and thud against my shins.

"Ow, dammit," I groan, rubbing my leg. "That's one way to make an entrance."

She blinks up at me and says an "I'm sorry," then stares in disgust at the mess at our feet. She stoops to pick them up, and I can't help but notice the oversize men's blue dress shirt she's wearing, belted at the waist and paired with heels. Hot.

Our eyes meet, and there's this electric jolt, a silent reminder of what went down between us.

I squat to help her with the books. "Sorry about the mess."

Her cheeks flush pink, and her eyes dart everywhere but at me. Ah, she's still feeling shy. "It's fine. Just watch the water. Stand back, will you?"

I raise my hands and back away. Babs leans in, curiosity in her gaze. "Long time no see, Jasper."

I lean on the counter, trying to look casual. "Yeah, I guess you know that Jane convinced me to join Cupid's Arrow. I'm their star client. But these dates she picks? Yikes."

Jane bristles as she brushes down her dress. "As if. You practically begged to join. And what was wrong with Melinda?"

Melinda being the date I had last night.

I shoot Jane a look, my gaze lingering on the way her hair falls around her shoulders. It's a pretty color, a soft honey blond with lighter shades mixed in. It frames her oval face and contrasts with the forest green of her eyes.

Those eyes were soaked in desire when I made her come.

I shake the memory away. It's weird, you know? One minute you're just kinda sorta friends, and the next, there's this image of her burned into your brain, an image you're not supposed to think about but do. The way her hands clung to me, the sound she made when she came, the vanilla scent of her skin—

Focus, Jasper.

Forget Jane and her scowly Jane-ness that makes her irresistible. She's clearly not interested. Otherwise why would she immediately set me up on another date *after* the orgasm?

I clear my throat. "Melinda likes to write poetry."

Jane nods. "Right. And you minored in poetry. It says so on your application. The database loved you guys together."

"I don't like *bad* poetry," I mutter. "The database had it wrong,"

She moves past me and gets behind the counter and angles the screen toward me. "Melinda even wrote a glowing review. Don't worry. I'm the only one who has access to these. It helps me make better matches. Stop glaring at me and read it."

I look at the screen.

> Two worlds colliding, the stars aligning . . . I never thought I could find a perfect guy through a dating service, but I am absolutely bewitched, body and soul, by the most incredible person. Plus I love football. Thank you for matching me with Jasper! Oh, and the poetry themed wine bar was a great hit. Thanks for the recommendation, Jane.

My eyes go to the ceiling. There's a water stain up there that's more exciting.

Fine, Melinda loves football, points to Jane, but mostly she talked about how she'd redesign the uniforms with sequins. Yes, she is gorgeous. Yes, she likes poetry. But it just didn't work.

"That," I say, pointing at the screen, "is exactly the problem. She seemed cool at first, but then writes something like that? She's living in a fantasy."

"You're mad at me?" Jane puts her hands on her hips.

A little.

Because I was bored to tears on the date.

Because all I could think about was Jane while Melinda sat across from me.

"Are you taking my matches seriously?"

She nods. "I am. Truly. Melinda and I, we used to model together, and I've always thought she was great. How was the poetry-themed wine bar? I've heard good things about it."

I grunt. "It wasn't my scene. Very dark and moody."

She exhales. "Okay, I'll make a note of that."

"She made up a poem about me, you know. *Jasper, my gridiron king, In my heart, I wear your Super Bowl ring.*"

Jane bites her lip. "Really? Like she got up on stage?"

"Yeah. It's not funny," I say. "And I never should have given her my digits. She's been sending me little snippets all day. I might have to change my number." I shove my phone under Jane's nose and point out the last text she sent: You are the soft squishy center of my coconut.

Jane's lips twitch, but before she can break out in a smile, I glare at her.

She rubs her temples, her face drawn in concentration. "Okay, I get what you're saying. You just didn't connect with her. I mean, it's a cute little . . . metaphor? Not quite a poem there. Maybe if you'd known her better, it wouldn't seem so weird. But this is why people date, to find the right person. I'll let her know that it didn't work for you and to stop texting." She types on her computer. "Let me just make some tweaks to your data and update your profile . . ."

She talks under her breath for a moment, then sighs and turns the computer to me. "I think I have someone. Erin. She's wonderful. The software gave you an eighty percent chance of forming a long-term relationship with her."

I don't even look at the computer. "Uh-huh, what was the percentage with Melinda?"

She winces. "Ninety percent."

I run a hand through my hair. "See, that's the issue. Compatibility isn't always about what you have in common. It's about spark."

She nods. "Right, but we have to start somewhere. I'm not giving up on you, Jasper. I'll find you someone."

I exhale, crossing my arms as frustration eats at me. Of course she thinks I'm frustrated because of Melinda, but that's not it at all. The truth is, Melinda was fun. Just not my kind of fun.

"Erin is super sweet," Jane says quietly as she studies my face. "I really like her as a person. Let's give it a shot, okay?"

I glance at the computer screen. There's a woman with long, light-brown hair who's wearing a tank top that shows off tanned arms and a nice rack. Her smile is a ten.

But Jane . . .

That night with her—god, it was something else. It was intense and completely unexpected. The kind of night that plays on a loop in my head.

But now, I'm struck by an overwhelming sense of . . . uncertainty? Regret? It's hard to say. Besides the blushing, she seems completely unfazed by it all, as if our hookup was just another Saturday for her. And maybe it was. Jane's not the type to get hung up on things, not like me.

Maybe I stepped over a line by letting our kiss get out of hand. We've always had this sort of push and pull dynamic, a weird frenemy relationship. Now I'm left wondering where we stand.

Are we friends who just happened to hook up?

Or has that night shifted something between us?

The weirdest part is, I'm not even sure what I want the answer to be. Part of me wants more. But then there's the rational side, the side that knows how complicated things could get. She doesn't do complications.

I'm struck by a sudden desire to pull her aside and ask, "What are we doing?" But I hold back.

Still.

It's like we're caught in each other's gravity.

I see how earnest she is to make her matchmaking business work. I want to help her. Even if it means going on another date.

But what does she want?

Dammit, maybe the truth is, I'm not sure I'm ready to find out.

"Fine," I grumble.

I watch as Jane's fingers fly over the keyboard, setting up what I'm already labeling as "The Date I'm Going on Because I Don't Know What Else to Do."

Jane looks up, her eyes bright. "Done! I'll let you know when Erin is free. You'll like her, Jasper. She's a lot of fun. Maybe this time we can do a daytime coffee date? Keep it short and sweet?"

"Sure," I mutter, trying to muster enthusiasm I don't feel. The truth is, no matter how fun or beautiful Erin might be, she's not Jane. And that's the problem.

I walk closer to the door, ready to leave, but hesitate.

"Jane," I start, turning back to face her. "I—"

She waits, her expression open and expectant.

Never mind. The words lodge in my throat, refusing to come out.

"Thanks for setting this up," I say lamely, hating how dumb it sounds. "I mean, you're right. You have to keep trying before you find someone. Thanks for letting me vent in person."

She nods, though there's a flicker of something in her eyes. Disappointment? Sadness? She quickly masks it with a professional smile. "Of course. I'm here to help."

We stare at each other, longer than is comfortable. I'm thinking about how different she is from Rae-Anne. How fierce she is when it comes to taking care of Londyn. She's the kind of woman you'd want by your side when life goes sideways, because you know she's gonna fight the battle with you. She's tenacious and vulnerable all at the same time. It's fucking sexy.

But I don't say any of those things.

I nod and tell her bye before heading out the door.

Chapter 11
JANE

On the morning of Erin's date with Jasper, I wake with dread in the pit of my stomach. It only gets worse as I go through the morning, getting Londyn ready, dropping her off at preschool. By the time I get to the bookstore to start my shift, I'm more worried than ever.

"Why do you look like you're about to throw up?" Babs asks me.

I groan. "Why do you think?"

She follows me out to the sales floor, where I turn on the lights and power up the register. "By the way you're freaking out, you'd think you're the one going on the date."

I sit down on the stool behind the counter and unpack a book delivery from yesterday. "I'm trying not to think about the fact that I set Jasper up with one of Londyn's preschool teachers."

Babs helps me stack the books on the counter.

I sigh. "It's someone I might run into. If this date goes south, it could be really awkward the next time I pick Londyn up." And if it goes well? How will I feel then? I shove those thoughts away.

Babs shrugs. "It's just coffee, right? Not even a real date."

I press my lips together. A lot can happen in a forty-five-minute, midday coffee meetup. Babs does not know the power of Jasper. He bewitches women. Even Abigail sent me an email after her date and told me how charming he was. Even though he wasn't a long-term prospect for her, she was impressed by the match and left a review on the website forum for others to read. She also said she'd enjoy having drinks with him again if he wanted.

Babs pats my shoulder. "Don't worry about it. You've spoken to her about him, right?"

"Yeah."

"What did she say? Is she a sports fan?"

"Huge, and yes, she's super excited."

Before I can get another word out, the door chimes and in walks a man. He's in his forties, sporting a mullet that's battling baldness on top. He pauses next to our foyer's old manual typewriter and caresses the keys with a dramatic flair, like he's channeling his inner Hemingway.

What really catches my eye is his attire. Despite the summer heat, he's wearing a long beige overcoat, and from what I can tell, that might be all. His legs are bare, and he's in flip-flops.

Babs leans over, her voice a conspiratorial whisper. "Are you thinking what I'm thinking?"

I nod, feeling a sense of impending doom.

"Flasher alert?" Babs asks.

I press my fingers against my temples, foreseeing the headache this day is going to bring. "Let's not jump to conclusions. Maybe he's just odd."

With glee, Babs eyes the direction the man goes. "Remember that guy last year? The one you chased down the street? Think it's him? Should we tail him? I've always wanted to be in a spy movie."

"Just stay on alert. DEFCON 1, Babs."

She nods, scanning the store like a hawk. "Ready. Operation Flasher is a go." She grabs the microphone we use to make store announcements.

"Ladies and gentlemen, attention please," she says over the speakers, her voice dripping with false cheerfulness. "Today, we'd like to welcome the NYPD to the Darling Bookstore. They're here to keep literature safe! What a wonderful group. We give them free coffee with every visit. Please say hello when you see them. Also, employees, we have a possible F in the store. I repeat, a possible F. Be alert, and thank you for shopping with us!"

F means "flasher."

Or it could mean "fucker."

It just depends on who has entered the building, according to Babs.

The announcement echoes through the bookstore, causing a few customers to glance around with raised eyebrows. The man in the trench coat pauses in his tracks, his head cocking as he looks around, maybe searching for a cop. He walks to the science fiction section and browses. Then he looks over at us, and even from several feet away, I see the gleam in his eyes.

"Babs? I don't think he's buying the NYPD. I think he's gonna do it," I mutter, starting to move from behind the counter, but she pushes me aside.

"You had your fun last time with the twig and berries. This one's on me. You can thank me later." She sounds like she's gearing up for a race.

I watch in amazement as she dashes toward the man just as his fingers start to fiddle with the buttons of his coat. I wince when I see his furry chest and big stomach.

"Stop it, motherfucker!" she yells, her voice echoing around the first floor.

The man's eyes widen in alarm, his hands freezing mid-unbutton, right at his crotch, as he backs away from her. Babs launches herself at him, tackling him to the ground. Books from the nearby shelf rain down around them.

I leave another employee at the counter as I jog over to them, hoping I can prevent anyone from seeing what's going on. I've got my phone out to dial for the police.

The man lets out a yelp as Babs pins him down. "Sir! No one wants to see your naughty bits! You are disgusting!"

The bookstore goes silent before a few customers erupt into cheers and applause. I guess subtlety is out the window now.

Trying to break free, the man wriggles around, eventually sliding out from under Babs. He scuttles away on his rear end, while I pray no one sees his genitals. He then leaps to his feet and dashes through the aisles. "You haven't seen the last of me!" he yells over his shoulder as he disappears out the door.

"And it's only ten in the morning," I muse.

Babs, unfazed, brushes herself off and checks her reflection in a pocket mirror. "Still got it," she says with sass as she smooths her hair back into place.

I can't contain a snort of laughter. The flasher is gross and terrible, sure, but in the world of retail, it's just another day.

She sashays back to the counter and grabs the microphone like a seasoned MC. "Attention, darlings! Code F is officially over. Our flasher has fled. As a token of our appreciation for your ordeal, please enjoy a complimentary pastry on us. Remember, at the Darling Bookstore, we protect your right to read in peace!"

I shake my head, chuckling. Only here would a flasher become an incident for a pastry giveaway.

Around lunchtime, I sling my heart-shaped purse over my shoulder, ready to dash out for a while.

Babs looks up from a summer-reads display. "Off to spread the word about Cupid's Arrow?" she asks, her tone light but eyes sharp.

"Yep."

"And where might that be?" Babs prods, leaning on the counter.

I glance at my phone, buying time. "Cool Beans," I say nonchalantly, pointing down the street. "They make great sandwiches."

Babs raises an eyebrow, a knowing look crossing her face. "Isn't that where Jasper's date with Erin is?"

I shrug, feigning indifference. "Coincidence."

But Babs isn't buying it. She strides over to me. "Jane Darling, are you planning to spy on Jasper's date?"

"Why would I do that?"

"Maybe because you two got a little too close recently?" she says, a playful smirk on her lips.

I let out a frustrated sigh, wishing I had kept that night to myself. "Okay, I may have influenced their meeting location, but it's only because I'm worried about my professional relationship with Erin."

Babs opens her mouth, no doubt ready to rip apart my excuse, but I'm already heading for the door. "I really have to go," I call over my shoulder, fleeing.

I step out onto the street. Am I really concerned about Erin, or am I just looking for an excuse to keep an eye on Jasper? The thought of him with someone else tightens something in my chest, a sensation I'm not ready to examine too closely.

Walking briskly toward Cool Beans, I tell myself it's all about protecting my business interests, but deep down, I can't shake the feeling that it's personal.

I slip into the coffee shop, the aroma of freshly ground coffee beans mingling with the scent of baked goods. It's a cute place with lots of bohemian charm. It's busy, but I manage to find a secluded spot in a little alcove. It's partially hidden by a decorative folding screen, offering me a place to observe without being seen.

Settling into the chair at the table, I pull out *Jane Eyre*. As I pretend to read Brontë's words, my gaze scans the entrance.

Erin walks in. Her long brown hair cascades over her shoulders, framing a face with striking blue eyes and a sweet smile. Today, she's the picture of casual grace, her movements poised yet relaxed. She has a degree in early-childhood education, and she's only twenty-three, yet there's a maturity about her I've always liked. Londyn adores her and must be disappointed the bestest-teacher-ever took a half day off today.

As Erin's gaze sweeps the room, likely searching for Jasper, I slink into the shadows behind the screen. But she's too preoccupied to notice my presence. I watch as she selects a table near the window.

From my nook, I have an unobstructed view of her table, a perfect spot to observe. My heart twinges with an emotion I can't quite place as I wait for him to arrive. The anticipation of watching them together is unsettling.

Ugh. I'm officially a creeper.

And why? Because, apparently, my orgasm with Jasper really got under my skin.

I mutter under my breath, "Is this what my life has come to?"

Why am I so invested in Jasper's date? The questions gnaw at me, but I push them aside. I remind myself this is about protecting my professional integrity, about ensuring Erin's experience with Cupid's Arrow is a positive one. But deep down, I know there's more to it than that.

Erin pulls out her phone and starts to scroll through it as a waitress comes up to her.

Erin glances my way, and I hold my breath for a good ten seconds, until she says something to the waitress and the waitress walks away.

I look up and realize that she was looking at the menu, which is on the wall right over my head. Whew.

Letting out a relieved breath, I'm about to turn to my book when the same waitress comes over to me. "Hi," she says, pen and pad at the ready. "What can I get you?"

But right at that moment, the door opens and Jasper walks in.

I forget to breathe, because he looks . . . well, perfect. He's wearing more than the gym clothes I saw him in last time. It's like he's making an actual effort, in slim jeans, casual loafers, and a tight-fitting T-shirt. He removes his sunglasses, scrapes a hand through his wayward hair, and I swear, every jaw in the place drops. It's such an entrance that I roll my eyes.

I want to hate him. I want to find something to dislike about him. But other than possessing more perfect DNA than any single human being should have, there isn't a damn thing. Sure, I give him a hard time, but it's my defense mechanism. I'm attracted to him. Who wouldn't be? It's nothing.

The clock on the wall above him says 12:00 p.m. exactly. He isn't even late. I watch closely as he catches sight of Erin. The corners of his eyes crinkle a little, and the smile that spreads across his face is genuine. Like he's really happy to be in her company. She stands up and gives him a hug, and why do I wish he'd greet me that way? I'm sure it must be amazing to feel those muscles, and I know he smells fantastic.

Focus, Jane.

He slides into the seat next to her, not across from her, without any hesitation, as if he wants to be extra close so he can really connect with her.

"Hello?" the waitress says, actually snapping her fingers in my face.

I forgot she was waiting for me to order. "Oh, um . . ."

"Your order?" she says, sounding annoyed.

"Hot tea and a chicken melt." The words come out in a low mumble. I don't want to call attention to myself.

"Huh?" She's louder now. "I can't hear you?"

At that moment, Jasper looks around for the waitress. His eyes sweep dangerously close to me.

I stiffen.

"Hello, lady?"

"Hot tea and a chicken melt," I say softly, punctuating every word.

"Swiss or provolone cheese?"

I don't answer, because I'm too busy trying to read lips.

She clears her throat.

"Surprise me," I hiss.

She lets out a huffing sound and heads off. I'll apologize with a big tip. Right now, I have work to do.

I watch as the two of them converse. It's easy, friendly. A little flirtatious, from the way she keeps giggling. I strain closer, wishing I could hear what they're talking about. At one point, she throws her head back and laughs, slapping the table.

Oh, yes, how droll. You're just so funny, Mr. Romeo.

My surveillance mission feels increasingly like self-inflicted torture. I can almost feel my blood pressure rising, irritation, and . . . jealousy?

No, can't be.

Then, disaster strikes. As the waitress delivers Erin's coffee, Jasper glances around the café and his eyes lock onto mine. In a panic, I hoist my copy of *Jane Eyre* like a protective barrier. Really smooth.

Peeking over the top of my book a moment later, I see that Jasper has turned his attention back to Erin. But now, he's holding her hand on the table, his thumb tenderly stroking her skin. My jaw drops slightly.

Hand-holding? Already? They've barely been here fifteen minutes!

The sight sends a jolt through me, and I find myself grumbling under my breath, "Damn bewitcher." The words slip out louder than intended, drawing a curious glance from a nearby patron.

I sink back into my seat, my grip tightening on the book. This is ridiculous. I'm supposed to be observing, not getting upset about whatever Jasper's doing. But there's no denying the twinge of something more than professional interest at the sight of him with Erin.

The waitress returns with my order, sliding it in front of me with a snippy "Enjoy," as if she'd rather I choke on it.

"Thanks." I lift the tea to my mouth without thinking and burn the crap out of my lower lip. I wince and pull away, sloshing some of it on my hand. "Mother—"

I bite my tongue and pluck at the napkin dispenser, trying to get one. Instead, I get an entire pile, which I clamp over my hand.

Peeling the napkin back, I see a blister already starting to form in that fleshy part between my thumb and forefinger. Perfect. Erin gets the touch of adoration, and I get this. I should really run it under cold water before it gets worse.

The restroom is behind me, but if I get up, I'll have to leave the protection of the screen. And they'll probably see me. Or maybe they won't, since they seem to only have eyes for one another.

I sit there, grimacing in pain as Erin now leans into him, twirling a lock of her hair around her finger.

She shows him a picture on her phone, and he inches closer. I grip my book, bracing for a coffee shop kiss. Then my mind goes to the worst-case scenario, a restroom hookup.

It's his life. He can do what he wants, but if they go to the bathroom, they'll stroll right past me. I'm practically a human land mine they're about to step on.

Not that it matters. I'm like a ghost in my own stakeout.

I should be cheering them on. A successful match is the goal. That's why I'm in this business. I should be throwing confetti.

I take a deep breath, forcing my shoulders to relax. As the matchmaker, I've done my part. Now it's time to step back and let whatever happens happen.

The waitress walks by, balancing a tray. I snag her attention. "Any chance of a back exit?"

She squints at me. "What?"

I gesture toward the rear hallway, raising my voice a notch. "Back exit?"

"Employees only," she replies curtly before moving on.

I can't help myself as I reach out, clutching at her arm. "Please, just this once—"

She shrugs me off, annoyance etched on her face. "Absolutely not." She strides away to another table.

It's futile anyway. Jasper and Erin are already rising from their table. My eyes dart to him as he scans the café, then down the hallway. I shrink back, a sinking feeling in my stomach.

Instead, he pulls out his wallet, casually placing a bill on the table. He assists Erin with her cropped jacket.

I shove my book into my bag, eyes still glued to them as he opens the door for her. I inch toward their abandoned table, stealing glances through the front window. They walk away, side by side, until they vanish from my sight.

"Whoa, nice tip," a voice says beside me.

I turn to see the waitress, smiling as she eyes the fifty-dollar bill Jasper left.

Mr. Big Spender . . . I think, wanting to find something to get pissed about. Flashing his money around. I bet it's because . . .

Of course.

It's his reason for everything. *Sex.*

But not in the restroom. Somewhere else.

I rush for the door. Just as I'm about to push it open, I realize I never paid for my own stuff. So much for that big apology tip. Turning back, I reach into my bag and pull out the first bill I find. The waitress is confused as I grab her hand and thrust the money into it. "Here. I have to go."

She looks down at it. "A dollar? Your order was $12.79."

"Oh." I fumble through my purse and find no cash whatsoever. Shit. I hand her my credit card. "Can you ring this up real fast? I'm kind of in a rush."

"You don't say," she deadpans as she moves like a snail back to the counter.

"Put fifty percent on for a tip," I say, hoping that'll make her go faster.

I don't get the same praise Jasper got. She takes all the time in the world, handing me the receipt and my card, glaring at me.

On the sidewalk, I look as far down as I can, but they're gone.

By the time I've walked another block, I come to my senses and exhale. I slow to a stop and shake my head.

I'm an idiot. Completely.

Why do I care so much?

I'm not his boss.

But a part of me thinks that if he did hook up with Erin, then it would prove everything I believe about him.

I've just turned to head back to the bookstore when a big hand clamps over my wrist.

It's Mr. Big Spender himself, a knowing little smirk on his face.

He leans in close to my ear and says, "How was your stakeout, angel?"

Chapter 12

JASPER

Jane looks up at me, wide eyed, and places her free hand over her chest. If she were wearing pearls, she'd be clutching them.

She'd never make it as a spy. She sucks at it. Not to mention that she's too beautiful to get lost in a crowd. And she's damn cute when she's blushing after getting caught red handed.

I let her wrist go and smirk. "You all right?"

She nods. "You scared me. I was just—"

"You were following me."

She blurts out, "What? I was just having a lunch when I saw—"

"And that's why you were hiding in the back behind that screen. Sorry, but you stick out, angel." I'm beyond delighted that she was there, watching. It was the best part of the date.

I can't help but feel a surge of anticipation tingling inside me. There's something about her that gets under my skin, making me crave more than just her banter. It's as if she's deliberately pushing me away, only to leave me wanting her even more.

I quickly shake off these thoughts, reminding myself that this is just a dance we've been engaged in since the moment we met. But now it feels different—more charged, more dangerous. The line between attraction and irritation has blurred since the Jane Orgasm.

When she doesn't respond, I add, "You knew we were going to Cool Beans."

She looks away and tucks a lock of hair behind her ear. "Was your date today? You have to realize, I set up dozens of meetups all—"

"Yeah, yeah, yeah. Okay."

"It's true! Anyway, I don't have time for this. I have to get back to—"

"I get it. Work, right? Don't let me keep you from making the world a more loving place." I move aside to let her pass. "See ya, matchmaker."

Chin up, she stalks past me. I watch her leave, taking in the dressy shorts that hug her heart-shaped ass. No stockings. Heels. Little sweater. Goddamn.

It's almost a shame that she whirls around, just as I'm trying to commit that back view to memory.

She wags a finger at me. "If you must know, it was a professional matter. That's all. I often look in on dates to make sure they're going all right."

"Sure." I don't believe that for a second.

Her cheeks pinken. "I do!"

"And how did ours look?" I ask, tilting my head.

"Well, to tell you the truth . . . I was concerned," she admits, her eyebrows knitting.

"About what?" I play innocent, but I know exactly what she's getting at. "Ah, maybe that it was going too well, is that it?"

She hitches a shoulder slightly. "Well . . . you got up so fast . . ."

"You thought I was taking her home. Is that it?"

I can just about see her pulse, going crazy beneath that creamy white skin of her throat. Her breathing gets more rapid, and she looks away. "Well . . ."

"You're right. It was. We got on like a house afire." I look behind myself, at the alley there. "We decided, why wait to get to my place? We did it right here in the alley."

Ah, and there it is. Her mouth opens, and she looks horrified for a second, before her lip curls. "Fast finisher, I guess?"

"Then I told her to get lost and kicked her to the curb."

She stares at her shoes, then looks up at me, those green eyes making my heart twinge. "I know you're just giving me a hard time. I swear I was at Cool Beans to promote my business."

I lean against the side of the building and cross my arms. "Lie detected."

She looks at her shoes again. I smile because it's her tell when she's guilty.

Sure, I like getting laid. But it would be better with someone I'm really into. I'd even wait for the third date for that. Or the fourth. Hell, if it was Jane, I might even wait as long as she wanted. Something tells me she's worth it.

Jane stares at me. "So are you going to see Erin again?"

I decide not to answer right away, because that's the only thing I have, keeping her dangling. Erin was a sweetheart. She talked mostly about the new puppy she recently got to help her get over her ex. She even teared up a little talking about the lawyer who broke her heart, so I held her hand.

"First I need to rate my date with you, don't I?" I reach into my phone and open the app. It's already prompting me to provide the rating. Thankfully, the rating system is only for Jane to see how it went and help her make better matches.

She comes closer to me, watching as I hold my phone. She gasps. "Only three stars? Seriously?"

"For a reason," I say, thumbing in the rest of the review. "She's still recovering from a breakup. She didn't even ask me anything about myself."

"Oh, it's all about you. I see."

"Not at all. She really just needed a friend to vent to."

She presses closer, leaning in, and I inhale her scent, sweet like honeysuckle. It must be her shampoo. When I finish, she grabs the phone. "'And she looks like George Washington with long hair'? What?"

I shrug again.

"She's beautiful! You're so mean!"

True. Erin is gorgeous and doesn't look like a dead president, but I freaking love getting a rise out of Jane.

"We just didn't connect," I try to explain. "She was more like . . . vanilla. Nice, but meh. And I want chocolate-brownie explosion. You know, the orgasm-in-your-mouth type of thing?" I clearly recall Jane's orgasm. Under my tongue.

She hands me the phone. "You two really looked like you were getting along well. You were flirting. Leaning into each other."

"Yeah . . . I do that. Even the lady with the mustache at my dry cleaner's. It's called 'charm.'"

"But you don't do that to someone you're not interested in," she says heatedly, waving her arms and accidentally poking a passing runner in the ribs. She winces and calls after him, "Oh, sorry!" but he keeps going and doesn't look back.

"I do," I say with a shrug. "That's why everyone likes me. You should try it," I suggest. "Maybe more people would like you."

This time she pokes me in the chest with her finger. "You know what that's called? Being a phony. No one likes a phony. Trust me. They might, at first, but when they find out it's all an act, they won't like you anymore. I'm real. What you see is what you get."

I grin. "You're hot when you're angry, angel."

Her eyes narrow as she backs away. "Don't call me that."

Before she can turn to run off, I say, "So . . . do I get another match?"

"Your three are up, which means your money is mine."

"Is that a yes?" I ask as she marches away, taking that beautiful ass with her.

No response.

I say, "I'm telling you. You just have to have a date with me."

She glares.

I grin. "I really feel bad about making you have to work so hard to find me a match. Why don't you come over to my place tonight, and I'll make you dinner? I might even let you put a tiny little photo of me on the website."

Before she can open her mouth to deny me again, I add, "I'm kind of a celebrity. That's probably why I have a multimillion-dollar sponsorship deal with Gatorade and more on the way."

She rolls her eyes. "So what?"

"Just that I'm sure you're looking for positive reviews about your little side hustle, huh?" I say lightly. The reviews for the business itself go on the website for everyone to read.

"Well, one from me . . . would probably be worth a lot. Then again, a negative review . . . not so good."

She gasps. "You wouldn't!"

"Jane Darling." Her name drips from my lips. "Just say yes."

"Fine," she says. "I'll come." She winces and then adds, "For dinner. Just to talk business."

I suppress a laugh and smile. "You can peel me back, layer by layer, find out everything you need to know. It'll be . . . fun."

Chapter 13
JANE

In my apartment, I'm rummaging through my closet, searching for the least appealing outfit I own. Babs is sprawled on my bed and watches me with a bewildered expression.

"You do realize you're supposed to look nice when you go out, right?" she asks, flipping through a magazine.

I pull out a baggy, faded T-shirt and a pair of old jeans with a questionable stain on the thigh that I could never get out when I washed them. "I'm going for the just-rolled-out-of-bed look."

Babs puts down the magazine and stares at me. "Why?"

I toss the clothes onto the bed and start searching for shoes, settling on a pair of old sneakers. "It's strategic. If I look like a mess, maybe Jasper won't be so Jaspery around me."

Babs snorts. "Honey, Jasper could probably find charm in a potato sack. You dressing down won't change a thing."

"I swear, Babs, it's like walking into a lion's den every time I see him."

I pull my hair into a messy ponytail with strands falling down and examine myself in the mirror. "Perfect. I look like I've given up on life."

She shakes her head. "He's going to think you've been cleaning house for a week."

"Exactly," I say, nodding with a sense of accomplishment. "It's foolproof."

Babs gets up and adjusts the old, striped cardigan I pulled on. "Well, you definitely look sad. I'll give you that."

I grab a tote bag that used to belong to Gran, ignoring my stylish purses. "I haven't shaved my legs in a few days. I'm a complete man repellent."

As I head to the living room, where Londyn is, Babs calls out, "Hey, maybe you should smear some dirt on your face?"

I consider it for a moment. "No, that might be too much."

Londyn looks up from the race car she's running over the carpet. "Where are you going, Mommy?"

I kneel down. "I'm just going to see a friend. Jasper. Do you remember him?" She's been around him a few times at social events, but it's been a while.

Londyn shakes her head, her big eyes curious and innocent. She scrunches up her nose. "Boys are silly. Andrew makes funny faces."

"Yes, boys can be silly."

Londyn nods earnestly, then holds up her race car. "Will you bring this to Jaspie? He can play with it. It's superfast."

Jaspie? So cute. Wait. Not cute. I can't get gushy about what Londyn calls Jasper.

I take the car, feeling a flutter in my chest at her thoughtfulness. "Of course, sweetie. Jasper will love it."

She beams, then looks serious. "But make sure he gives it back. It's my favorite."

I stand up, tucking the car into my bag. "I'll make sure he takes good care of it."

Londyn runs up and wraps her small arms around my legs. "Have fun, Mommy."

I bend down and hug her back as I give her a kiss on the top of her head. "You have fun too. Be good for Babs, okay?"

Stepping out the door, I take a deep breath. Jasper may be expecting the polished, put-together Jane, but tonight, he's getting the real me. Let's see how he handles that.

◆ ◆ ◆

I approach Wickham and take in the elegant facade, rising majestically.

As I step inside, the doorman offers a courteous nod, his uniform crisp and tailored. My gaze drifts across the lobby and sitting areas, the gold sconces adorning the walls, the floral arrangements. It's a world that seems almost surreal in its extravagance.

I've been here before to visit Emmy and Graham. It's fancy with a capital F.

I feel a little out of place, and I don't miss that the girl at the desk gives me a hard look. I just smile and wave.

Jasper waits next to the elevator with an air of confidence as he watches me approach. I think his lips twitch.

He's wearing jeans and a white button-up shirt that seems tailored to highlight the golden tones of his tan. His hair is up in a man bun, accentuating his gorgeous bone structure.

"Hey. You made it. I'm shocked you didn't cancel," he teases with a playful edge.

"I keep my word," I retort lightly.

He rubs his hands together in mock anticipation. "So, is this a date?"

"It's a meeting about your next match."

"Sure."

He holds the elevator door for me, and I step inside. We're alone, and the air crackles around us. Or maybe it just crackles for me. I don't know. I really don't. I feel him giving me subtle looks, but I keep my focus on the mirrored wall in front of me as I clutch my tote bag.

Pretending I'm confident, I stride into Jasper's apartment, anticipation buzzing under my skin. I've heard rumors about how big it is, but I've never been inside. I stop in the foyer, taking in a wide-open space that's all sharp lines and minimalist chic, with a den, kitchen, and formal dining area. Heavy wooden beams crisscross the ceiling. "Wow, Jasper, compensating for something with all this space?" I say as I look around.

He chuckles, leading me through an area with concrete. Everything is decorated in white and beige and gray, the kind of place you see in magazines and wonder if anyone actually lives there. It's a shrine to masculinity, from the leather couch to the massive flat-screen TV on the wall above the fireplace.

He gives me a tour of the kitchen, then moves to three different bathrooms, then pauses at a double door.

"My bedroom," he says in a husky tone, and I give him a glare.

I'm half expecting more of the same. Instead, he opens the door to reveal a moody room draped in burgundy and black, with an ornate king-size four-poster bed that wouldn't look out of place in Dracula's castle. There's even a black canopy over the top.

"Welcome to the chamber of secrets," Jasper says, a grin evident in his voice.

The room has an intimate feel.

Against one wall stands a massive antique dresser, its surface hosting a collection of candles. Their scents linger in the air.

Artwork hangs on the walls, but it's not the kind you'd find in a typical bedroom. There's a framed painting of a moonlit night over a forest. Another frame holds a painting of a castle on top of a mountain. A huge standing mirror in one corner seems to be the only piece in the room that reflects light.

I can't help but gape. "Should I be worried about a coffin in here?"
He chuckles. "Funny."

I run a finger along the back of an antique-looking chair. "This is unexpected. It's so different from the rest of your place."

"It's my private domain. Plus, it's a great conversation starter."

"Do you have lots of conversations in here?" I picture him rolling around in that bed, his broad shoulders and long legs intertwined with the black sheets as he fucks someone.

I push the image out of my head.

Without replying to me, he leads me back out to the den, with floor-to-ceiling windows that frame the Manhattan skyline.

I hear giggling and glance over to see the two girls from Carson's coming down the hall toward us.

Jasper sighs, a bit of dread on his face as he looks at them. "Jane, meet my nieces, Macy and Lacy."

"I'm Macy," the one in the ponytail says with a smile.

"And I'm Lacy," says the slightly shorter one. Her hair is down, and I make a mental note to remember which one is which.

"You're really pretty," Lacy says as she throws a playful look at Jasper. "Uncle J., you're stepping up your game."

He rolls his eyes in mock exasperation. "Don't start. Jane's just a friend."

"Great to meet you," I reply, suddenly feeling nervous. They're his family, and maybe a tiny part of me wants to make a good impression.

Jasper heads toward the kitchen. "Can I get anyone something to drink?" he calls out over his shoulder.

The twins ask for sodas, and Jasper hands them over.

They begin a spirited recounting of their day at a dance camp they've been attending at one of the theaters.

Soaking it all in, I make my way to the kitchen island, taking a seat on one of the high stools. On the island is a huge plate of bacon, already cooked, with thick slices of sourdough bread.

"We're having BLTs," he says. "One of my specialties."

Macy flits around, helping him. "Where's the mayo?"

"Fridge. Where else?" he says, grabbing a piece of already-cooked bacon and popping it into his mouth.

She pokes her head up from the fridge. "I can't find it!"

"What are you, blind?" he says, moving her out of the way. "Stand aside."

A second later, he pulls a squirt bottle of mayo out of the fridge. "If it were a snake, it would've bitten you, dude." He sets it down.

"You didn't slice tomatoes?" Lacy says, with her hands on her hips.

"Tomatoes are the devil's fruit," Jasper says. He picks one up off the counter and tosses it to her. "If you want it, you cut it." He pauses. "Jane, do you want tomato? I'd cut one for you."

I shake my head. That's one thing we can agree on. Tomatoes are yuck.

In the bright light of the kitchen, it's obvious the girls are super young. Lacy is actually filming herself as she makes a sandwich, and the other is twerking to Taylor Swift and mouthing one of her songs.

"Cut out that music, and leave something for our guest," Jasper says, getting in the video and making a face.

Giggling, they grab their sandwiches, Cokes, and phones and sit down at the island.

It's all so casual that I feel relaxed.

I go up to the counter and start to make a sandwich. He stands across from me, doing the same, piling lettuce atop a piece of bread.

"Pickle?" he asks. "It's so good with bacon."

"They are worse than tomatoes," I say, taking too much bacon for my sandwich.

He opens the lid, and I wince. He notices. "What?"

"The smell. So gross."

He brings the jar to his nose. "I don't smell anything."

I laugh and push him away.

He quickly puts the lid back. "Better?"

I nod, feeling shy that he's so sweet. We settle in around the island, and the girls ask me questions about the bookstore and Londyn. The questions really start when I tell them that I'm Jasper's matchmaker.

They look at Jasper and giggle. "Why do you need someone to find you a date? What about all those girls that tuck their numbers in your hand every time you go out?" Lacy asks.

I swing my head toward him, eager to hear his response since I've been asking myself the same question.

He wipes his mouth with a napkin. "I've been doing that, and it hasn't worked out. Figured it was time to try something new."

Macy leans in. "So, Jane. How are you going to find our uncle a date?"

I swallow the bite I've been chewing. "I have to ask him a bunch of questions to form a profile, and then based on that, I feed it into my system and it gives me possible matches."

Jasper nods. "Apparently, I filled it out badly the last time. Which landed me Abigail."

"Oooh," Lacy says, making a face. "We heard about her. She's a viper."

"How did he fill it out?" Macy asks. "Did he talk about how he likes *Vampire Diaries* way too much?" She giggles.

I smile at them. "What is his deal with vampires, am I right?"

They nod.

"He's into folklore. He digs old stuff," Macy tells me.

"So what kind of questions do you ask?" Lacy says, nibbling on a piece of bacon.

"Well, maybe you can help me with that." I reach into my bag and pull out my laptop. "Sometimes, a person doesn't know themselves as well as other people know him. Maybe you could give me a better picture."

The girls bounce on their seats, excited, but Jasper is less enthused. "Whoa, whoa, whoa. I don't think that's a good idea."

Lacy claps her hands. "No, it totally is! We can help."

"Good," I say, opening up a blank profile and typing in his name. I honestly have everything I need from Jasper since our convo at my apartment, but it's fun to play along. "So, girls, what are your uncle's bad habits?"

They look at each other, grinning slyly.

Behind me, Jasper warns, "Nope. Don't gang up—"

"He snores. So loud. Like a bear in hibernation," Lacy says, then mimics a loud growly sound from her throat.

"Oh my god, it shakes the house! And every time he sees us doing our TikTok dances, he feels the need to jump in and be our backup dancer," the other says, with an eye roll.

I laugh.

"And he is the worst twerker ever," Lacy says, nodding. "He looks like a duck. And when he comes in the room and it's too quiet, he always has to announce, 'Jasper is here.'"

"Lie detected!" Jasper calls out. "I do not talk about myself in the third person."

"Right!" Macy reaches over and grabs her twin's hand excitedly. "Or what about how he can't ever say anyone's actual name? He has to call them by a nickname. Usually, a really clichéd one. He calls us 'Thing One' and 'Thing Two.'"

I laugh. "He calls me 'angel.'"

Jasper blows out a breath. "You had a costume on. What did you expect?"

"He can't even tell us apart, really," Lacy says. "We're not even identical. I don't have a dimple. I'm Lacy."

"I can too," Jasper mutters. "Macy is an inch taller."

"Right," Macy says, shaking her head at him, then turns to me. "And you should hear him sing in the shower. He usually sings Disney songs, and he doesn't even know all the words, he just makes them up."

At that, Macy starts to sing in a terribly high falsetto, miming holding a microphone.

Lacy grins. "He loves sweet and salty snacks. If you dig around in his bed, I bet you'll find SNICKERS-bar wrappers or ALMOND JOY. Those are his faves. Once I caught him eating CHEETOS in bed. He tried to hide it, but I saw. I'm a teenager, and even I don't eat in my sheets. He cleaned his room before you came over."

I can't help it. I'm giggling, too, and when I look at Jasper's steely expression, it makes me giggle all the more. These girls are a blast.

I'm typing in his pretend profile when Jasper looks over my shoulder and warns, "Don't put any of that in there."

"Why? This is great stuff. It's good to keep it real." I swat him away. "Okay, girls. Enough of that. What are some of your uncle's best qualities?"

"His best quality?" Macy says, in all seriousness, "He can burp the alphabet. Really fast."

"All right, all right! That was one time in college. One time!" Jasper says over her. Who would've believed it only took a couple of seventeen-year-old girls to put a crack in his ego.

Macy sighs. "He sends his mom flowers every month. That's pretty cool."

Jasper shrugs. "She deserves it after putting up with all us kids."

Lacy smiles. "He's got a big heart. He special orders bracelets for each football player at the start of the season. He loves to have people around him. He's just a big old teddy bear."

Jasper shoos them away. "All right, you're just trying to butter me up for something. Get out of here." He checks his phone. "You told Francesca you'd babysit. Jump to it."

As they grab their plates and toss them in the garbage, Jasper explains that former player Tuck Avery lives in the penthouse with his wife and two kids, and it's been good for Macy and Lacy to babysit for them. He gives each girl a playful tug on the hair as they vacate the room, scamper down the hall, and out the door.

I'm perched on the edge of Jasper's couch, and he's across from me.

"So I read you majored in world history?" I ask, genuinely curious. "That's not something you hear every day."

"I love history, but my favorite topic is folklore."

"Hmm, like what?"

"Old fables and even fairy tales like 'Snow White.' Folklore can be songs or art or anything that reflects a culture."

He points out a couple of books about Pandora's box on some shelves behind him. I get up to see them. "Impressive," I murmur.

I glance back at him, finding his gaze on me, an intense look in his eyes. It's disarming, and I quickly divert my attention back to the bookcase, noting the classic fiction nestled among the books.

He continues to surprise me.

The silence between us stretches like a rubber band.

I dart my eyes at him and catch his gaze, a flutter of something twitching in my stomach. It's ridiculous, really. One night of passion, and here I am, trying to decode his every look, every move. It's as if that night added an extra layer to what we are.

Sure, we've always danced on the fine line between friends and, well, not enemies, but certainly not allies. Now, though, every interaction feels loaded. It's strange how one orgasm can alter the dynamics of a relationship I thought I had pegged.

And what bothers me most is my own reaction to it all. I actually followed him to his date with Erin!

Part of me wishes we could reset to before things got so muddled. But there's another side of me that wonders what it would be like to cross that line again.

Ugh. Reality snaps me back. Jasper and I, we're like fire and ice. He's a wealthy, famous quarterback that even Abigail wanted to see again, even though she knew he wasn't a true match. And me? I'm struggling to make ends meet. I don't have time for a man in my life.

So why did my heart race on the way here?

What is this hungry feeling inside me, for him?

I tell myself to snap out of it, to remember what I want. The only thing I should be passionate about is my business. It's my future. And Londyn's. I don't need a man to complete me. But as I steal another glance at Jasper, that conviction wavers.

He tosses me a smirk, and I smile back at the teasing glint in his eyes. Here we are, alone, and it does feel like a date. Dammit. He's so hot. And, yes, he's fun to be with. Those tarot cards he read for me? I mean, it wasn't even a big deal, but he made me feel important and valued, and maybe a tiny piece of me wanted to believe the words he said, about good things coming to me. I kept the three of them—the Star, the Ten of Cups, and the Lovers—on my nightstand, and I've looked at them each day, wondering about some of the things he said, about family and emotional bliss, about love.

With a mental shake, I push the thoughts away. He's just Jasper. We're sort of friends, and that's all we'll ever be. Anything more spells disaster. After all, he's friends with Graham, and if we dip our toes into whatever is brewing between us and it blows up in my face, I'll still have to hear about him and see him at get-togethers.

No. I can't let my guard down.

I clear my throat. "Um, I think I need some water."

I move to the kitchen, but he moves to block my way. I brush against the solid wall of his chest, feeling the warmth radiating from him.

"You're running away, angel." His voice is a low murmur, and I can't help but look up. His hand touches my arm, just a featherlight touch, but it might as well have been a bolt of electricity.

The air around us thickens. I can barely draw a breath. There's something in his eyes, a depth of emotion like he's on the edge of revealing something significant, something that's been weighing on him.

"Yes?"

The intensity in his gaze doesn't waver. It's as if he's peering straight into my soul, searching for something. The room falls away until there's nothing but the two of us.

I wait, heart pounding, for whatever revelation is about to spill from his lips. But the words don't come. Instead, we remain locked in this silence, a push and pull of emotions.

He shakes his head. "You know, forget it. It's not important."

It was. I know it was. I point toward the kitchen. "Water. Do you want some?"

"Jane, wait."

I'm in the hallway and turn around, and he's right behind me. He smirks. "Your hair is falling down. I'll fix it," he says as he reaches for my scrunchie and tugs at it. My hair spills around my shoulders.

A breathless moment passes as he runs his fingers through my hair, arranging it into a messy knot. Tingles dance over my skin.

My throat moves. "Does it look better?"

He makes a humming sound in his throat as he turns me to face him. "I'm going to kiss you."

I feel lightheaded, clearly recalling what his last kiss led to. I should say no, I really should, because he's waiting, pausing, giving me the chance to pull away.

Okay, pull away.

Now, Jane. Do it now.

"I'm waiting," I say, and it's all he wanted to hear. He pushes me against the wall and presses his lips to mine.

My hands move from his chest to circle his neck as I tug him closer, eliciting a low groan from him that reverberates through my body. His arms snake around my waist, pulling me flush against him, and I can feel every hard inch of him.

He deepens the kiss, his tongue exploring my mouth with an urgency that matches my own. His hands roam up and down my back, tracing the curve of my spine before settling on my ass. I gasp as he squeezes me.

"Jane," he breathes, breaking the kiss. His forehead rests against mine. "You're making it hard for me to stop."

"Don't stop."

With a growl, he lifts me up, and I wrap my legs around his waist. He carries me down the hallway toward his bedroom, our lips never leaving each other's.

We reach his bedroom, and he kicks the door shut behind us with a force that makes me laugh.

"What about the twins?"

"They won't be back for a while." He pauses. "We don't have to do this, I mean, but if you think about it, this might help you write the profile."

"Totally," I agree as I press my lips back to his.

It's dark in the room, but he flicks on the light, casting the room in a warm glow. We stumble toward the bed, our hands never breaking contact.

I'm pushed onto the soft mattress and feel the bed dipping beneath me. Jasper's lips find my throat while his hands roam down to cup my shoulders. "Why the hell are you wearing this sweater?"

"Just wait until you see my hairy legs."

He laughs into my neck, the warmth of his breath making my body sing.

He whips off my sweater, then my shirt, and gazes down at my lacy demi-cup bra.

I bite my lip, watching him and feeling nervous. I'm not well endowed, and I haven't had proper sex in years.

"You know you've got me hooked, right?" he growls, his fingers lightly tracing the line of my bra. I flush with heat, my breath catching in my throat as he undoes the clasp, letting my bra fall to the side.

His hands explore me, his fingers tracing the curves of my body, sending shivers down my spine. I arch my back, eager for more. "You're so beautiful. So receptive," he says, kissing a trail down my neck and across my collarbone. He sucks a nipple into his mouth and cups my breasts, burying his face in the valley as he lavishes them with attention. The scruff from his jawline sends prickles of sensation over me.

This is so good. So fucking good.

My heart races as I feel his hands slide around to cup my ass, his fingers brushing against the sensitive skin of my thighs.

I want to see him, all of him. I unbutton his shirt and spread it wide, inhaling his smell. His chest is firm and warm, covered in a light dusting of hair that I run my fingers through. I trace the lines of his abdomen, feeling his tension and anticipation.

He groans, his hips thrusting toward me. "We need to be naked. Now."

A moment of hesitation hits. "Do you have condoms?"

"Hold on," he says, springing up and rushing to the nightstand. He comes back with an open box and tosses them on the bed. "They're pink. Is that okay?"

"You're seriously asking me if I care what color they are?"

He shrugs. "I want it to be good for you. Pink is my favorite color."

I like him so much. Especially when he says things I don't expect. "Pink is perfect."

I lean up on my elbow and watch him undress. It's been so long since I've seen a man naked that every movement is like a revelation. His shirt is already on the floor. He unzips his jeans and pushes them down, his dick thick and long. I really try to keep my cool at how big he is, but he notices and chuckles. "Like what you see?"

He goes commando. I nod. Apparently mute at the moment.

"You ready to get off, angel?"

I gaze into his sultry eyes and nod as my breath hitches in antici-pation. Yes, orgasming can be addictive.

"That's right. I'm gonna bring you there." All smirky, he smiles and does a little move like one of his touchdown dances as he kicks his jeans away.

He stalks to me and helps me slide down my jeans. He stands over me, making me squirm as he looks at my white underwear. They're nothing fancy, but at least they aren't granny panties. If the hungry look in his eyes is anything to judge by, I won't have them on long anyway.

He leans down and runs a finger from my cheek, past my breasts, to my hips, all the way to my toes, then comes back to my waist. His hand slides inside my panties. His eyes heat, a fire growing as he dips into my pussy and fingers me.

"Jasper," I say breathlessly.

He chuckles, using his other hand to gently pull my panties down, baring me entirely to his gaze.

"You're so gorgeous," he says, his fingers continuing to explore me. He dips a finger inside me, pumping in a slow, steady rhythm that makes my core clench.

I make a sound in my throat, arching my back to get closer, to get more.

He leans down to kiss me, his tongue darting into my mouth as he continues to finger me. I whimper, my body trembling with need.

He pulls away, his chest rising rapidly as he crawls between my legs, his eyes never leaving mine. He plants kisses along my inner thighs, his tongue tracing the lines of my upper legs.

His warm breath washes over my center, the anticipation building with every passing second. I grip the sheets beneath me, my heart pounding as I watch him.

"Promise you won't regret this," he says, his voice husky.

"I want this more than I've ever wanted anything in my life." I wanted this to happen. I admit it.

Jasper is so much more than the person I thought. He's a family guy, taking care of his nieces; he's worried about football, hoping he still has his team family even with a new quarterback; plus he's dealing with his biological mother.

"What?" he asks. "You just went somewhere else, and I can't have that."

The truth is, Jasper and I have more in common than I realized. His mom left him, for whatever reason, and my mom left me too. We share abandonment. And for some reason it makes this moment special.

"I'm a little worried I'm too inexperienced for you," I murmur as I reach up and kiss him, my teeth dragging against his bottom lip, making him pant.

"Jesus, don't even think that. You're awesome, baby. So damn hot," he says, then dips down to my center, his tongue tasting the most intimate part of me. I gasp, my head thrashing back and forth as he licks and sucks at my clit. The pleasure is intense, and my body writhes as shock waves radiate through my body, building at the base of my spine.

"That's it, angel," he murmurs. "Enjoy every lick."

Just as I'm about to reach the peak of my orgasm, he leans up and kisses me, his tongue sliding into my mouth as if to mimic the pleasure he was giving me elsewhere. The ferocity of his kiss catches me off guard, but I return it eagerly.

"Let me taste your pussy again," he says in my ear.

My breath hitches as I nod, unable to speak.

He slides down my body, his hungry eyes locked onto my center. I quiver, so ready to be devoured.

He licks me, long and slow at first, savoring as I moan, my pleasure building back up again, my hips bucking against his mouth. Using his hands to hold me open, he thrusts his tongue inside me, deeper and faster now, and I grip the sheets with white-knuckled hands.

He sucks on me, creating a vacuum that sends shocks of pleasure up and down my skin. I'm so close, so fucking close, feeling my orgasm approaching with every second, electricity pulsing through my veins. My muscles tighten, my breathing becomes ragged.

"Please, Jasper, I'm going to . . ."

"That's it, baby," he growls, his voice deep.

And then, it happens. The pleasure peaks inside me, so intense that I can barely stand it. My whole body shakes as the orgasm rips through me. My body explodes with pleasure, my muscles tightening and releasing as wave upon wave of bliss washes over me.

I gasp for air as Jasper slowly pulls away. He looks up at me, his eyes full of satisfaction as he smiles softly. "How would you rate that?"

"Shut up," I pant, gasping for air.

He cups my cheeks, his thumbs brushing softly against the skin below my eye. "Suck me."

I nearly pass out with the heat that spears through me. I like a man who tells me what to do in bed. I laugh, and he laughs with me when I tell him.

The laughter makes everything exponentially better. As if we're easy with each other and able to say what we want and need.

He pulls me up to sit on the edge of his bed and stands in front of me. I look at his cock. It's perfect, long and thick, veins running along the length of it, the head glistening with a drop of precum. I lick my lips and take him in my hand, stroking him slowly, my fingers brushing against the sensitive skin at the top. He groans, his hips bucking slightly.

"Yeah," he says. "Show me how much you want me."

I lean forward, my lips parting slightly as I take the head of his cock into my mouth. He tastes salty, the scent surrounding me as I take him deeper, his girth filling my mouth.

I suck him, my tongue swirling around his shaft, my mouth moving up and down, my hand pumping his dick. He groans, his hands tangling in my hair, holding me in place.

I suck on the head, running my tongue around the ridge, savoring the feel of him in my mouth.

"Oh, fuck, Jane," he calls out, his hands threading through my hair.

His cock thickens as he pushes me off him. "Wait, angel. Wait. I want to be inside you for this."

He gently lays me down, then reaches for the box of condoms, pulls one out, and slides it on. He crawls between my legs, his blue gaze holding mine. He positions himself at my entrance, the tip of his cock teasing me as he slides into me inch by inch. He stops to press my hands down on the mattress, interlocking his in a strong clasp.

Oh, I like that. The intimacy. He pushes deeper, and I get lost in the way he feels, the way his hips thrust slowly, every inch of him finally hitting home. I wrap my legs around his waist, pulling him closer.

"You feel so good," he says as he slides out, then back in. He gazes down at me, the intensity of his eyes making me catch my breath. "Never want it to end."

His pace quickens as he stares down at me, his eyes lingering on my lips.

"Your hands," he gasps, tugging at my wrists. "Hold on to your legs, Jane."

I do as he asks, my hands gripping the back of my legs and giving him access to go deeper. He hits a spot inside me that sends pleasure everywhere.

He makes a primal sound, his pace quickening even more. "That's it, angel."

The room spins. I feel desperate every time he pulls out of me, just to go back in. He grinds against me, swiveling his hips to touch my clit. He's panting when he slows down, his lips sucking at my neck. "Doggy style. I want you at my mercy, baby."

I want to *be* at his mercy.

He helps me flip over and runs his hands down my back, a growl of appreciation coming from him as I arch my back for him. His fingers play with my pussy, tapping at my clit. "You're so wet," he says in my ear, and I nearly combust.

With his hands on my ass, he slides inside me, filling me up with every inch. My arms shake from holding on to the pillows as our bodies collide.

My pussy clenches around him, my walls pulsing with each thrust. I'm in a haze of lust and need.

He grips my hips tightly, pulling me closer to him. His hips pound against me, every strike of his cock deepening my arousal. The bed creaks beneath us, keeping time to the beat of our bodies.

His hand reaches around my waist to play my clit like a guitar string.

He keeps calling me "angel," over and over, the timbre of his voice low and needy, and it only ratchets up my need.

My climax builds, tighter and tighter. My breasts bounce wildly with each thrust, and I cry out, the echo bouncing off the walls.

My entire body freezes as my orgasm hits, wave after wave of ecstasy shattering me. My body convulses around his, my pussy clenching his cock in a viselike grip.

His body shudders as he comes right after me.

I collapse onto the bed on my stomach, my body spent, my mind reeling from the intensity of the experience.

He collapses on top of me, his heart pounding against my back. He lifts my hair out of the way and kisses my neck, my shoulder, anywhere he can reach, leaving a trail of heat.

He pulls out of me and flops down next to me and gathers me into his arms.

I feel deliciously languid as I melt into his chest.

The earlier tension between us has vanished, and now all I feel is a wonderful sense of relaxation. "We should probably clean up," I manage to say several minutes later. I don't want to move, but I need to get back to Londyn.

"No, we should stay like this," he says, his voice thick. He leans up on his arm and gazes down at me, satisfaction on his face.

I laugh at his goofy expression. "What are you staring at?"

He kisses me slow and sweet, his tongue dancing against mine in gentle strokes. "You're so repulsive that I'm ready to go again."

I laugh, then sober as I look down at his cock. I frown. "Wait. Where did the condom go?"

He gets up and looks around, lifting pillows and checking under the duvet. "It's missing, but I think I had it on," he says in a casual tone.

He thinks?

Panic hits me immediately.

"It's not like it grew legs and walked off, Jasper. It's not a caterpillar."

He stops searching and gives me a glance. "Hey. No need to get upset. I had it on when I came. I'm positive."

I sense uncertainty in his tone.

My heart races.

I mean, really, universe? After five years of celibacy, the one time I throw caution (and clothes) to the wind, the condom disappears?

Getting up, I look under the bed, but it's not there.

He runs his gaze over me, ending at my crotch. "Is it still inside you?"

Oh. That's weird.

I move away from the bed and dash to an open door that I assume is his bathroom.

My reflection is wild in the mirror, my face flushed and my hair sticking up in all directions, but who cares about that? Where is the condom? I bend over, feeling around. It's not in my vagina. My breathing quickens, and I sway on my feet.

What if he came inside me?

"Found it!" Jasper calls from the bedroom, and when I walk out with a towel wrapped around me, he's holding it like a trophy. "It was at the foot of the bed."

I must have missed it. I lick my lips, nerves flying in all directions. "Jasper, are you sure you didn't come inside me?"

He puts on his jeans and zips up, a small frown growing. "I don't think so."

My head replays our sex. He did flip me over, and what if it fell off then or got pulled off—

"Jane," Jasper says as he strides toward me. "Angel. Baby. You've got panic all over your face."

"I'm not even on the pill. It makes me moody, plus I've never had to worry about using precautions." Sure I've had a few dates since Tomas, here and there, but nothing that came close to sex.

"Okay. Let's think about this, just in case it did come off. Is this the time of the month when you ovulate?"

I start.

He shrugs. "I have four older sisters. I know a lot about cycles."

I shake my head. "I don't know, I need to think. I'm not a twenty-eight-day-cycle girl. It's always different. I'll need to go home and look at my calendar." My voice shakes. "But you're not a hundred percent sure, are you, about the condom?"

He runs a hand over his jawline. "I mean, it felt *really* good. Like maybe it came off? I don't know."

Okay.

I'm already scrambling into my clothes, my heart pounding against my rib cage. All I want is to get home and try to recall the last time I had my period. And I can't think straight here. I reach for my cardigan and drape it awkwardly over my shoulders.

He reaches out, his hand gently rubbing my back. I allow myself a moment to relax into him, hoping to calm the anxiety. The rational part of me knows we were careful, but fate sometimes has other plans.

Jasper looks into my eyes. "How do I make you feel better about it? Should we take extra precautions?"

I gulp. "Like what?"

"Plan B," he suggests with a gentle seriousness. "Just to be safe."

I nod, the logic in his words resonating. "Of course. I just didn't think of that." Because I haven't had sex in years. "I can get it."

"No, I'll come with you. It's the least I can do."

"Now?" I ask, disbelief in my voice. Is he really that worried about a possible pregnancy?

He quickly dresses in shorts and a shirt and sneakers. "Yes, now. Let's go."

I grab my tote from the kitchen. Memories of my pregnancy five years ago come flooding back, the fear, the uncertainty, the sense of being utterly overwhelmed.

And how Tomas left me.

Jasper's hand rests on my lower back as we leave his apartment.

In the lobby, he speaks to the doorman, who quickly hails us a cab. The ride to the pharmacy is a blur. Once there, we navigate the aisles, Jasper leading the way.

He pays for the medication, his actions swift, gripping my hand as we leave the pharmacy. The weight of the small box in my hand feels huge.

"I can walk myself back to my place," I say, but he refuses to listen.

We walk in silence. My mind is a whirlwind of emotions, the condom thing a shadow over the great sex.

Maybe it was a wake-up call. To stay away from Jasper.

As we approach my building, the familiar sight of home causes a long exhale to come from my chest. Finally, I can decompress. I glance at Jasper, his profile illuminated by the dim streetlights. He seems deep in thought, his usual confident demeanor replaced by a more somber one.

He insists on walking me to my door, a gesture that I can't refuse even though every part of me wants to get away. As we stand at my doorstep, an awkward silence envelops us.

"Jane, you've barely spoken."

"Sorry. Really. It's just that's the first time I've been with someone in a long time, and then it got confusing with the missing condom. It makes everything muddled."

"I'm sorry about earlier," he murmurs, his voice sincere. "I shouldn't have made a joke about losing it. It's a big deal to you. It's all I could think about on the way over."

"It's fine. We took care of it." My words are brisk.

He shifts his weight, looking down at his feet before meeting my gaze. "I want to see you again."

"Oh."

His words send a jolt through me. Part of me yearns to say yes, to dive into whatever this is between us. But the rational part, the part that's been through heartache, slams on the brakes.

If only the condom hadn't gone missing.

"I don't think that's a good idea," I say, staring down at the brown bag in my hands. It's the reminder I need. I need to end this conversation before I lose the resolve. "Good night, Jasper."

Without waiting for his response, I unlock my door and slip inside, closing it softly behind me. My back presses against the door, and I let out a shaky breath. The quiet of my apartment wraps around me like a cocoon.

What am I doing? Jasper is everything I've avoided, yet he's awakened something in me, something I'd buried deep.

I slide down to the floor, my head in my hands. This is madness. I can't let myself fall for him. He's a client, for goodness' sake.

The sound of footsteps pulls me from my reverie. It's Andrew, home from the bookstore. His concerned eyes find mine as he sees me on the floor.

"What's wrong?" he asks.

I shake my head, trying to play it cool. "It's nothing, just a long day."

He glances at the closed door. "Didn't you go see Jasper for work?"

I nod. "Yes. I'm just tired."

He frowns as I get up and drink a glass of water, then head to my room.

Alone, I feel like the walls are closing in on me. The weight of my decision presses down, suffocating. I did the right thing by pushing Jasper away. I have to protect my heart, my daughter. I can't afford to get lost in a romance.

But as I crawl into bed, the emptiness around me pulls me down.

Tears prick my eyes, and I let them fall silently.

Pushing Jasper away is the safe choice, so why do I still feel so lonely?

Chapter 14
JASPER

The next day, I step into my apartment after training, and the place is too quiet. "Lacy, Macy!" I call out, but there's nothing. Not even the sound of their favorite pop band blasting from their room.

I make a beeline for their bedroom, pushing open the doors, only to find their phones abandoned, the screens lit up with missed calls and messages.

A note is on the fridge: "Gone to Jane's bookstore. Back soon."

I get a bad feeling. They never leave without their phones unless they don't want me to know where they are.

I leave and go back to the street in front of Wickham and walk through the evening crowd. When I reach the bookstore, Jane is already locking up. My gaze takes her in, noting the shadows under her eyes. She looks like she slept as well as I did.

She smiles. "Hey. What's wrong?"

"It's the twins," I say. "They left a note saying they were here."

She shakes her head. "They weren't here today. I'm sure they would have said hi."

I nod, my hands clenching as I look around. The city is so big. "If they aren't hurt somewhere, I'm going to be pissed for real."

She comes closer. "I can help you check around. Maybe they're nearby."

I scan the street as I start walking. "Okay, thanks. They might be at Carson's playing pinball."

She follows me, her pace quickening to keep up.

I glance at her, surprised she's helping. Honestly, I thought she'd want to keep her distance from me for a while.

"Are they usually like this, just going off on their own?"

"They've always been a handful," I say, recounting the escapades they've pulled since I took them in. "Their mom needed a break, but I didn't expect it to be this hard."

She smiles a little. "Single parenting is tough. I'm shocked they're causing so much trouble. They seemed so sweet."

She checks her phone.

I wince. "This isn't your problem. I'm sure you have to get Londyn."

"It's better not to be alone when you're worried. Besides, Andrew's got Londyn. He just sent me a text."

"Rayna, their mom, she's been doing it all alone since their dad passed away a few years ago. I thought I understood what it meant to be a single parent, but this . . . ," I trail off, my gaze fixed on the bar's entrance as we approach.

She nods, her expression softening. "Being a single parent is like juggling. It's never just one thing. It's everything all at once."

We enter Carson's and split up. After a thorough search turns up nothing, we regroup outside. "They're not here," I mutter, frustration evident.

She scans the street. "They're smart girls, Jasper. They'll be okay."

My phone buzzes. It's Herman, the doorman at Wickham. He watched me leave in a rush earlier and is calling to tell me that he saw the twins leaving around five, chattering about a place called Scandal. I thank him and end the call, urgency and frustration rising. A club? Dammit.

As I look up the address on my phone, I fill Jane in on the details. "It's a club for eighteen and up, and it's four blocks from here."

She nods. "Lead the way. I'm going with you."

"Seriously, I can't believe them," I mutter under my breath as I dodge pedestrians, with Jane in tow. "A club? At their age? I'm going to skin them alive."

Jane smirks. "Did you think it would be easy watching them?"

I exhale. "Maybe. My own sisters were tricksters, too, so I should have known better."

She nods. "They probably have fake ID's. They aren't hard to get."

Ugh. Another worry. What if something happens to them? The city's a jungle at night, and they're about as prepared as a pair of kittens. The mental image of them, wide eyed while trying to blend in with the club scene, makes me anxious.

Jane's strides become shorter, and I notice her wincing with each step. "Hey, you okay?"

She grimaces, stopping to remove her heels. "Just a blister."

I shake my head, crouching down in front of her. "Hop on. I'll carry you."

She hesitates. "Jasper, I can walk. Really."

I grin, trying to lighten the mood. "Come on. Let's not waste time. I promise I won't drop you."

With a reluctant chuckle, she gives in, wrapping her arms around my neck as I lift her onto my back.

We continue, me carrying Jane piggyback; the absurdity of the situation isn't lost on me. I laugh, and she does too.

"I didn't realize you offered a taxi service."

I adjust my hold on her, making sure she's secure. "Only for special clients. And you are definitely special."

We approach the club's entrance, the thumping sound of music reaching the sidewalk.

I put my hands on my hips. "I'm going to ground them until they're thirty. I'm giving their inheritance away. I'm going to tattle on them to their mom, and boy, let me tell you, she will yank them hard."

"It doesn't seem to be open yet," Jane says as we scan the faces waiting in line at the entrance. She hops off and immediately goes up to a girl and starts talking. She comes back with a smile as she holds up two Band-Aids. She puts them on her heels, then slips into her shoes.

We decide to split up, with her taking the back of the line and me taking the front, and then we'll meet in the middle.

I go toward the entrance, where a bouncer is guarding a red-roped-off area. "Hey, any chance you've seen two blond teenage girls here? Twins?"

The bouncer, muscles bulging, frowns. "We check ID's. Strictly eighteen and over. But we haven't even opened the doors yet."

Jane's urgent voice catches my ear. "Jasper!" She's pointing toward a section of the line.

There are Macy and Lacy, deep in conversation with two guys who look like they walked out of a midlife crisis. One's sporting an unconvincing comb-over, while the other is decked out in gold chains. They're both far too close for comfort, and my blood boils.

I storm over, inserting myself between Macy and one of them. "If you're fond of that hand, move it now," I snap.

The two men recoil. One says, "Hey. Aren't you the quarterback—"

"No time," I cut him off, herding the twins out of the line with a hand on each of their wrists. "Let's go, now."

The twins pout, but I keep a firm grip on them, leading them away from the club and to a quieter part of the street. I stop and face them with my hands on my hips.

"You're no fun," Macy grumbles.

I did want to be the fun uncle, and I gave them plenty of leeway. But now I'm tired.

"You want to see no fun? Wait till you get home. You are in so much trouble. How could you think this was okay? Didn't you know that I'd be worried sick?"

Macy exhales. "We just wanted to get in line and pretend for a little while."

Her sister nods in agreement.

"You don't have fake ID's?" I ask sharply.

They drop their shoulders.

Caught.

Macy pleads with me, "Okay, okay, we do, but I promise we just wanted to get a peek inside, then come back. We're going to be college freshmen this fall, Uncle J. We've never been to a real club back home, and we just thought we'd see what it was like. I promise."

Lacy nods. "Plus, we'll be eighteen in a couple of weeks."

I shake my head. "Don't care. You lied to me about where you were going. I'm the one responsible for you, and if something happens, it's my fault." I sigh. "You'll have plenty of time for clubs when you're older. Another thrill is seeing if you can escape your bedroom when I lock you two in," I add.

"You really worried him," Jane tells them.

They keep their heads down, sheepishly mumbling apologies about how they didn't mean to make me worry and how they thought they'd be back in an hour or so and how they planned to admit where they'd been once they got back. They toss in several "pleases" and "you are the best uncle in the world." It goes on for a few minutes, and I let them.

Jane and I exchange glances. She nods as if to say, "They look sorry to me."

Their remorse does seem genuine. I know they're just kids, testing boundaries.

"Let's go home," I say.

We head to Wickham, and Macy says, "I'm super hungry. You're not going to starve us now, are you?"

I shoot her a stern look. "Considering the stunt you just pulled, maybe a little starvation is what you need."

Lacy's eyes well up with tears. "I'm hungry too."

"Okay, okay, no one's starving tonight," I say at the sight of a nearby food truck cooking up what smells like Mexican. "Who wants tacos?"

They squeal in unison.

Jane hesitates, probably about to make her exit.

Her first instinct is always to run away. I grab her bag from her arm. "Hang out with us a little longer."

She shakes her head. "I have to go—"

"Please." I don't hide my disappointment. Because shit. If she leaves, I'm . . . shit. Alone. "Eat with us?"

"Come on, Jane. Stay for a bit," Macy pleads, tugging at her sleeve. "We hardly know you."

Jane laughs. "You just met me."

Lacy joins in. "Tell us about your little girl. Oh, we're following you on TikTok, by the way. You have a nice platform."

I decide to step in. "It's just a quick bite. Besides, the twins may not be back for another summer visit once they go off to college."

She smiles. "It's Andrew's night to cook at my place, so Londyn is taken care of. I guess it wouldn't hurt to stay a little longer."

We find a nearby table and sit to eat tacos and cheesy rice.

I watch Jane as she listens to the twins recount their day at dance camp. She's got this way of making them feel heard, laughing at their stories, and asking questions. She fits right in.

"Please, Jane, can we meet Londyn?" Lacy pleads, her eyes wide with anticipation as we leave the taco truck behind and head to Jane's apartment.

Jane hesitates for a moment, then smiles. "Okay, but just for a little while. It's close to her bedtime."

As the twins skip ahead of us, Jane and I fall into step beside each other. Our hands brush, sending tiny jolts of electricity through me each time.

I try to ignore it. Jane and I . . . she wants no part of me.

Andrew opens the door. "Looks like you brought the party home," he tells Jane.

"His nieces wanted to meet Londyn," she explains as she does the introductions of the twins.

"Hey, Jasper. Didn't expect to see you here," Andrew says, extending a hand.

I shake it.

"How's the new season shaping up for you?"

Before I can reply, a small figure in polka-dot pajamas dashes out, wispy blond hair bouncing with each step. She's a mini Jane.

Londyn's eyes widen with excitement as she takes in our presence.

"Mama!" she exclaims, running toward Jane and hugging her legs tightly. Her curious gaze then shifts to us. "Who are they?"

Jane smiles down at her. "This is Jasper. He's a friend of mine. You've met him before, but it's been a while."

Londyn looks up at me with big blue eyes. "Jaspie," she says.

The sound of my name in her sweet voice sends a twinge through my chest. I crouch down to her level. "Hi. It's really nice to meet you."

"Do you have my car?" Londyn asks, her head tilted to one side, a serious look on her face.

"I forgot to bring it because I didn't know we'd be coming over here. Can I bring it next time?" I ask, recalling the car Jane handed over the night before.

She nods. "Okay. It's my favorite."

"I promise," I assure her, struck by how trusting her world is.

Lacy and Macy come bounding over. "Hey, Londyn, wanna see a cool dance?" Macy asks, grinning.

Londyn's eyes light up with excitement. "Yes!"

"Come on, we'll show you in your room," Lacy says, taking Londyn's hand.

As the three of them dash off toward Londyn's room, I stand up, watching them go. A warm feeling spreads through me, mingled with envy. I think about Tomas, about how he walked away from this. Just like my mom did.

"Jasper? You okay?" Jane's voice brings me back to the present.

I turn to her. "Yeah, I'm good. Just thinking."

She studies me for a moment, her eyes seeming to read my thoughts. "Kids have a way of making you think, huh?"

"Yeah."

"We'll come again, right?" Lacy asks when we get ready to leave a few minutes later. "We can even babysit."

I scoff. "Like Jane would ever trust you!"

"You can," the twins say in unison.

Jane laughs. "We'll see," she says, her gaze meeting mine.

As we say our goodbyes, I linger at the door. "Thanks for helping me find them," I tell her.

Our eyes lock for a moment longer than necessary, the air charged.

She nods, her eyes avoiding mine. "It was really the doorman. Maybe give him a bonus at Christmas. Besides, that's what friends are for, right?"

"Right. Friends." I start again. "About last night . . ."

"I've got an idea for a match for you."

What the hell?

Another match?

After everything?

I frown. "Why? I've had three. It's enough."

Her expression is unreadable. "It's my job, Jasper."

I glance at the twins, who are pretending to be engrossed in a conversation.

"Yeah, but—" I start, but she cuts me off.

"Freida," she blurts out, as if the name is an escape hatch.

"Who?"

She forges ahead, her voice gaining an artificial cheerfulness. "You like travel, right? You mentioned Vermont. And you'd probably love running a B and B?"

The idea of running a B and B is as foreign to me as knitting a sweater. But she doesn't give me the chance to respond.

"I actually thought of her last night, after, um, I came home . . ." She clears her throat. "Anyway, the database says you two have a sixty-eight percent chance of matching as far as interests go, but of course, you'd have to meet her to know for sure. She might be the one," she says.

"And why's that?" I ask, already knowing I won't like the answer.

"She's been on dates before but never clicked with anyone. She runs an online fashion magazine. She knows everyone in town and likes sports. She likes nature, running, and spending time with family, like you. She just went through a bad experience with a date and gave up. I'll send you her profile." She taps away on her phone, a mechanical motion that feels like a barrier going up between us.

The text arrives, and I glance at the profile of Freida. She's attractive, with long dark hair, but everything feels wrong. Fine, she likes sports and nature and exercising. That's the same for tons of people, but a bed-and-breakfast enthusiast? Sure, I have a dream of living out of the city, but why the hell would I want a stranger staying in my house using my towels and eating my breakfast?

"I can watch the twins for you."

She thinks my reluctance to go out with Freida is because of the two terrors.

But if that's the way Jane wants to play this, fine.

I'm tired of chasing her. It's time to give up.

"All right," I say, my voice flat. "I'll give it a shot."

Jane gives me a tight smile, but her eyes are sad. "I think it'll be great."

I take a step back. "I should get going."

She nods, her gaze lingering on me for a moment too long. "Good night, Jasper. Night, girls."

I turn and walk away, my hands clenching.

Then I hear Londyn call out, "Night, Jaspie. Night, Lacy and Macy."

It makes my heart do a funny flip. I turn around and throw her a big kiss.

Chapter 15
JANE

A few days later, I'm lost in a sea of spreadsheets and inventory lists on the third floor of the shop when Babs's voice crackles over the intercom. "Attention, we have an X alert on the main floor. I repeat, an X alert. Jane Darling, this is for you."

X is a new one. With a groan, I leave my paperwork and make my way down the staircase.

Babs is in the bestseller section talking to a customer. I wait until she's done, then poke her in the arm. "What's up?"

"Look to your left."

I scan the room. Customers browse quietly, a kid is entranced by a picture book, and then I spot him.

"Dr. Romantic, in the flesh." She makes a gagging sound.

Tomas. My *ex*. I wince.

"I thought you'd want a heads-up," she continues. "Also, I've been waiting to use the intercom for something dramatic."

"Like the flasher incident wasn't enough for you."

"I like a little spice every day."

Of course she does.

She nudges me with her elbow, a glint in her eye. "He started in the cooking section, and now he's moving to the medical books. I bet he needs help deciphering all that lingo for the show." She huffs. "I've watched it. I mean, how many times can a man furrow his brow and look pained as he operates on someone? He's so over the top. Is that good television?"

"Apparently." It even won an award. Tomas isn't over the top, though; he's actually quite shy until you get to know him.

"Yeah, but can he do this?" Babs clutches her chest and mimics a terrified expression. "Oh, the anguish of love, the despair of losing a patient! I need a woman to fuck me in the doctor's sleep room. Stat. So. Are you gonna go talk to him?"

A long sigh comes from my chest. I've been dodging his calls and texts like they're the plague. Yet, here he is, stepping into my safe space.

I eye his attempt at going unnoticed, the casual shorts, a plain T-shirt, and a black hat tugged low, with sunglasses. He's trying to blend in, but I recognize his hesitant stance, the way he tends to lean to the right, the shape of his shoulders.

I'm not in love with him anymore—no, those rose-colored glasses were ripped off years ago. But, before my pregnancy, our relationship was sweet. He used to gaze into my eyes and swear I was the most beautiful woman he'd ever laid eyes on. He loved to surprise me by cooking dinner and making me guess what he'd made.

As I watch Tomas browse through the aisle, more memories trickle in. Long walks in Central Park holding hands and laughing, the way he loved to twirl my hair in bed, a surprise dinner he organized on my birthday on the roof of my old apartment. Then there was the time he stayed up all night nursing me back to health when I had the flu. Every hour he'd check my temperature and bring me an ice pack. He'd joked that he was auditioning for a role as nurse. I guess he wasn't far off, considering his current TV gig.

He said he was deeply in love with me, but when reality hit, he only thought about his dreams.

I guess he got what he wanted, so why is he tracking me down?

I grab Babs's arm and move us over to the hallway where there's a mirror, checking my appearance. My linen shorts and blouse are blah, but I grabbed a bright-red cropped cardigan this morning to dress it up. It's cheerful at least.

As if reading my mind, Babs opens her purse and hands me a red lipstick. I slide it on.

My hair is styled in a low bun at the back of my head, and I yank it down and run my fingers through it.

We walk back out into the store, and Tomas looks up and starts making his way in my direction.

Taking a deep breath, I steel myself and walk to meet him.

"Welcome to the store," I say, trying to be normal.

Babs has gone back to the front counter and comes over the intercom again. "Jane, please report to the drama section. You're living it."

I glare over my shoulder at her, then exhale as I meet Tomas's eyes. "That's Babs. She thinks she's a comedian."

He clears his throat as he tucks his hands into his shorts. "Right. I guess I'm not very popular around here. Look, I hate to just show up, but you haven't returned my texts. I want to talk about Londyn."

My gut clenches. "I'm at work. I can't do that here."

He follows me as I head back up the stairs. "Wait. Jane. Just give me some time, okay? How about dinner tonight? Are you free?"

My jaw tightens. Of course I'm free. I don't have a social life.

"'Free' doesn't mean 'willing,'" I say as I take the stairs up two at a time, hoping to put physical distance between us.

"Jane, please. Before I head back to LA, I want to settle things between us. I'm trying to make things right for you and her." His voice holds a note of earnestness I hadn't expected, throwing me off balance.

I turn to face him, my arms crossed. He takes the steps to reach me and stops at the one below me, a nervous expression flitting over his face.

He exhales slowly, his gaze meeting mine. "Please. Let's meet at Leo's at eight tonight or tomorrow. You used to love that place. You always said they had the best pesto. Have dinner with me."

My heart drops, anxiety tingling down my spine.

Everything inside me wants to say no and retreat.

But as I stand there, locked in his eyes, I come to a decision. "Okay, fine, tonight."

I can't keep pushing him away as if he doesn't exist. He does.

And if he wants to talk about Londyn, then isn't it my responsibility as her mom to listen?

She's already asking questions in her innocent way. She's wondering who he is.

Someday, when she's older, she'll want to know why I pushed her father away when he finally showed up.

"Good, that's great. Thank you. I mean it." His relief is palpable as he reaches out and takes my hand and clutches it.

There's not even a spark between us as we touch, just lingering nostalgia.

"Okay. Goodbye," I say as I pull my hand back and turn to go up to the third floor. With each step, I'm already bracing myself for the dinner later, armoring myself to face what's ahead.

Later that night, I get out of a cab, wearing a strapless red dress, one I kept from a runway event years ago. My hair is curled and falls around my shoulders, and my makeup is heavier than usual.

Still, it doesn't make me feel confident. I'm a bundle of nerves.

I push open the door to Leo's, the yummy scent of garlic wrapping around me. Despite the years, this place hasn't changed. It's been around forever, and he used to save up his money for us to come.

I spot him immediately, sitting at a table near the back, his posture tense, his eyes tracking every person who enters. When his gaze lands on me, there's a flash of relief on his face with a smile. I steel myself, drawing on every ounce of composure I have, and walk toward him.

"Jane," he says as he stands. He's dressed up, wearing navy slacks and a dress shirt. Of course, he's handsome, and I notice several patrons eyeing him, perhaps recognizing him from the show. To me he just looks like a stranger. I recall the young man with longer hair and faded jeans, band shirts, and Converse.

"Hi," I reply, my voice steadier than I feel. He pulls out a chair for me, a gesture familiar yet weird.

We sit, and an awkward silence envelops us. The soft glow of the light above our table does nothing to ease the tension zipping between us.

The waiter comes by, and I order a glass of red wine, something to calm the nerves. Tomas opts for water, his eyes never leaving the menu, as if the answers to our situation might be between the lines of appetizers and entrées.

"So, the pesto pasta here is still the best?" he says, glancing up at me.

The truth is, I haven't been to this place since he left. I nod anyway.

The waiter returns with our drinks, and we place our orders, pasta for me and eggplant parm for him.

I take a sip of my wine, gathering my thoughts. "Let's talk, Tomas."

He sucks in a breath as he squares his shoulders, and I almost think he's a little scared of me. It makes me smirk.

He clears his throat, and out come words that sound as if he's rehearsed them a few times. "I've thought a lot about talking to you. About Londyn," he says, his voice lower than usual. "I want to be part of her life. I know that it's awful of me to ask because I've had no contact with you or her since she was born. Here and now, I deeply apologize for it, for not communicating with you, for pushing you away as if neither of you existed. I'm not the best human. I'm deeply flawed, and I'm sorry for it. At the time, I thought I was making the right choice. You know, career and timing."

His eyes hold mine as I keep my face impassive.

"And now? What's changed?"

He hesitates, sipping his water like it's a lifeline. "Savannah. She has nieces around the same age as Londyn. Every time I see them, it reminds me of what I missed out on. I've kept up with you through social media. I've seen photos of her. She's truly beautiful. She has my dimples."

"Ah, so a wedding's on the horizon, and suddenly you remember you have a daughter."

"I always knew," he insists. "But I was in another world. I had to make sacrifices. And now, I want to do right by Londyn."

The audacity.

"And how do you plan on doing that? You think you can just walk back into her life?"

He leans in. "I'm not asking for forgiveness. I don't deserve it, but I wanted you to know that I am sorry and I've thought about you over the years."

I arch a brow. "I guess the tabloids would rip you apart if they knew you'd deserted a daughter."

His lashes flutter. "That's not the reason I wanted to see you."

"Okay, fine," I say with a shrug, letting that angle go for the moment. "You're sorry. What else?"

He shifts in his seat, seeming uncomfortable, but there's no denying the determined expression on his face. "Things are going well for me. The show just got renewed for another season, and I'm doing a movie next year. I'm buying a house in Malibu with my fiancée. And I thought, well, maybe Londyn could spend some summers with us. Get to know her other side of the family. Savannah wants to meet her too. She adores kids."

"It's nice that you have such a perfect life."

He reaches across the table, attempting to take my hand, but I pull away. He exhales in exasperation. "I'm sorry, that came out wrong. My life isn't perfect, Jane. I just want to make amends. Perhaps I can just be a friend to her? We don't even have to tell her I'm her father until you're ready."

I cross my arms. "So you want me to uproot her life because you've decided to play dad?"

He winces. "I know it sounds abrupt, and I know you have your life here, your family who's supported you when I didn't." He looks down at the table, his brow furrowed. "I was flat broke back then, Jane, remember? I was waiting tables, doing catering gigs, delivering food just to keep a roof over my head. I couldn't fathom being a dad then, but I can help you now. In fact, um, I'd like to give you money, you know, for all the time I've missed paying for things Londyn and you needed."

I have to look away from him, recalling how hard Emmy worked to keep us going. Andrew too. I had savings from modeling, but it ran out fast.

My fingers clench around the cloth napkin, the fabric twisting in my hands.

How dare he assume that his money can make up for missed birthdays or the countless nights Londyn was sick.

Money doesn't buy time.

But as I look at him and see the strained expression in his eyes, the slouch of his shoulders, my anger eases. Perhaps he's grappling with his own guilt.

"Money doesn't cover your guilt. If you want to see Londyn, it's forever," I say sharply.

"I know. I do. It's time I stepped up." He lowers his voice and mentions a seven-figure number he wants to give me right now. I don't even twitch. I don't care about the money because I have made it work, but dammit, I'm still pragmatic.

That amount would secure her college and offer her opportunities that I couldn't do, like dance class and music lessons. A kernel of bitterness rises in my throat at the idea of accepting it.

Tomas brushes a hand through his dark hair. "It's not about the money. I just want a place in her life."

My mind spins as I try to focus. Can I allow him this, knowing it comes with the risk of another abandonment? Or do I deny Londyn the father she might come to cherish?

"I'm not a bad guy, Jane," he murmurs gently. "I loved you. I guess, I loved myself more."

"Is that still true? Are you still the number one person in your life?"

He lets out a long breath. "Probably. I'm self-centered, this is true, but I also know it and try to think of others now."

"But are you a good father?"

He looks down, tracing the rim of his water glass. "I want to be. Growing up, my mom was an alcoholic. Home was the last place I wanted to be."

I nod, recalling his stories about a tough upbringing in Indiana.

"My older sister gave up her dreams to take care of the rest of us. I saw how much it cost her, and I swore I'd chase my own dreams someday and not let anyone get in the way."

I listen, part of me empathizing. "And your dreams led you to Hollywood, away from us."

"Yes, and I won't lie—it's what I wanted. But the guilt . . ." He pauses to rub his forehead. "It eats at me. Missing out on Londyn growing up, not being there for you. I can't undo the past, but I can try to make things right."

His sincerity tugs at me, a reminder of the complex person he was when I knew him. He's not a hero type, but he isn't a villain either. He was a bit wishy-washy, a bit shy, but he was kind to others. In our relationship, I tended to make the big decisions. He was the dreamer; I was the realist.

"And if we agree to Londyn spending time with you, what's to say you won't just disappear again? What if your career goes kaput or you get a divorce or really anything that makes you run? Londyn isn't a toy you can pick up when you feel like it. She's a little girl, with feelings."

He meets my gaze, his eyes earnest. "I've realized something. Dreams aren't just what you achieve; they're about who's by your side when you chase them. I want to be a father to Londyn."

Still. How can I just let him waltz into our lives when he hurt us so much?

I stop, my mind spinning. Am I being especially hard on him because of my anger, at the fact that he left not just Londyn, but *me*?

The food arrives, and we eat in silence. My thoughts are going a mile a minute, and I barely touch my pasta. He doesn't eat much either. I watch him surreptitiously, trying to see beyond the mask to the man underneath.

He is older, now thirty. He has a stable career and a fiancée. He has a home.

But can I trust him with the heart of my daughter?

The waiter clears our plates and brings me another glass of wine.

Tomas gives me a small smile. "I know you're over there thinking about how to deal with me. You're wondering if I'm worth the trouble."

"Yes," I admit.

He gives me a hopeful look. "Does that mean you'll give me a chance? I'll do whatever you want. I don't want to change your life. I want to make it better—if I can. You made a commitment to her. I didn't. But I want to change that, if you'll allow it."

The silence that follows is heavy as I process his words.

The clamor of the restaurant fades into the background, leaving only his request echoing in my mind. A chance. He wants to be a part of Londyn's life, and my initial reaction is to guard her fiercely from the man who, by his own admission, couldn't prioritize her when it mattered.

Fear—and anger—looms large in the back of my mind. The risk of him flaking again, of him disappearing when Londyn gets attached, terrifies me. The potential for heartbreak, for Londyn's questions turning from innocent curiosity to tearstained confusion about why her dad doesn't want to see her anymore, is a scenario I can't bear.

I've been the one to hold her, to soothe her questions with stories and distractions.

There's also the part of me that bristles at Tomas's presumption. At the suddenness of it all. After all these years, he wants to step back into her life.

I pause, thinking. I'm the one who always says surprises can be good. They help us grow.

This is definitely a surprise.

I think about second chances and mending bridges.

People can change.

Whatever I decide will change everything. If I accept him, then there's a chance he'll hurt her, but if I don't, Londyn may never forgive me when she discovers it.

Tomas catches my gaze, the softness there reminding me of the sweet person he used to be. "I'm sorry to throw this at you, but well, I had to. I hope someday you'll forgive me."

I nod as I signal the waiter and ask for the check, even though Tomas tries to take it from me. It's defiance, I guess. I don't want him to think I can't pay my own way. After it's paid, we rise together and head to the exit. He walks next to me, opening the door for me to leave first. I hail a cab and turn to him as he thanks me for dinner.

"I have a lot to think about," I say.

He nods, sticking his hands into his pockets. "I'm here for a few more weeks. Maybe we can talk before I go?"

"I have your number." I pause as a cab pulls up next to the curb, and he opens the door for me. I brush past him. "Also, congrats on the wedding. I mean it."

Chapter 16
JASPER

There's a pink satin bendy thing in my bathroom.

I pick it up and go into the game room, where the girls are in a game of air hockey. "Time out," I say, holding it up. "What is this thing?"

The girls keep playing until Lacy glances my way and Macy uses that moment of weakness to her advantage and sends the puck into the goal.

"Yesssss," Macy hisses, arms wide in victory. "I win!"

Lacy looks at it. "Hair wrap. For curls."

I chuck it at her. "Why are you curling your hair in my bathroom? In fact, there's a lot of crap in my bathroom. What the hell happened?"

"You have the best light, Uncle J.," Lacy says. "We did a get-ready-with-me video in there."

Macy gives me a searching look. "So, forget your bathroom. We're wondering what's going on between you and Jane? Are you going to ask her out for a real date?"

"Nope."

"Aw, why not?" they say in unison.

My phone buzzes on the nearby table. I glance at the caller ID, and it's Andrew.

"That's Jane's brother on the line. Gonna take it?" Lacy's nosy, like she's tuned in to some drama channel.

I grab the phone, feeling that jolt in my chest. "Yo, Andrew. What's the deal?"

Yeah, I called him this morning to check in on Jane. My pride stings that she pushed me away, but I get it. Yes, she arranged a date between Freida and me, but in the end, I canceled it on the app.

The twins are eyeballing me, picking up on the tension as I step aside with the phone glued to my ear.

"Jane's out with Tomas tonight." Andrew cuts straight to it, knowing I wanted the heads-up if he showed his face again.

I stiffen, playing it cool. "Oh, yeah? Where they at?"

He hesitates. "You're digging for dirt on Jane? Since when?"

I rake a hand through my hair, cornered. "Not dirt. Just worries. She's been all twisted up about this Tomas crap since he showed up at her place."

Andrew laughs, not buying it. "And you're what? Her hero?"

I shoot a look at the twins, who are still listening. "It's not black and white."

"Jane's tough. She's got this," he says like it's that simple.

I exhale, annoyed. "Sure, she's tough. It just bugs me, thinking she's stressing over him."

Andrew goes quiet then. "Just tread lightly, man. Jane's had her share of rough waters. I don't know what's going on between you two, but she's my sister, and if you hurt her, I'll be pissed."

"We're friends," I say, downplaying the real deal going on between us.

I want her. She doesn't want me.

"Fine. She's at Leo's with Tomas."

I tell him goodbye and hang up, facing the twins' curious stares.

"All good, Uncle J.?" Lacy's got that look, all eyes and ears.

"Yeah, all good," I lie, plastering on a grin. Inside, it's a whole different story. My chest twinges, and I know exactly what it is. Jealousy. Which is dumb. The dude is getting married, but still, right now, he's with Jane.

A few minutes later, the doorbell cuts through the silence, and I swing it open to Rayna. Tan, a bit windswept, and wearing one of those easy smiles that says she's been doing more relaxing than worrying lately. Makes me think that's what moms like her need—breaks, not just a day here and there.

Like Jane. I'm starting to get why she's often got a scowl on her face. Between her job, Londyn, and dealing with Tomas, she's got a lot on her plate.

Rayna steps in, and her smile kicks up a notch, lighting up the place. Man, I love her.

"Jasper!" she says, throwing her arms out. We crash into a hug, her laughter ringing in my ears. "I missed you, little bro!"

Her energy's infectious, always has been. It's good to have her back.

"Missed you too," I chuckle as I pat her on the back. The twins crash into us, turning it into a noisy, squirming group hug.

As we break apart, Rayna's all lit up as she shares stories. "Italy and France were insane! The food, the sights! We did the whole gondola thing in Venice. And Paris? I ate so many croissants." She rummages through her bag and pulls out a key chain with a tiny Colosseum on it. "Figured I owed you for keeping an eye on the munchkins."

I scoff as I inspect the key chain. "Feels like I'm getting the raw end of the deal here."

She grins. "I'm so happy to be back! But spill, how were the twins? Give me the dirt."

I shoot a look at the girls, who suddenly seem very interested in their shoes. "Well, 'lively' would be putting it mildly," I say, trying to keep it light. No need for Rayna to start worrying the second she's back.

She shakes her head. "'Lively,' huh? I'll squeeze the truth out of them later."

171

After hearing a few more stories about her trip, the girls zip off to continue their hockey match while Rayna and I settle in the den.

"Actually, there's something we gotta talk about," I tell Rayna as she gets cozy in an armchair.

She raises a brow. "Woman troubles?"

I let out a dry laugh. "Nah, it's about my birth mom. She showed up, and we had coffee."

Rayna looks genuinely shocked. "After all this time? That's heavy. How are you dealing?"

I give a halfhearted shrug. "I'm all over the place. Angry, confused, you name it."

Worry flits over her pretty features. "It's a lot to process."

"She's got a new family now. They live in Philly."

Rayna gets up and paces around the den. Being upset on my behalf is pretty much a given with my four sisters. They've always been super protective of me since I was a little kid and they were teenagers.

She's the closest in age to me, with only ten years between us. She attended the same K–12 private school with me in Millwood, a neighborhood outside Salt Lake City. We rode the bus together, and even though she had friends to sit with, she always sat next to me like my protector.

Once on the playground, when I was in first grade, an older kid thought it'd be hilarious to use my backpack as a soccer ball. Rayna marched into the fray, her eyes blazing with that don't-mess-with-my-family fire. She liked to use her razor-sharp tongue, and she didn't mind using her fists either. Messing with me meant an encounter with her.

Then there was my struggle in school. Math was my nemesis, and Rayna, bless her, would sit down with me at the kitchen table when she was in community college, night after night, breaking down problems into something I could actually understand. She had the patience of a saint, no matter how many times she had to explain what x stood for.

She huffs. "The nerve of her. I mean, how did she explain never calling or writing?"

"Exactly," I say, the bitterness seeping through. "She moved on, and now she's back, acting like we can just pick up where we left off."

She pokes me, trying to lighten the mood. "Look at you, though. I bet the twins kept you busy, didn't they?"

"Ah, you know I'll never tell on them."

"So they were awful. I knew it. One on one, they're okay, but together . . ."

I laugh. "Nah. I enjoyed them."

"But Sunflower . . ." She puts her hands on her hips, her eyes steely. "I'm worried about you seeing her. Are you sure it's okay?"

I exhale. "It messes with my head, you know? Especially with the season coming up."

"I'm sorry, Jasper."

I clasp my hands together, clarity hitting me. "It's weird, but I've got this fear that I'm just like her. I don't necessarily bail, but I tend to disappear into a shell when things get tough. Maybe I do that because she dumped me."

Rayna watches me. "You don't bail. Look at how you've stuck with football. Look at all the friendships you've made over the years on the team."

I sigh.

Still.

I may be my own worst enemy when it comes to holding on to women. My college girlfriend, Amanda, is an example. We could have had something real, but at the first sign of trouble, when she wanted to talk, I retreated and became passive. It wasn't that I didn't care about her—no, it was the opposite. I cared too much and that terrified me.

It's like there's this voice in the back of my mind, whispering that everyone I love will eventually leave. So I leave first. Not with a dramatic exit, but by fading away so that they have no choice but to move on.

It's a defense mechanism. I rub my jaw.

Amanda deserved better. They all did. Each woman I let slip away because I couldn't commit to climbing over the walls I've built around my heart.

I glance at Rayna. She thinks she knows me, but deep down, I'm wrestling with this fear of turning into Rae-Anne.

Later, the girls and Rayna order a pizza for dinner, and I slump into the nearest chair, my thoughts drifting back to Jane. With Tomas shaking up her world and my own life turned upside down by my mom, our situations feel similar, and if I'm struggling this much, Jane's situation must be even more daunting.

Maybe she's got a point pushing me back.

Could be I'm not cut out for the deep end.

Not the type to plant roots. Because of my mom.

But then, every time Jane pops into my head, there's this buzz.

A vibe that's got nothing to do with sex.

It's all her.

The way she is.

That scowl that means business.

I've been with plenty of women, but she's a whole different league. She's different.

Feeling an urge to move, to try and make sense of my thoughts, I stand. A walk might do me some good. I grab a hat and head out, wondering if I'm making a mistake by letting Jane keep me in the friend zone.

Yet fear nags at me, whispering that perhaps it's wiser to step back now, before I risk causing hurt to her and Londyn.

I find myself walking to Leo's, my feet moving of their own accord. I know I'm crossing a line, but something in me needs to see her.

I shouldn't.

Every logical bone in my body screams to turn back, to stay out of it. But then there's that gnawing feeling, hating the thought of her dealing with Tomas alone.

The night's alive with people as I near Leo's. I halt outside, my hands clenching.

Am I about to crash her dinner? It feels wrong, yet I'm drawn to her like a magnet.

I push through the door and make a beeline for the bar. My eyes sweep the place, hunting for Jane.

And there she is at a corner table, facing Tomas. Even from this distance, I can spot the tension in her posture. I move toward them, then freeze. What's my game plan? I've no right to invade her space, no matter how much my gut tells me to pull her out of there.

If she looks over at me, if she seems like she's in distress, then I'll go to her.

I order a whiskey, but my stomach is too weird to drink it. I toy with it as I watch them.

She never takes her eyes off Tomas. It's as if they're having a silent war between them.

Dammit. I need to go. She doesn't need me. I lay out cash on the bar and bail, the city lights a blur as I try to shake off this feeling of uncertainty when it comes to her.

Chapter 17
JANE

As I step out of the cab, the night air is cool against my skin. I pull out my phone, scrolling through the notifications. There, among the clutter of messages and alerts, is Jasper's text. Sent an hour ago.

Jasper: Hey, you okay?

My fingers hover over the keyboard. What should I say? I decide to keep it simple.

Me: Yes, I'm fine. Just got home.

Almost immediately, another text from Jasper comes through, and my stomach flutters.

Jasper: Was thinking about you. How did it go with Tomas?

I hesitate. How did he know about my dinner? Do I want to open up about it?

Me: How did you know?

There's a brief pause before his reply pops up.

Jasper: I talked to Andrew. Want to talk about it?

A small smile tugs at my lips. Jasper, showing his caring side.

Me: I'm exhausted.

Jasper: Understandable. Rain check then. Whenever you're ready.

Me: Good night.

Jasper: I'll protect you if you'll let me.

I stop in the lobby, reading the words. My throat tightens as I pocket my phone. I can't reply to that. I just can't.

Because I like it way too much.

With a sigh, I make my way up to my apartment.

I get off the elevator and freeze at the sight before me. It's Jasper, sitting with his back against my door, with his head tilted back and eyes closed.

"Jasper?"

His eyes snap open, and he stands up swiftly, relief in his gaze.

"I, uh, wanted to make sure you got home and were okay," he says, scratching the back of his head, looking slightly embarrassed.

"Since when do you wait outside doors?" I try to keep it light, but my heart pounds in my chest.

He shrugs. "Since I realized I care about what happens to you."

The confession hangs in the air between us. We stand there for a moment, just looking at each other, the tension palpable.

His eyes never leave mine. "I guess I just needed to see you to make sure you were really okay."

His honesty catches me off guard.

"Thank you," I finally say softly.

"Can I come in? Just for a minute?"

The invitation is tempting. But I hesitate, aware of the complexity of our situation.

"I don't think that's a good idea," I say, although every fiber of my being says otherwise.

He nods, understanding. "Okay, I get it. Take care of yourself, okay?"

"I will," I assure him.

He lingers for a moment longer, then turns to leave. As I watch him walk away, a part of me wants to call out to him, to invite him in, but it's a line I'm not ready to cross.

Something inside me twists.

This isn't right. I can't just let him go. It's only talking. Londyn is fast asleep, and a conversation can't hurt.

"Jasper, wait," I say. He stops and turns, a question in his eyes.

"Come in. Just for a talk," I add quickly.

A small smile appears on his face. "Yeah, I'd like that."

He follows me inside, and we move to the living room.

Babs is asleep on the couch with a book in her lap. She stirs as we close the door, blinking herself awake.

"Jane? And Jasper? What a surprise," she says, sitting up and rubbing her eyes.

I feel a blush creeping up my cheeks. "Hey. How was everything with Londyn?"

Babs stretches, yawning. "Oh, we had a blast. We built a fort in the living room and pretended we were on a safari. I read her *Where the Wild Things Are*. She loved it."

Jasper chuckles. "Sounds like a fun night."

"It was," Babs agrees, standing up and gathering her things. "By the way, Andrew called. He's out with some friends and won't be home."

I nod, grateful for the update. "Thanks for everything tonight, Babs."

"Don't stay up too late, you two," she teases with a sly grin. "And remember, no trouble."

I roll my eyes playfully. "Good night, Babs."

She heads toward the door. "Have fun," she says, and then she's gone, leaving Jasper and me standing awkwardly in the living room.

I glance down at my red dress, the one I agonized over wearing earlier when I got ready to go to Leo's. I excuse myself from Jasper's presence and make my way to the bedroom.

I quickly change into my joggers and shirt, feeling a sense of relief at the coziness of the fabric. It's like shedding Tomas and stepping back into the real me.

I check on Londyn, and she's asleep, her little chest rising and falling in a steady rhythm. I lean down, brushing a gentle kiss on her forehead. She is what matters.

I think about Jasper waiting in the living room. He makes me feel alive, but can I really afford to let that take root? Am I ready to open my life to the possibility of something more?

I run my finger down the Lovers card. Do we have a chance?

I give another glance at Londyn, her presence grounding me. No matter what happens, she's my priority. Jasper, whatever this thing is between us, it can't change that.

I sit on the couch, tucking my legs under me, while Jasper chooses the armchair across from me. The distance feels necessary, and a little frustrating.

"So," he says, running a hand through his hair, "how was your meeting with Tomas?"

I sigh. "Complicated. I'm afraid he really doesn't know how to be a parent." I stare down at my clasped hands. "He wants to see her and get to know her. He's also self-centered, so I'm afraid that when she really needs him, he might flake."

He leans forward, his eyes intense. "If he does, you can handle it. You're strong, independent. You've built a life here, for you and Londyn. Don't let him shake that."

"He won't."

He leans back, the lines of his face softening. "My adoptive mom became mostly blind when I was a kid and never lost her spirit. My dad, he's her rock. He rearranged the entire house for her, installed tactile guides, and learned braille. He made it seamless. He would read to her every night, describe colors and sceneries. He even took cooking classes to make her favorite meals."

"That's incredibly sweet," I say, imagining the love between his parents. I peek at him from the corner of my eye. "Tell me more about them."

"Really? I thought we'd drag Tomas through the mud first."

I laugh. "Nah. I don't want to think about him. Tell me good things."

He mulls that over, then chuckles. "Okay, once Dad took us all on a cruise to Antarctica. Wanted us to see something out of the ordinary, and he delivered. Picture this: my four sisters, their husbands, a bunch of kids, and us all arguing at every meal on the ship. We took up the top level of the boat with our suites."

He shakes his head. "It was chaos. At one point, we're on this smaller boat for whale watching, right? Macy, ten or so, decides she's gonna sing to the whales. She starts belting out these howls, trying to talk to them."

"Did she get a reply?" I'm already smiling at the thought.

"They didn't exactly chat back, but we did get a curious whale to check us out, probably wondering what the racket was. And just as it surfaces, my sister—Rayna, the twins' mom—jumps so hard she falls backwards. Ended up needing stitches on her head."

"And you're laughing?"

"Hell yeah. Rayna's made it into one of those legendary family stories." He pauses. "She just got back from her European trip, so she and the twins will be Utah bound soon."

Realization hits me. "You're going to miss them."

"Yeah," he says, his voice dropping. "A lot."

He seems to push the sadness I saw away and continues with the story. "On the same trip, we went out on the ice as one of our excursions. Demy, my oldest sister, instigates a massive snowball fight. Dad's guarding Mom, I'm rallying the kids, and it's all-out war. Dad's building forts, the kids are launching snowballs like pros, and our guides are begging us to stop."

"Let me guess. Someone got hurt?"

He smirks. "My brother-in-law, more of a city guy, decides he's gonna storm dad's fort. Ends up slipping and rolling down this hill. He came face to face with a penguin. Of course, we all go chasing after him, and he was fine. We ignored him to check out the penguins. It's a wild place to go, really. Very windy and dry. The ice is so thick that there are mountains under the ice. Also, there aren't any polar bears there. They're in the Arctic. You know, the best part wasn't the ice or the penguins. It was being in this remote, untouched part of the world with my family. Sharing that experience with them."

"Wow. I need to sign up for your vacations."

He gives me a quick look, and I glance away. Ugh, why did I say that?

"I bet Londyn would love to see a real penguin," he says softly. "Nothing beats the sight of those little guys waddling around. They own it."

"She would love that."

He reaches into his pocket and pulls out the toy car. "Speaking of Londyn. I've been carrying this around."

My heart warms at the sight of it in his large hands. "You should keep it and give it to her yourself."

His eyes widen. "Oh?"

I nod.

"Maybe I can tell her about those penguins then."

His words do something to me, stirring emotions inside me. It's like every sentence he utters is a thread, tugging me closer, weaving something together that I can't seem to resist. There's something about him, beyond his charm and the easy smiles, that reaches out to the emptiness in me.

I chew on my bottom lip. He's so warm. So fun.

It's in the way he sees the world, his passion for the simple things, and how he talks about his family. It's in the way he looks at me, like he really sees me—not just as Jane, but as a woman with a heart that's guarded.

This pull toward him is like stepping to the edge of a cliff and gazing down at a beautiful view.

Do I take one more step or run away?

"Jane?"

I glance up, and he's standing, a look on his face I can't read.

"Yeah?"

He takes a deep breath. "I don't want to leave, but I've been here for an hour and I'm sure you need some sleep."

"I'm not sleepy."

Our eyes lock, a silent conversation passing between us. My breath hitches slightly at the intensity in his gaze.

He moves closer, and there's a question in his eyes, and my heart is pounding so loudly, I'm sure he can hear it.

He stops in front of the couch and takes my hand and pulls me up. His hands come up to frame my face. I close my eyes, leaning into his chest.

Finally.

It feels right.

Like everything is going to be okay.

I gaze up at him, his face that's sculpted by the hands of a god. His hair falls in soft waves, framing a face that carries the faintest hint of stubble. His blue eyes, like an endless expanse of sky, hold a depth of emotion.

Moving slowly, he presses his lips to mine, hesitant and soft. Little brushes of heat that make me gasp.

My hands find their way to his shoulders, instinctively pulling him closer. There's a rightness in the way we fit together.

His kiss isn't demanding. It's heartbreakingly sweet.

As we part, our foreheads rest together, our breath mingling. I open my eyes to Jasper's gaze, filled with an emotion that sends a shiver down my spine. In that kiss, we shared more than just affection; it was vulnerable.

"What was that for?"

He looks into my eyes. "I don't know," he admits softly. "I shouldn't have done that. I mean, with everything going on . . ."

I shake my head slightly, silencing his doubts. "It's just complicated."

But life is *always* complicated.

An exhale comes from his chest. "And I don't want to make things more difficult for you."

I pause, then I find myself saying, "It's not about making things complicated. It's about what feels right. And that felt right."

His finger tugs at my bottom lip. "It did."

We kiss again, and I feel the heat of his breath on my skin and the rasp of stubble against my cheek. My fingers tangle in his hair while his hands hold me firmly at the waist. Our mouths move in perfect rhythm as if we've done this a million times before.

I don't worry about Londyn asleep in the other room.

I don't think about the Plan B still sitting unused in my bathroom.

I just want him.

"Is this just us having fun?" I gaze up at him. Part of me wants him to say yes; the other side yearns for something I can't say.

Jasper pauses for a moment, his gaze searching my face. His hand gently caresses my cheek, his touch leaving a trail of electricity in its wake.

I shake my head. "Don't answer that. Don't say anything. Just kiss me again."

He leans in, his lips begging mine, coaxing them, adoring them.

My fingers grip his shirt, pulling him closer as if trying to merge our bodies into one. I want to lose myself in him.

"I want you," he says huskily as he kisses down my neck.

He takes my mouth again, our tongues intertwining. His teeth lightly nibble on my bottom lip.

"We'll take it one day at a time, angel."

I press my lips to his jawline, kissing my way to his ear. I bite down, making him groan.

I can't predict the future, but I can control what happens right now, in this place, in this time. I tell him this, whispering in his ear as my hands drift down his chest.

"Live in the moment," he says. His voice is low and velvety, sending shivers down my spine. "I want to feel you here with me, right now."

I close my eyes and surrender to the feelings coursing through me, trying to push aside any thoughts of what tomorrow might bring.

I bury my face in his neck and inhale.

I'm intoxicated by him. Drunk. With every breath, I'm falling deeper into the spell he weaves.

He swings me up into his arms and carries me to the couch.

I can't help the giggle as he kicks a few toys out of his way.

"Don't step on a LEGO," I warn, and he dodges it.

He lays me on my couch and just stares down at me, his chest heaving. "I don't know what I want to do to you first."

"Anything."

Heated eyes caress my curves as his hands grip the ends of my T-shirt and whip it over my head. With fumbling fingers, I help him take off my bra. He drinks in the sight of me, his eyes dilating.

He's unbuttoning his shirt, and it's off in a heartbeat—then he's unbuttoning his jeans. My mouth waters when I see he's commando again. His cock is hard, standing erect and demanding attention. I reach out and take it, feeling the firmness beneath my fingers. He moans softly as I stroke him, my eyes locked on his. His body is perfect, muscular, lean, and covered in a light dusting of hair.

I lick my lips, my eyes never leaving his. "Do you like that?" I ask, my voice husky with desire.

"Fuck, yes," he growls.

I release him and sit up, slipping off my jeans. I leave my underwear on, stopping.

"What?" he says, clearly disappointed.

I dash off the couch, grab a chair from the kitchen, and walk with it down the hall. I hear him following.

He peers at me. "Um?"

Ignoring him, I arrange the chair a few inches away from the door. I lean the chair back till it's resting against the closed door. It won't keep Londyn from opening it, but if she does, the falling chair will alert me that she's coming out of the room.

"Ah," he says. "In case she wakes up."

"I don't want her to be scarred for life if she sees me having sex. What would I even say?"

"Londyn, Mommy and Jaspie were wrestling," he says as he sweeps me up in his arms and carries me back to the living room. He sits on the couch and arranges me to straddle him. He holds my gaze as he cards his fingers through my hair.

"Jesus, you're beautiful," he tells me gently, rubbing his fingertips over my eyebrows, the curve of my cheeks, then down between my breasts.

My breath catches at his touch.

"But we need some ground rules."

Jasper nods. "All right, what do you suggest?"

"We can't do this if we're not honest with each other," I say firmly. "No secrets, no hiding how we feel. This is just fun."

There's a long pause. "I can do that, but I'm not going on another date you set up, angel."

"Okay." I laugh, caressing his stubble as I take a kiss. "Also, condoms."

"One in my wallet."

I wrinkle my nose. "You always have it? Is it old? Don't lose this one."

He gives me a mocking look. "We fucked so hard, baby. It couldn't keep up."

I pretend glare at him. "Don't do it again."

"Yes, ma'am," he says as he leans in and snatches a kiss.

I relax against him, letting the moment wash over me, feeling something weird, something strange, something like happiness.

He kisses my lips, then my neck, moving down to my chest, leaving a trail of open-mouthed kisses that makes me breathless. He toys with my nipples, his hands kneading them.

"Lean back, angel," he murmurs, and I do, positioning my spine on the tops of his legs. The friction of his skin feels incredible against my bare skin. I bare myself to him, no trepidation in me, as he rubs his fingers over my clit, then enters my pussy with his finger. It takes balance, but it's worth it.

I moan softly, feeling the waves of pleasure coursing through me as he slowly moves his finger in and out. He rearranges me on the couch and deftly slips off my underwear. He kisses a trail back up my naked body, driving me wild with desire.

"You're so wet," he says, his voice low and gravelly.

My nerves are electrified as his lips make their way to my nipples, where he gently sucks and bites, sending shivers down my spine.

I watch his face. The flush on his cheeks, the heat in his gaze, the intensity of his desire. God, he's so unbelievably beautiful. I feel myself slipping away, consumed by the pleasure he's so skillfully giving me.

He adds another finger inside me, and I gasp.

The sensation is overwhelming, and I arch my back, trying to push against him, wanting more.

"You like that, baby?" he asks, his voice sultry.

"Yes," I gasp, feeling my arousal build with each thrust of his fingers.

I grab his head, urging him to go deeper, to take more from me. He complies, his fingers moving faster. I'm building toward my orgasm with each plunge of his fingers.

He pushes the coffee table out of the way, and we get on the floor. We end up between the couch and the table.

He lies down next to me, placing my arms above my head, pinning me in place. His lips are on my neck, his teeth gently nibbling and his tongue licking, sending shock waves of pleasure through me. My hips buck, desperate for more.

He puts his fingers back in my pussy, leaving me feeling filled, yet still aching for more. I whimper, but he silences me with another deep kiss. "No crying out, remember? That's right, baby," he growls, his fingers finding my clit, rubbing it in circles, sending me into a frenzy. My legs tremble as he exerts just the right amount of pressure, getting me closer and closer to the edge.

"More," I beg, my breath coming in ragged gasps. My walls clench around his fingers, the pleasure building to a climax. "I'm going to come," I say in his ear, the words spilling from my lips.

He keeps up the rhythm, knowing exactly what to do to push me over the edge. His fingers slide in and out of me, his thumb on my clit.

I go over the edge, and he keeps going as I convulse, my body shuddering with release. Sensations rocket, first building in my spine, then spiraling out over my body.

My eyes roll back in my head. The pleasure radiates from my core, spreading outward until it envelops me entirely. I feel like I'm floating, weightless and free.

I feel myself reaching the edge again, the tension building and building until I can't take it anymore.

"Please," I gasp. "Please."

Finally, he pulls away, his face wet with sweat.

"Perfect," he says, a satisfied grin on his face. "Now it's my turn." He gets up to find his jeans and pulls the condom out of his wallet. I admire his body, the broad shoulders and trim waist.

I watch as he rolls the condom down his length, feeling a surge of desire at the sight.

"Put your back against the couch. That way you won't scoot away and I won't give you rug burn," he tells me, and I obey. He lifts my leg and lets it hang in the crook of his elbow. He kisses me softly before positioning himself at my entrance.

"Are you ready?" he asks, his voice a breathy whisper against my lips.

"Yes."

With one swift thrust, he's inside me, filling me completely. I gasp, my body adjusting to the feel of him.

His eyes lock onto mine as he begins to move.

He goes slowly at first, his hips rocking gently, eliciting soft moans from me as his cock slides in and out. I wrap my legs around him, wanting more of him.

He picks up the pace, his thrusts becoming faster, the muscular cord of his body taut as he works to please me. I meet his every thrust, our bodies slapping together in a rhythmic dance of desire.

"Take all of me."

I do, my hips bucking to meet his every stroke, my nails digging into his back as I cling to him.

He leans in, his mouth finding my neck, his teeth gently scraping against my skin.

His hips rock forward. I can't really move but try to meet his rhythm. The pleasure builds, my senses heightened as he hits just the right spot.

"Jasper. Don't stop."

There's a wicked glint in his eyes. "Trust me, I won't." He picks up the pace, his hips moving faster, his hair sweeping my skin with each thrust. My breath hitches in my throat, the intensity overwhelming.

His gaze holds mine. Sweat glistens on his skin, his eyes hooded with desire.

I'm lost in the sensation, my mind foggy.

"I'm going to . . ." I gasp, my voice hoarse.

His thrusts become erratic, his body shaking with the intensity of his own arousal.

"Fuck, I'm so close," he says, his lashes fluttering against his cheekbones. "I'm not going to last much longer."

I wrap my legs around his waist, pulling him closer, wanting him to feel every inch of my body. "Then don't."

The pleasure builds, becoming almost unbearable, and I know that we're both on the edge of something incredible. I grip his hair, my walls tightening around him.

"Oh god," he groans, his eyes opening wide as he gazes into mine. "Fuck."

I fly over the cliff, my body combusting. It feels like my entire body is alive with pleasure, every nerve ending tingling with ecstasy.

"I want you to come on my dick every fucking day." He watches me writhe and goes with me, then collapses, his body shaking with the aftershocks.

He pulls out of me and looks between us. "Condom is still on," he says as I gulp in air, my chest heaving.

"Come here, angel." He pulls me close, his arms wrapping around me as I melt into his embrace. We're both sticky.

"That was incredible," I breathe.

He hums in his throat and reaches over to turn my face to his. His kiss is achingly slow and sweet.

My heart races at the touch.

I trace the line of his arm, feeling the solid weight of him next to me, and it's terrifying how right it feels. I told him our hearts weren't involved, but this isn't just physical attraction. Part of me is daring to dream of a future where I don't have to face everything alone.

But I'm scared.

Falling for Jasper isn't part of the plan.

He presses a kiss to the side of my head, and I hear him inhaling the scent of my hair. I burrow closer, and he lets out a sigh of contentment.

I keep my eyes closed to hide the emotion I'm feeling.

Tears want to fall.

And I don't know why.

But I do.

He's broken down all my walls.

He's opened the door to my guarded heart and walked right in.

Chapter 18
JASPER

Sprawled out on Jane's floor with couch cushions and throw blankets, I feel content. Jane's head is on my arm, her hair brushing against my face.

I tease her a bit. "Is this a regular thing, having people over for floor sleepovers, or am I just lucky?"

She shifts to give me a look, one of those half-amused, half-serious glances. "I save the living room floor for the elite."

I give her a gentle nudge, chuckling. "Maybe next time we could use a real bed?"

The question floats between us, and I watch as her long lashes brush against her cheekbones. "We talking about a next time?"

There's a pause, and I wonder if I've pushed too far. But then she cracks a smile. "I'd like that."

I catch the significance. She's rolling the dice on us.

We hit a quiet moment, the kind that feels right. I switch gears. "Are you working tomorrow?"

Her hands play with my hair almost absently as if she's not even aware of it. "Nope. I promised Londyn a day out in Central Park. They've got a fair this weekend."

"I've never really checked out the park."

She flicks me on the forehead. "Bull. Your place is right there."

I shoot her my best wounded look, which I know works wonders. "All right, busted. But what do you say to me crashing your day out? I'll even throw in dinner, my treat."

"I don't know. It's supposed to be a mom-daughter thing . . ."

"It'll be a blast. And I swear, I'll behave. Plus, I'm pretty good at those carnival games. How about I win Londyn a giant stuffed animal? Maybe a penguin? It will be just us having fun."

She thinks on it, and I can't stand the wait, so I tickle her and get her to laughing as she pleads for mercy. "Fine, fine. You're in. But keep that competitive side under wraps."

"Deal."

She settles back against me, and we soak up the quiet.

"I'll snag the fluffiest beast they've got. We'll have to make room for it," I promise.

She smirks. "Great, another obstacle for the floor."

I lean in, dropping my voice. "It's not about the prize. It's about the fun. Just two friends and Londyn enjoying the day."

Her look softens, and I know I've played my cards right. "All right, but you better come through for Londyn."

"I'll get her the top prize, even if I have to hit up every booth."

The silence stretches between us, comfortable, yet tinged with something else. Happiness?

The question is, Am I up for being just a friends with benefits guy with Jane? I shove that aside for now as she tells me more about her dinner with Tomas and how she's considering letting him see Londyn. I tell her more about the history of my bio mom and how I grew up in a cult. I mention how she's been sending me text messages, which I've ignored. Around two, I kiss her goodbye and leave, still buzzing from being with her.

In the morning, Rayna and the twins and I have breakfast at a local place, and then I send them off to the airport in a town car, counting down the time until I see Jane.

Dressed in shorts and a T-shirt with a hat and sunglasses, I hit Central Park's entrance. It's midday Sunday, and the place is swarming with people.

The sun plays hide-and-seek through the trees, and some street performers are doing their thing near Bethesda Fountain.

I spot Jane and Londyn by the entrance near the Plaza Hotel. Jane's wearing a cute blue sundress and a straw hat. Londyn has her hair up in pigtails, practically vibrating with excitement.

"Jaspie!" she shouts as she runs toward me.

I catch her and swing her around. "You pumped for today? Got a whole day of park adventures ahead."

Her head bobs like one of those dashboard dolls. "Picnic and ducks and the lake!"

Jane gives me a shy look and smiles hesitantly. I don't kiss her or even try to hold her hand. We're going to move at a snail's pace to protect Londyn.

We weave through the park and pick a spot by Bow Bridge where the view's pretty.

Jane's got lunch sorted in a basket and spreads it out for us on a small blanket—sandwiches, strawberries, chips, and bottled water.

Londyn talks nonstop about her preschool. When she mentions her teacher Miss Erin, I have to keep my face straight as Jane smothers a laugh. Afterward, we head over to the boats, and Londyn picks out a purple one with yellow oars.

As I paddle us, Londyn perches at the front of the boat, taking it all in. Jane sits across from me, a smile on her face as she watches her.

"Jaspie, are you sure you know how to drive this boat?" Londyn asks.

I grin, giving the oars another strong pull. "Trust me, kiddo, I've got this. We won't end up swimming."

"I can swim!" she tells me proudly. "Mama taught me at the gym."

Jane smirks at me. "That's right. Honestly, I wouldn't mind seeing Jasper take a dip. Should we push him in, Londyn?"

She giggles. "No, Mama. We need him to row!"

"Hey now, no mutiny on my ship," I say playfully, the rhythm of the boat in the water making a soothing sound.

Londyn laughs, then turns her attention to the water, trailing her fingers along the surface. "It feels like we're flying!"

I agree, feeling a weird sense of pride that I'm contributing to her happiness. "You see any fish down there, Londyn?"

She leans over slightly, peering into the lake. "I think so. Hey, can fish hear us?"

Jane leans in. "They might. Why don't you say hello?"

Londyn cups her hands around her mouth. "Hello, fishies! What's your favorite color? Mine is blue! Do you like to draw? I do." Then she goes on to tell the fish about a conversation she got into with another kid from preschool over who's drawing was the best. Hers was, of course.

"Did they talk back?" I ask.

"I heard them. They think I'm a mermaid," Londyn declares, settling back down with a satisfied nod.

As we glide over the lake, I catch myself looking over at Jane. She's got Londyn tucked in next to her now as they soak up the sun.

My heart does something weird in my chest, and I have to glance away from them just to gather my thoughts.

Jane is incredibly beautiful and not in just a physical way. It's the way she gazes at Londyn with a fierce kind of love.

After we finish on the lake, we walk along the path, and Londyn's eyes light up at the sight of carnival games stretching out ahead. "Can we?" She pulls at my hand.

"Sure, let's check them out," I say, eyeing the lineup. We zero in on a dart game. It looks straightforward, just pop balloons and win stuff. The catch? The cool prizes need more balloons popped.

The guy running the show is all smiles and smooth talk. "Give it a shot," he tells me, waving us over.

I lay down some cash. Should be easy, right? Wrong. My first three darts miss by a mile.

"Bit off your game, huh?" Jane says to me with a giggle.

"Just getting started," I reply, throwing down more cash for round two. This round's a bit better; one balloon pops, but it's still not enough for a decent prize. Ugh.

The man running the game laughs at me, his eyes knowing. He gets that I have to win for Londyn. "Third time's a charm," he says.

"Watch this," I say, more to myself than anyone. I'm not about to let a bunch of balloons best me. I can throw—hell, I'm a quarterback.

This time, it's like the darts are part of my arm. Pop, pop, pop—the balloons don't stand a chance. Londyn squeals as Jane laughs. I do my quarterback dance, then give them both high fives.

The man digs out the day's top prize—a massive fluffy unicorn that's almost as big as Londyn.

She wraps her arms around it, then me. "You're the best, Jaspie!"

Jane gives me a playful shove. "Looks like you're the champ after all."

I feel ten feet tall.

Sure, it's just a carnival game.

But seeing them happy, hearing their laughter, hell, this whole day, it's about the best win I could ask for.

Chapter 19

JASPER

While I'm walking out of the training facility, my phone buzzes with a call from Graham—Emmy's husband and Jane's brother-in-law.

"How's that baby girl doing?" I ask him. Emmy and Graham have a one-year-old named Hazel. They've been in Greece for a few months staying at a villa he bought.

Graham's voice is all laid back. "Good. She's taking a nap at the moment."

I picture them there, the ideal little family under the sun in Santorini.

"Magic's turned into the local star. He roams around and makes friends with the neighbors," he adds, chuckling as he mentions their cat. "How are things with the team?"

I slide into my car, thankful for the blast of AC. "I'm sure you're keeping up with the news. Dalton Talley arrived for training. He's got potential but needs to adjust to the switch from college."

"You showing him the ropes?"

I laugh, shaking my head even though he can't see. "Trying to. Kid's a bit cocky, but he's not hopeless. We've been working out together and going through tape."

"Good, good. Hey, so . . . Emmy says you and Jane have been getting close. You took them to the park?"

I pause, my head adjusting to the change in topic. Emmy and Jane talk, so he knows about us, obviously. "Yeah, we've been hanging out."

Hanging out. Or more specifically, I've spent most nights at her place since Andrew moved out. I usually show up after Londyn goes to bed, and we end up sleeping on the couch. I then slip out around five, before Londyn wakes up. Tonight she is getting a sitter and coming to my place.

He clears his throat, as if gearing up for a hard convo. "Look, Jane's solid, you know? After the hand she's been dealt, she doesn't need anyone stirring up trouble in her personal life."

"It's not some game for me," I say, my grip tightening on the steering wheel. "I like her a lot."

Graham hesitates, then hits where it hurts. "I'm sure you do, but it's just your history. You tend to just let things fizzle out when it comes to relationships. Or am I wrong?"

His comment reminds me of my own fear, the one where I'll end up hurting Jane.

And I can't think of one thing to say to defend myself.

He clears his throat. "She has more than just herself to think about."

"I know."

"She needs someone who's all in."

Defensiveness rears its head. "Wow. I thought you were calling just to chat, but this feels like an interrogation. And my relationship with Jane isn't really your business."

He tsks. "She's my sister-in-law, so yeah, I have a say, and if you're not ready for what she needs, you've got to own that. Dating someone so close to my family changes things."

"It's not something I entered into lightly. I've known her for a long time."

"I know, but if things don't work out, it could put everyone in an awkward spot. Not just you and Jane."

Fine, that thought has crossed my mind, but hearing it from Graham makes me even more anxious.

"What about your friendship with me?" he asks.

"I value our friendship, you know that."

"Yeah, but if things end badly? If you end up hurting her, I'm not sure how to handle that."

My throat feels dry. "Believe me, I'm trying to navigate this as carefully as I can."

"This whole situation could get messy."

"Yeah, I get it," I say sharply. "You keep repeating yourself."

Graham exhales, the sound heavy with frustration. "I didn't call you up to pick a fight. I'm worried about Jane, but I'm worried about you too." His voice softens. "I called because I care, not to lecture."

I hear Emmy's voice in the background, and Graham says something to her. "Hey, I gotta go. I'm here if you wanna chat."

Then he's gone, and I exhale, his words swirling around in my head.

Being with Jane isn't simple. Not when every moment with her feels like I'm walking a tightrope between wanting more and fearing just how much I could cause her to lose.

Graham's call is a reminder, illuminating the fears I've been shoving into the corners of my mind. Jane and I started this with a clear agreement, but lines are starting to blur. After we have sex, all I want to do is hold her close. I want to make her smile. I want her to *need* me.

And the idea of hurting her, of being the reason there is pain in her life, knots my stomach.

Then there's Londyn.

Jane deserves someone who won't retreat when the going gets tough.

Can I be that person?

Chapter 20
JANE

After a long day at the bookstore, I'm excited and nervous for the evening ahead. Babs, ever the lifesaver, agrees to pick up Londyn and take her for a sleepover. "Make sure she eats something green, and not just a Skittle," I remind her as I leave.

I arrive at Jasper's apartment, my heart skipping a beat as I knock on the door. He answers, and I'm momentarily lost for words. He stands there, all casual yet undeniably sexy in dark jeans and a fitted shirt that accentuates his broad shoulders. The faint scent of his cologne hits me.

"You look amazing," he says, his eyes appreciating my silk-blouse-and-dressy-shorts ensemble.

I find myself blushing and have to tear my gaze off him.

"Come on in. I've been working my ass off cooking for you. Welcome to our first official date night."

I arch a brow. "Did you really cook?"

"No. Sorry. I ordered in from a steak house. Are you disappointed?"

"Not at all. I'm hungry."

He takes my hand. "I did set up a table on the balcony, though. Herman, the doorman, helped me out."

Jasper leads me through his apartment to the balcony, where a table set for two awaits.

"Wow, Jasper, this is . . ." I trail off, words failing me as I take in the view, the soft glow of candlelight. It's romantic, and it's been so long since anyone has made such an effort for me.

He pulls out a chair for me, a gentlemanly gesture that makes me smile. "I'll bring the food out from the kitchen," he says softly as he takes in my awe.

He brings the plates, fillets with creamed spinach and salad. As we eat, with the city sprawling beneath us, fear wants to trickle in. That it's too much too soon, or that it won't last, or that this is all just a dream.

"Cheers," he says, raising his glass of red wine.

I clink my glass against his, shoving down my reservations as I allow myself to lean into the possibility of us. I allow myself to dream of what could be.

"You know," I say, slicing a piece of my steak, "I made a match that went super good, and it's funny because the computer didn't give them a good chance, but something about them made me want to see them together."

"What happened?"

"Well, she's an introvert, an astronomer who spends a lot of time studying. She's really passionate about stars and the universe, and well, he's a professional bowler, a former fraternity guy who's super outgoing."

He laughs. "Yeah, those don't seem to go together."

"Right, but he's also a big bird-watcher."

"I didn't see that coming. So, she likes birds too?"

I shake my head, musing as I smile. "No, that's the crazy bit. She just loves being outside and looking at the sky. So, on a hunch, I suggested they give it a shot, and they called me today, gushing about their date at the planetarium. They're going to the zoo on their next one."

He watches me, his gaze lingering. "They made your day?"

I blush. "It's nice when things work out."

He nods. "It was a surprise. A good thing. A little bit of magic."

"Yes!" I say, thrilled that he gets it. "It makes all the failed attempts worth it." I take a sip of wine. "Tell me about your day."

I relax into the evening as he talks. Our conversation flows naturally, and with each word, each laugh, I feel the tug toward him, toward falling in love.

◆ ◆ ◆

After we've eaten, he pours me a glass of wine and gives me a long look. "Are you enjoying yourself, being alone with me?"

"Eh."

His face falls. "'Eh'?"

"Well, I'm a little disappointed. I was told by your nieces that you love to sing Disney tunes. And I have yet to hear a single one."

"Ah." He pushes away from the table, then stands and makes a big show of cracking his knuckles. "You want to hear some singing?"

I nod. "And dancing. Don't forget the dancing."

He holds up a finger. "One moment."

He disappears into his apartment. A moment later, when he returns, music swells from somewhere inside. I expected "Can You Feel the Love Tonight," but it's "Open Arms" by Journey.

He extends a hand to me.

I blink. "What?"

"You think I can dance alone?"

He finds a spot, turns to me, and holds out his arms, leaving a space for me. This is where I'm supposed to slip between them, and we glide away, as if on air.

I hesitate.

He wiggles his fingers, like, *Get over here, woman.*

I go to him.

"You're doing pretty well," he says smoothly, sweeping me around the balcony and into the living room. His steps are sure and gentle, leading us into a slow sway that feels like we're the only two people in the world.

I laugh. "I'm waiting for the singing."

"Getting there. Didn't want to overwhelm you with my magnificence all at once."

I roll my eyes as if he's annoying me. But it's the opposite. With his arms around me, I feel safe, and yet I'm on a roller-coaster ride, waiting for the loop.

His hand climbs up my back, grazing over my skin with whisper-soft touches. It's all I can do not to shiver uncontrollably. He leans in and starts to sing under his breath.

I giggle at one point, and he huffs. "You aren't impressed?"

"You're full of surprises," I say, my head resting against his shoulder as we move.

The lyrics of "Open Arms" take on a new meaning as they're woven with the warmth of his voice.

As the song comes to an end, we linger in the embrace, neither of us eager to break the spell.

"I think this qualifies as a real date now," I say softly.

His eyes meet mine. "Best date ever," he says, pulling me closer.

We stand there, inches from each other, something needy pulsing between us. Then his hands reach out to scoop me toward him, and he presses his lips against mine.

I surrender, my knees going weak as I sway against him, but he holds me firm.

It's too much, and not enough. My mind spins and my body tingles with a drunken giddiness as his hands encircle my waist.

He tears his lips from my mouth with a ragged breath, pressing his lips down my throat. I cling to him, desperate, twining my fingers through his hair as his mouth continues descending my neck, dragging his hot tongue over my skin. I arch up against him, offering more of myself to him.

"Jasper," I say, my voice weak as I reach for his T-shirt, grabbing fistfuls of material.

He grabs both my wrists with a sudden fierceness and stares into my eyes. We gaze at each other, trading breaths, until he opens his mouth, and I'm sure he'll say something hot in reply.

"But I haven't finished singing to you," he says instead.

I giggle.

But then he says, "Screw it, I want you more," and covers my mouth with his lips.

He leads me into his bedroom and pushes me against the door.

As he works his way down my body, I whimper softly. His touch is electrifying, sending shivers of anticipation through me. I'm vibrating with need. I lean against the door, helpless in his grasp, as he pulls me closer, nuzzling into my neck.

"You're mine now," he growls, his voice rough. He slowly traces the curve of my hip, his touch sending shivers down my spine.

His lips find mine again, his tongue demanding entry. My arms wrap around his neck, pulling him closer to me. His hand slides into my shorts as his fingers trace the line of my panties, sending a jolt straight to my core.

Jasper's hands slide lower, his fingers brushing against my clit. I gasp, the sensation sending a firestorm of pleasure.

"Please, let's get on the bed," I say, my voice shaking with desperation.

He smirks against my lips, his hands still teasing me. "I'm not done with you yet."

His tongue explores my mouth as his hand moves to cup my breast through my shirt. I moan into his mouth, my body arching toward him. I want him to touch me everywhere, to make me feel this way all over. He undoes my shorts and pushes them to my feet. Slowly, he takes off my heels.

I'm standing there in a silk shirt and my undies.

"Just wait and see," he says as his hands trace my legs, sending shivers down my spine, his fingers grazing the sensitive skin on the inside of my thighs. I can hardly stand, wanting him to touch me everywhere all at once.

"I want to show you how good it can be, even when I go slow," he says, his voice low. With that, he slowly pulls my panties down, revealing everything to him. I can't breathe, my heart pounding in my chest as he looks at me, desire burning in his eyes. He unbuttons my blouse and eases it off slowly. He unclasps my bra, lets it dangle for a moment, then drops it. His hands touch me gently as he reveals my skin, as if he's unwrapping a precious gift. I feel exposed, but also vulnerable in a way that I've never felt before. This man is making me feel more alive than I ever thought possible.

"You blow me away," he murmurs, his fingers tracing the line of my hips, his thumbs brushing over my skin.

"I'm naked. Why aren't you?"

He smiles and lifts me up. He carries me to his bed, my legs wrapping around his waist as he lowers me onto the mattress.

"It's the anticipation that's the best. Especially for you. You've been on a sex vacation, so you need to take it slow."

I laugh. "You're teasing me."

He presses his forehead to mine. "Want to know a secret?"

My heart skips a beat. Do I? I'm not sure. What if his secrets draw us closer? At all costs, I must protect my heart.

"Sure," I say as I kiss his lips lightly.

"I was a virgin until I was twenty-one. She was my college girlfriend."

I am surprised. "Oh. Did she break your heart?"

He cocks his head thoughtfully. "It was a hard time for me. I was about to be drafted, and we drifted apart . . ." He frowns, and I wonder if there's more to this story.

"So she's your first love?"

He cups my face. "I don't know why I thought of that, and I didn't mean to ruin the mood, but I wanted you to know that I'm not really a sex fiend. I need connection too."

A long breath comes from his chest as he gazes down at me on the bed. His hand gently traces my spine, sending waves of pleasure coursing through me. "I kept pushing her away, little by little, until one day she dumped me for someone else."

"Why did you do that?"

"Fear. The future was uncertain. I was leaving for New York, and she still had another year of college. It felt right to let her break up with me." He lies down on the pillow next to me and turns to face me. Our gazes hold. "Then she got married a few years later, and I got over her."

"Do you regret it?"

He threads my hair through his fingers. "We never would have made long distance work, not with me being so busy in the NFL. My whole life changed when I moved to New York."

"We all have a first love. We all get broken hearts."

"I don't want to break your heart."

His words make my breath catch in my throat. A resolute feeling grows inside me. I won't let him. I can't.

"This is just sex, Jasper. Something I've been missing for way too long. If it wasn't you, I might find someone else." It's not true but . . .

His jaw flexes, and he presses a hard kiss on my lips. "Don't say that."

He whips off his shirt and tosses it at the foot of the bed. His jeans are next. Naked, he gets up to light some of the candles in the room, the light flickering against the dark walls. It feels like we're separate from the world in here, just me and him.

He hops back on the bed, making me laugh. He gives me a wink before trailing kisses down my neck and collarbone toward my breasts. His tongue swirls around one nipple while his hand massages the other.

"Angel," he says as he places me on top of him so I'm straddling him while he sits with his back against the headboard.

We stare at each other. Feeling shy at the intensity of his gaze, I trace patterns on his chest.

"Look at me."

I lift my gaze, and he cups my cheek. My breath quickens as the moment stretches between us, full of emotion.

His breathing, slow and even, chases away the doubts that itch to get inside my head. That I'm treading on thin ice with my heart in his hands. This moment is all that matters.

I rest my head on his shoulder.

His hand cards through my hair. "Kiss me, angel," he whispers as his fingers find mine, entwining them.

I do, reaching up to brush my mouth against his sweetly.

He kisses down my neck, his lips leaving a trail of fire on my skin. His fingers then slip inside me, and I gasp, my breath caught in my throat as he begins to explore. He moves slowly, savoring me.

I reach over and grab the condom sitting on the nightstand.

His deep voice vibrates against my neck as he murmurs his approval. I roll the condom down his thick length, my fingers tracing every ridge and vein as if they're sacred. The head of his cock brushes against my entrance. He groans, and with one long stroke, he penetrates me fully, stretching me out so exquisitely.

His eyes lock with mine, filled with something I can't define. His hands roam across my back, tracing every dip and curve as he guides us both into a rhythm that feels intimate.

I lean down to capture his bottom lip between my teeth, tugging gently as I grind against him. The friction makes us whimper, our breaths becoming ragged as our pace picks up.

The sheets beneath us rustle softly. Our skin slapping against skin creates an erotic sound against the silence of our room. He cups my ass cheek in his hand, pulling me closer still while driving deeper inside me. Every thrust causes a spiral of need inside me.

My muscles tense up and release with each of his thrusts, making my toes curl. His muscular chest flexes beneath my hands as I rest them on his shoulders for support, feeling the play of muscles beneath his skin. The headboard thuds against the wall in time with us, ratcheting up the intensity.

His lips find my jawline, and he nips softly as he groans into my skin. "Fuck, you feel so good," he says hoarsely against my ear. I gasp as his scruff tickles my skin as he nibbles at it hungrily while thrusting, claiming me completely.

I grab on to his thick biceps for leverage, digging my nails into his skin slightly as I'm lost in the feeling of him.

My inner walls grip him tightly, clenching around his cock in an effort to draw out every last drop of pleasure. His teeth graze my collarbone, leaving goose bumps in their wake. His fingers dig into my hips.

My nipples brush against his chest with every move, sending electric shock waves through both of us.

Pleasure builds in my spine as he rubs my nub.

I arch my back, meeting him stroke for stroke while he continues to circle my clit.

My climax builds, a tidal wave of desire, until I'm at the edge of madness.

The edge of the cliff waits, and I tumble over as I orgasm, my muscles fluttering around his cock. He watches me, soaking in every expression I make. I watch as his lashes flutter and he goes over with me. He presses his forehead against mine, panting heavily as he holds on to me tightly.

My breath catches in my throat at the tenderness in his eyes. He kisses me softly on the lips, then wraps his strong arms around me protectively.

"You can stay, right?" he murmurs.

I nod. Babs is taking Londyn to preschool in the morning.

Pure boyish glee lights his face as he pulls back the covers and helps me get under them. After getting rid of the condom, which I checked to make sure was still on, he jumps back in bed and snuggles in behind me. He pulls me against him and throws an arm around me, then yawns.

"You're going to sleep? It's not even ten o'clock."

"Hmm. I feel good. You feel good. We sleep."

I'm ready for more, for a night without worrying about Londyn in the next room. Yet he wants to sleep. It's cute.

I snuggle closer to his warm body, feeling the steady rise and fall of his chest against my back. Comfort floods over me, and I bask in it.

I've been so lonely, and this feels so right.

As we lie there in the quiet, a thought tugs at the edges of my mind. It feels like I've known him for a lifetime. There's something about the way he holds me, the way he looks at me, that tells me this could be more, but . . .

"How is it that you make me feel so safe?"

He shifts slightly behind me, his arm tightening around my waist. "It's because you are safe with me," he replies gently. "I will protect you. From Tomas. From whatever you need."

But he'd protect anyone.

A surge of emotion wells up in my chest, and I turn in his embrace, facing him as I search his eyes for the truth. "But why? Why me? What is it about me that makes you want to keep me safe?"

"When people are meant to know each other, they just do. That's it, plain and simple. Me and Tuck were always meant to be friends. Graham too. Now you."

He brushes his thumb across my lips, silencing my doubts with a gentle touch. "Why all the questions?"

"Sex makes me energized, I think," I finally say.

"Hmm, I like holding you. If I snore, just elbow me, yeah? Can you wait for round two until the morning?"

I take a deep breath, allowing his words to sink in. He wants to hold me? How could I have missed that Jasper truly isn't the macho jerk I thought early on when we first met?

Leaning in, I capture his lips with mine, conveying the depth of my feelings through the simple act. As our mouths move together in sync, it's as if everything else fades away.

Minutes or hours could pass as we remain lost in our own little universe. Eventually, our lips part, but the feelings I have for him remain unbroken.

"Angel," he murmurs sleepily, "thank you."

Chapter 21
JANE

The door closes behind Mitch, the peanut-digging guy from Carson's I met almost six weeks ago. I sit back in my chair, feeling a rush of excitement. He's genuine, charming, and has a quirky sense of humor that will resonate with the right woman.

I jot down notes on my laptop, detailing his preferences, his career as a graphic designer, and his love for indie music and art shows. His ideal partner, as he described, would be someone who appreciates creativity and isn't afraid to let loose and be silly sometimes.

As I put together his profile, I smile. He even brought a box of chocolates as a thank-you for the interview. It's clients like him that make me love my job. I pause at that thought, my mind churning. A trickle of clarity seeps in. When I first had the idea for Cupid's Arrow, it was because of a gap in the market. It was about strategy, a way to bring in money while holding down my bookstore job.

But I'm realizing that the connections I make matter.

There's a bit of magic in the matches I make.

Maybe it's teaching me about myself, that someday soon, I can find my own happiness.

It makes me realize that the path we start on for one reason can lead us to entirely unexpected places.

I lean back, already flipping through my mental catalog of clients, trying to match Mitch with someone fantastic. Perhaps Erin from the preschool? I make a mental note to call her later.

The bell above the door of the Darling Bookstore tinkles, announcing a new arrival. Catching sight of an elderly gentleman making his way into the store, I notice his slow shuffle, supported by a polished cane. He has white hair and is dressed in a tweed jacket paired with a flat cap. Glasses perch on his nose.

"Good afternoon, sir," I say. "Welcome to the Darling Bookstore."

He lifts his gaze. "Ah, thank you, young lady. I'm Mr. Darden. I believe I have an appointment with you."

He's not just any visitor. He's a heavyweight from Wickham, practically owning the place. His visit is the latest in a series of men, all sent by Jasper. First, it was Dalton, then Coach Duval, and now Mr. Darden. Jasper is looking out for me.

I guide him to my office, ensuring he's comfortably seated before offering him tea. Babs swings by with a tea service and some scones, shooting me a thumbs-up before she waltzes out the door.

"So, Mr. Darden, Jasper tells me you're interested in finding a match?"

After a thoughtful sip of his tea, he chuckles. "Well, that's Jasper's version. Truthfully, I've come to like the young man. He's a bit of a nuisance, but in an endearing way. Always has something nice to say. And he spoke so highly of you and your daughter. When he suggested I might want a girlfriend, I wanted to laugh, but decided I'd like to meet you."

"Ah."

"My days of romantic pursuits are behind me. I couldn't bear to let Jasper down, though. He's quite set on seeing you succeed."

I smile warmly. "I'll be sure to tell him you dropped by."

His focus sharpens, capturing my attention with the deliberate placement of his teacup. "I'd like to know more about your match-making venture, though," he says, leaning in. "In an era where digital dominates, the value of personal connections can't be overstated. How did you start?"

I dive into the origins of my matchmaking service. I admit the journey has included its share of missteps and learning curves, emphasizing that even unsuccessful matches provide valuable insights.

Mr. Darden listens intently. "Remarkable," he finally says. "There's tremendous growth potential in what you're doing."

"I hope so. I like doing it, more than I even realized."

He gets to the point. "I'm pressed for time today, but I'd like to talk more about your operations, review your financials if you're open to it. I might want to invest."

I struggle for words. His interest in investing could transform the matchmaking service. My mind swirls with ideas of a better website, of more marketing, more ads, heck, maybe even a commercial on TV. "Mr. Darden, that's incredible. I'm very interested."

He nods. "Great. I'll be in touch to discuss this further. Now, I must collect my order at the counter. I called earlier in the week and had your staff do a search for books on honey badgers. I'm quite fond of those little devils."

And then he's out the door while I sit in stunned silence.

I'm still riding the high a few days later, especially after a dinner at Jasper's apartment. Londyn went with me, and we ordered in pizza. Afterward, he walked us back to our place, then left early so he could be focused for his quarterback meeting with Dalton.

It's been a busy day at the store. I'm just finishing checking out a customer when I get a notification on my business phone.

A refund request has been initiated from . . .

I haven't had one of those in months. Of course, they do happen from time to time.

I click on the notification and blink at the name.

Freida?

Oh no. Wait a minute. Jasper canceled his date with her. That was right in the middle of us figuring out what he and I were doing . . .

Eager to see what she wrote, I scroll down the form.

Freida did not mince words. Nor did she abbreviate. Under "Reason for Request," she's written, "READ MY REVIEW ON YOUR WEBSITE."

Shit. I scroll to the website and find it in the top position.

I joined Cupid's Arrow hoping for a genuine connection, but what I found was nothing short of disappointing and unprofessional. My first match was handsy and disrespectful, a terrible experience that should have been screened better. I canceled my contract with the owner immediately, then she called me back and said she'd found someone new and begged me to give it a shot. And my second match? A high-profile celebrity, Jasper Jannich, who stood me up! It's clear where the priorities are in this service.

But here's the kicker: the owner of the business, Jane, is allegedly dating Jasper herself! It seems like a conflict of interest and a clear disregard for clients. How can we trust a service where the owner is more interested in her own love life than providing quality matches?

This has been a deeply upsetting experience. I expected a service that values its clients, but instead, I feel used in a publicity stunt. I regret trusting Jane and caution anyone considering her service to think twice, especially if you're expecting professional treatment. Freida.

Rating: 0/5 Stars

Something hot begins to bubble in my veins.

How dare she? She didn't even pay the full fee, just a measly $200.

My phone buzzes again. A refund request has been initiated from . . .

It has to be a glitch. I'm being double notified.

But then I click on it and realize it's from a woman I signed up last week.

"Reason for Request"? She wrote, Apparently these "men" aren't as well-vetted as Jane promises. And any business owner who dates her clients is a no-go for me.

Ugh. This could get very bad.

I grab my phone and dial Freida. It rings through to voicemail. Instead of leaving one, I send her a text: Hey. Got your refund request and saw the review. I just want to talk. Call me back. Thanks.

Another buzz. Another notification that a woman wants a refund. I rub my temple. Freida knows all the same women I do, and at this rate she'll convince them to drop me.

"Excuse me, I need to check out," a customer says. I set my phone down and get it done. Then, my personal phone vibrates insistently on the counter. Glancing at the screen, I see it's a call from Londyn's preschool. My heart skips a beat—calls from the school in the middle of the day are rare.

I quickly pick up the call. "This is Jane."

"Jane, this is Erin from the preschool," comes the anxious voice from the other end. "There's been an incident with Londyn."

Instantly, panic hits. "What happened? Is she okay?"

"We think she had an allergic reaction to peanuts. She's never had one before, right?"

My mind races. "No, never. What happened?"

"One of the children accidentally brought in a snack with peanuts, and Londyn ate some. We were too afraid to use an EpiPen because we weren't sure what was happening. We called the paramedics, and they arrived immediately and took her to Manhattan General. I came with her. She's okay."

I feel like the ground is slipping away beneath me. "I'm on my way right now," I stammer, barely recognizing my own voice.

Without waiting to talk to Babs, I send her a text that I'm leaving and on my way to see Londyn.

I dial Andrew's number with shaking fingers. "Andrew, it's Jane. Londyn's had an allergic reaction, I'm heading to Manhattan General."

His voice mirrors my own panic. "I'm in class but on my way. Meet you there."

I barely register his words as I start running, my heart pounding in my chest. All I can think about is Londyn, so small and vulnerable, facing something scary without me.

I grab a cab and take off.

I clutch my phone tightly.

How could this be happening?

Every second feels like an eternity, every red light driving me crazy.

As I approach the hospital, the imposing structure of Manhattan General looms ahead. The sight of it makes my stomach swirl.

My breaths come in ragged gasps as I push through the hospital doors, my eyes scanning the signs for the emergency department. The clinical smell of the hospital fills my nose.

I approach the reception. "My daughter is Londyn Darling. She's four and was brought in for an allergic reaction."

The receptionist gives me a sympathetic look as she checks her computer. "Just a moment, ma'am. I'll find out where she is."

As I stand there, waiting for information, time seems to stand still. Every second is a battle against the worst-case scenarios playing out in my head. I clutch my phone like a lifeline, praying for a positive update, anything that will tell me Londyn is going to be okay.

With trembling fingers, I dial Jasper's number, but it goes straight to voicemail. "Jasper, it's Jane. I-I, just call me back." My voice cracks as I end the call, a knot of worry tightening in my stomach.

I need someone, anyone, to be here with me.

Tomas?

The thought surfaces reluctantly. He's her father, after all, despite the years of silence.

And he wants to be part of her life. Does he realize that being part of it also means being there for the hard things?

Since we had dinner together, I have softened to the idea of letting him in. The truth is, denying Londyn her father feels wrong.

It's not just about informing him; it's about reopening a door.

I'm torn between the need to protect Londyn from potential disappointment and the fact that she deserves to have her father in her life.

But what if he doesn't answer? What if he does?

I scroll through my contacts, hovering over his name. This isn't about me and my feelings toward Tomas. It's about Londyn.

I press the Call button. It's a leap of faith that maybe Tomas will prove to be the father she needs.

The phone rings, and Tomas answers immediately.

"Tomas, it's Jane."

"Is everything okay?"

"It's Londyn. She's in the hospital," I say, keeping my voice calm.

"What? What happened?" His voice spikes with worry.

"She had an allergic reaction to peanuts. We never knew she was allergic."

"I'm still in the city. Which hospital are you at? I'm coming right now—if you want me to?" he asks, even as I can hear the rustling of clothes, as if he's getting ready to leave.

"Yes, Manhattan General," I reply, surprised at his quick response.

"I'll be there as soon as I can." His voice is reassuring in a way I hadn't expected.

I end the call. A small part of me feels guilty for not being able to reach Jasper, for turning to Tomas instead. But right now, all that matters is Londyn. Everything else can wait.

When I finally reach the room, I see Londyn lying in the bed, so tiny. She's surrounded by an IV and other medical equipment. Erin, sitting next to her bed, looks up at me, then rushes to give me a hug.

"Londyn," I say gently, taking my daughter's hand in mine.

Her eyes flutter open, and she gives me a weak smile. "Mommy. So sleepy."

A nurse comes in, his expression kind. "Ms. Darling?"

I nod, and he smiles. "She's going to be fine."

Some of the tightness in my throat lessens. "The preschool said it was a possible allergic reaction, but she's never had any allergies before."

He nods. "It's not uncommon for allergies to develop at any age, even without prior symptoms. For my son, it was a honey allergy. The doctor will be in to talk to you in just a few minutes."

I clutch my hands together, trying to steady my shaking fingers as I stand beside Londyn's bed. She's asleep now, looking fragile under the thin hospital blanket.

A knock on the door breaks the silence, and a doctor enters, her expression somber. She's a middle-aged woman with a reassuring presence, which somehow makes the situation feel even more real.

She glances at Londyn and then back to me. "I'm Dr. Simmons. I've been overseeing Londyn's care." She pulls up a chair next to me. "She had a moderate-to-severe allergic reaction to peanuts. It's quite a serious situation, but she's stable now. In Londyn's case, her reaction included widespread hives, swelling, and respiratory distress. That's why we needed to act quickly."

"Respiratory distress?" The words echo in my head. It sounds absolutely awful.

"Yes. We administered epinephrine, and she is in the clear, but she is small, and we'd prefer to keep her for observation overnight."

"Is she going to have to deal with this for the rest of her life?"

"Peanut allergies can be lifelong, but with proper management, they can be handled. We'll arrange for an allergy test to confirm and to see if there are any other allergies you need to be aware of. It's also crucial she carries an epinephrine autoinjector with her at all times going forward."

I nod, trying to absorb it all.

"You, and anyone who takes care of her, will need to know how to use it. It's a straightforward process, and we can show you before you leave."

I glance at Londyn, her chest rising and falling gently. "And these reactions, could they get worse?"

Dr. Simmons nods gently. "It's unpredictable. A mild reaction in the past doesn't mean it can't be severe next time. It's why avoiding exposure is key."

No more peanuts. Ever.

I feel a surge of protectiveness, a fierce need to shield my baby girl. "Thank you."

Dr. Simmons offers a small smile. "We'll be here to support you through this. Let's talk more tomorrow after the tests. For now, try to get some rest. You're in good hands here."

As she leaves, the room falls silent again. I pull up a chair closer to Londyn's bed, watching her sleep. Erin tells me she has to get back to the preschool, gives me a hug, and leaves.

I'm right next to Londyn, giving her a gentle kiss on the forehead. "You're tough, kiddo," I murmur. "There's nothing I wouldn't face for you, love bug."

The door bursts open, and Andrew's in the room. "Londyn, oh my god, are you okay?" Andrew's all concern, eyes roving over her to make sure she's really all right.

"She's asleep," I tell him, then explain everything the doctor told me.

A few minutes later, the door to the hospital room opens again, and my heart clenches, anticipating the moment I've set into motion. Tomas steps in, seriousness in his eyes. He hesitates at the threshold, as if unsure of his right to enter, and I appreciate it. He looks around at the hospital room as if he's never seen one before, which is funny considering he plays a doctor on TV.

He whispers as he looks at her. His face is white. "Londyn?"

"She's sleeping," I say, keeping my voice low, feeling oddly calm.

"I got here as quick as I could. How is she?"

"Stable, now," I say, watching him closely as I run down the basics for him.

Andrew shoots Tomas a hard look. "And who are you?" It's for show; he knows exactly who Tomas is.

I fill in the blanks anyway. "Andrew, this is Tomas. I called him."

Andrew's face sets like concrete, but he lets it go, focusing back on Londyn.

Tomas, inching closer, can't take his eyes off Londyn. "Never seen her before . . ." His voice trails off. "She looks just like her photos. So pretty, just like you, Jane. I . . . I can't believe this happened. Is there anything she needs?"

"Just time to recover."

He nods. "Right."

"And maybe to meet you soon," I add. "Perhaps after your wedding and things have settled." It's only two months away.

There. I said it. And I mean it.

A long ragged breath comes from his chest as he looks at me then, really looks at me. "I can't undo the past, but I'm here now. For Londyn, for whatever. I want to be a part of her life, Jane. Really be there for her, and after the wedding is great. And I want to give you the money as soon as possible."

I nod in agreement. "Later," I say.

He stares down at her. "Thank you for calling me."

"Her life isn't perfect, and there'll be tough times like this," I say, trying to delicately remind him that it's not all kittens and rainbows.

His throat bobs. "I can't imagine all the things you've done for her. I'll do it, this, however you want. I need her in my life."

Oh. His words even make Andrew start; he gives Tomas a long, considering look.

From out of nowhere, I recall the nights my sister Emmy would read *The Secret Forest* to me when I was about Londyn's age. It was a story about an enchanted forest where trees were connected by thousands of roots that nurtured each other. When one hurt, they'd send comfort through the ground, giving support and love. It was a sweet story about never being alone, where the smallest sapling was taken care of by each tree.

Now, as I gaze at Tomas, I remember that story, that feeling it gave me, of being secure—that I had so many people around me to love me. Even though my mom had left, I had Gran and Emmy and Andrew and even Terry, the previous bookstore owner.

In life, we might not see the people who love us each day, but they're there in case you need them.

Maybe bringing Tomas into our lives is about giving her a network, a family with roots to support her. I shouldn't, and I won't, hold her back from those connections.

"Thanks for dropping by," I say a few moments later as I lead him to the other side of the room. "She's going to stay overnight, and I'm glad you came."

"I'll head out," he says, his eyes lingering on Londyn. He pauses at the door. "Need anything while I'm out?"

"No, we're good," I say, watching him leave.

Once he's gone, Andrew keeps tucking Londyn's blanket in and touching her hand. He sighs. "Are you sure it's the right thing to do, letting him in?"

I nod. "It's for her."

The ring of my phone pierces the quiet of the hospital room. I glance at the caller ID, and my heart skips a beat. Jasper. A part of me wants to answer, to hear his voice, but something holds me back. I let it go to voicemail.

Andrew raises an eyebrow at me, a silent question hanging in the air, but I shake my head, indicating that it's nothing important.

The timing feels off.

It's not like I expected him to drop everything and answer my call earlier, but a part of me had hoped he would.

Andrew watches me as I look at my phone, concern on his face. "Jane, if there's something going on . . ."

I shake my head again, forcing a smile. "It's nothing."

But it's more than that. It's the realization that no matter how much I want to lean on Jasper, to open up to him, there's always going to be uncertainty between us.

There's no clarification.

There's a gap between what I need and what he can offer. Yes, he said he wants to protect me, but does he really?

I turn my attention back to Londyn.

Later, around six, I dash toward the hospital cafeteria, needing a break. The quiet hum of the corridor follows me as I head for some

221

food. I grab a tray, loading it with whatever's in reach, my mind elsewhere.

Standing in line, a sudden wave of nausea hits. My stomach gurgles, and I feel faint. The cashier catches my concern. "Are you okay, ma'am?"

"I'm fine, thanks."

I hand over the money, then I rush back to Londyn's room, relieved to see her still sleeping.

I set down the food and sneak into the bathroom, closing the door with a soft click. As I'm leaning over the sink, the nausea peaks, and I'm throwing up before I know it, trying to stifle the noise.

Is this worry for Londyn, or something more?

My lashes flutter as the thought of possibly being pregnant flashes through my mind.

After rinsing my mouth and splashing water on my face, I catch my reflection in the mirror.

I sway on my feet, and my fingers cling to the edge of the sink as it dawns.

I don't have a clockwork twenty-eight-day cycle, but it feels like I'm overdue.

I've always believed in letting fate unfold but . . .

This is a curveball I'm not ready for.

Sitting on the closed toilet lid, I think about fate and choice. Buying that morning-after pill felt like clawing back some control, yet I never took it.

Why?

Because I had faith that I wasn't? Or faith that whatever happens, happens for a reason?

Ugh.

What was I thinking?

The first time with Londyn was unexpected, but now I only have myself to blame.

How could I have been so careless this time?

The weight of the responsibility, the fear all crash down on me.

Life is full of surprises, and sometimes, no matter how careful we are, things don't go as planned.

Still . . .

The thought of bringing another child into the world without planning fills me with dread.

My hands tremble as I fumble to unlock my phone. I dial Emmy's number, praying that the time difference won't keep her from answering.

"Hello?" Emmy's sleepy voice answers on the other end.

"Emmy," I choke out, my voice low, "it's me."

"Jane?" There's an immediate alertness in Emmy's tone. "Is everything okay? What's wrong?"

Tears stream down my cheeks as I huddle on the bathroom floor, my emotions threatening to overwhelm me. "It's Londyn. She had an allergic reaction to peanuts. They had to rush her to Manhattan General. She's okay, but we're still here." I sniffle and wipe away my tears. "They're keeping her overnight to monitor her."

Emmy takes a moment to process. "That's terrifying. I'm so sorry. I wish I could be there with you."

My heart aches with longing. "I miss you so much, Emmy. When are you coming back?"

She sighs on the other end. "Sweetheart. I'll be home in a few weeks. Until then, you have to stay strong for Londyn."

"I know. I needed to hear your voice. I needed some advice."

"Of course. What's on your mind?"

I hesitate, my thoughts full of doubt. Finally, I open up. "I called Tomas. I told him about Londyn, and he came to the hospital. Maybe he's not such a bad person, and I'm judging him over me not being the one for him. I've decided to let him in."

Her voice softens. "People can change, I believe that. You're a great mother, and Londyn is lucky. No matter what, she has you." Emmy pauses for a moment, then continues, "I can't wait to be back home. Hazel is growing so fast."

We shift gears, talking about Hazel, her new milestones, and I slowly feel better.

"Was there anything else?" Emmy says, and I can hear her yawning.

I might be pregnant.

I sigh. "No. Get some sleep. I'll call you tomorrow."

A few minutes later, Andrew slips back into the hospital room, phone in hand. He freezes for a second when he sees me curled up in the chair with my knees tucked under my chin.

There's a silence.

"Jane?" His voice is low. "What's up? Did something happen with Londyn?"

I blink away the moisture in my eyes. "No, she's fine. Just tired, you know? Hospital air and all."

He moves closer, perching on the edge of the bed opposite me. "Come on. It's me. What's going on?"

The dam breaks. "I might be pregnant, Andrew."

The words hang between us, thick with implications. His reaction is a slow dawn of realization. "Holy shit balls. Jasper?" He clenches his fists. "I knew there was something between you two."

I shake my head. "We're just seeing each other. It's not serious. We're just . . ."

"Fucking?"

I nod my head at Londyn. "Watch it, brother."

He sighs heavily. "Okay, first things first, we need to be sure. Have you taken a test?"

"Not yet."

He nods, as if ticking off a mental checklist. "Right. We'll do that first. Let me go buy one."

I sit up straighter. "Now? Here? No. I can't handle it today. I don't want to know right this second."

He sighs. "Fine. Whatever you need, I'm here, okay? Let me be there when you do it. Did you tell Emmy?"

"No. I just don't know how I feel about all this. I'm probably not. My period is never on time."

He leans in, lowering his voice even further. "Listen, whatever you decide, it's your choice. Jasper's a good guy, but this is your life. Your body. You're not alone, though. You've got me, you've got Emmy, and hell, you've even got Tomas now. I don't like him, but he did come and he is trying, I guess. I know it's overwhelming with Londyn being sick, but we've got this, all right?"

"All right," I say back as I get up. He wraps me in a big hug, and for a while everything feels like it's going to be okay.

Chapter 22

JASPER

Pacing back and forth in my apartment, I glance at my phone again. Still no callback from Jane. I shake my head, trying to ditch the worry gnawing at me.

I call Andrew's number, hoping he might have some insight.

"Hey," Andrew says, but there's an edge to his tone.

"Hey, have you heard from Jane? She's not answering my calls or texts."

There's a pause, then, "Yeah, I've heard from her. She's in the hospital with Londyn."

I start, shocked. "What happened? Is she okay?"

"They think it was peanuts. She's doing fine, but they're keeping her overnight."

"Damn, I had no idea. Is Jane okay?"

"She's shaken up, obviously, but holding strong. That's how she is. Tomas came by."

Tomas.

"I should be there," I murmur, mostly to myself.

There's a hint of warning in Andrew's voice. "I don't know if that's a good idea right now. Let Jane handle this her way, Jasper, feel me?"

His words seem like a warning, reminding me of Graham's opinion.

He tells me he has to go and gets off the phone. Afterward, I slump onto the couch. I want to be there for Jane, but I also understand that being supportive sometimes means stepping back.

I stare at my phone, the urge to call Jane still strong. Instead, I send her a simple text: Heard about Londyn. I'm here if you need anything. No pressure.

I don't get a reply.

If she wanted to see me, she'd reply.

The evening air is humid as I step out of my apartment and pull my black hat down to shadow my face. I need to clear my head, and a walk seems like the best way to do it.

I bury my hands in the pockets of my gym shorts, my mind replaying the conversation with Andrew.

I'm lost in thought when a woman approaches me. Her pace is quick, and there's an edge to her that puts me on alert.

"You're Jasper Jannich, aren't you?" Her voice cuts through the tranquility of the park like a knife.

I stop, trying to place her. She does look familiar. "Do we know each other?"

She rolls her eyes, irritation evident. "Seriously? It's Freida. From Cupid's Arrow. We had a date, and you stood me up."

Recognition hits me. I didn't stand her up. I canceled. "Freida, right. I'm sorry about that, there was a—"

But she's already pulling out her phone, her movements quick and agitated. "Save it. You're just another lying player."

I frown, lifting my hands up to stop her. "Hey, let's not do this here. We can talk about it."

But she's already recording me. "Oh, we're going to talk, all right. Everyone's going to hear about this."

Her voice rises, attracting the attention of those passing by. I feel their eyes on us and try to step back, to give her space, but she follows, her accusations growing louder.

"You think you can just use women and toss them aside? Parade around with Jane and her kid like you're some kind of family man?"

What?

The crowd grows, evening joggers and passersby, who sense drama and gravitate toward it. They're pulling out their phones too.

"Is that Jasper Jannich? What's happening?"

"Is he fighting with her?"

Freida's voice seems to echo around the entire park. "He's nothing but a fake!"

She steps closer, her finger pointed at me. "You think because you're some big-shot football star, you can treat women like they're disposable?"

I attempt to interject, to put a stop to this, but my words get lost as she barrels on. "Is this how you treat all women? Just toys for your amusement?"

Her words sting. I try to maintain my composure, but it's slipping away.

I hold my hand back up. "Please stop recording me."

She smirks. "I saw you, playing happy families in the park with Jane and her kid. What is that? Some sort of PR stunt? Are you really dating her?"

The crowd murmurs. Some nod along with Freida, while others look on with morbid curiosity.

"You don't care about anyone but yourself. You use your fame, your money, to get what you want."

I open my mouth to defend myself, but I don't know what to say. I did cancel on her, but it was a choice I made and I have the right, but I'm not sure that's how it will come across. So I keep my trap shut and just take it.

She ends the video and gives me a scathing look. "You'll find this on my social media." She turns and storms off.

Chapter 23
JANE

The sound of rustling stirs me from sleep in the hospital armchair. Blinking into the dimly lit room, I see a tall figure by the door. Jasper. Butterflies dance in my stomach at the sight of him.

"How did you get in?" I murmur, noting the late hour on the clock. It's nearly midnight, and visiting hours were over at six. Andrew has already gone home with a promise to call me first thing in the morning.

Jasper edges closer, his approach quiet so he doesn't wake Londyn. He gazes down at her softly, then looks at me, searching my face. "I went for a walk in the park and just decided to come and see you. Andrew told me about her allergic reaction. I was worried about you both. I couldn't get through on the phone, so I just came."

"I'm sorry I didn't call you back."

"It's fine," he assures me. "I'm sure it's been a tough day."

I rise from the chair, stretching my tired muscles. "It's just part of being a mom. I'll always run to her side when she needs me."

He steps toward me and wraps me in a hug, with his hand rubbing my back. "Ah, angel. Are you okay? Talk to me."

I sink into his embrace, craving the comfort. I don't have any words. I just soak him in.

He lifts my face toward his. "I hate seeing you all alone. And an armchair is not a good place to sleep. Let me take care of that." He presses a kiss to my forehead, then strides over to the nurses' station. I watch him talk to them, pointing back at me. Soon, he's back with a triumphant smile. "They're bringing a rollaway bed and pillows and blankets. I can sleep in the chair."

As he returns with that triumphant smile, something inside me shifts. It's not the relief I expected to feel. It's a knot of fear. His kindness should warm me. But it doesn't. It terrifies me.

What if I'm pregnant?

Would he want to be with me then?

Sure, he said he wanted kids, but he meant *planned* ones.

Would I be a burden to him, like I was to Tomas?

I've been down the baby road before, and the idea of placing that same weight on Jasper's shoulders feels wrong.

He's a supportive man, yes, but he didn't sign up for this when we started seeing each other.

Would he run, not physically, but emotionally retreating?

As I watch him charm the aide, something inside me breaks. This man, who could have anyone, doesn't deserve the mess that is my life. He doesn't deserve to be dragged into my complications and fears.

It's not just about protecting myself from potential heartbreak. It's about protecting him.

But how do I explain this? How do I tell him that it's not him, it's me.

How do I say goodbye to the best thing that's happened to me because I'm too scared of repeating the past?

Another wave of nausea hits me. Beads of sweat form on my forehead as I make a beeline for the bathroom. Hunched over the toilet, I throw up, the little I've eaten today making a swift exit.

The bathroom door creaks open. "Jane? Baby. Are you all right?"

"Fine," I lie, trying to put some cheer into my voice. "Just close the door, please."

But he doesn't. Instead, he steps in, concern on his face as he finds me on my knees. "Why didn't you say you were sick?"

"It's nothing. Just nerves."

He doesn't seem convinced but moves to wet a cloth at the sink, then comes over to wipe my forehead. The gesture is too much in the face of everything else.

It's going to hurt too much when he walks away.

I stand up, taking the cloth from him. I smile gently. "You should go home, Jasper."

He frowns. "No."

"You'll rest better for training. Londyn is doing great, she's just resting. I'm fine."

His blue eyes search mine, and I harden myself.

Everyone leaves.

My mom.

Tomas.

"Really, I'm doing fine," I say in my most reassuring voice. All I want to do right now is sort through the turmoil of possibly being pregnant without him clouding my thoughts and making everything more confusing.

He's quiet for a moment, then lets out a slow breath. The strong columns of his throat move as he swallows. "You're pushing me away. You think I don't understand? I do. Your mom and Tomas did a number on you. My mom did one on me too."

He leans against the wall in the bathroom. "I held out hope for years that she'd come back, even though I had an awesome family taking care of me. Little by little that hope died. It turned on me, and I guess what I'm trying to say is I don't want to be afraid of getting involved with you. I don't want to run away when you need me. I'm here, right now."

His gaze locks with mine, emotions swirling in his eyes.

I sit on the top of the toilet lid. "Yes, you're right, and I appreciate you showing up tonight, but I can't afford to talk about it right now.

Not with Londyn here. There's a lot on my mind, Jasper. The best thing for you to do is just give me some time."

He flinches, as if wounded. "Jane—"

"No," I murmur softly, interrupting him, needing to make him understand, needing to protect what little peace I've managed to carve out. "It's a lot, okay. Me and Londyn . . ." and maybe another baby. "There's things going on with me that I just need to think about."

"Like what?"

"Can you just go?"

His jaw clenches, and for a moment, he looks like he might argue, but then something shifts in his demeanor, a resignation.

He looks away from me and out the window. A tired expression settles on his face. "If that's what you want."

"I'll call you soon," I murmur, wondering if I will.

There's a heavy silence between us. Finally, he steps forward, closing the distance I've put between us.

He leans down and presses a gentle kiss to my lips. "All right. Take care of yourself."

With that, he turns and walks out of the room, leaving me alone with a heart that feels like it's been split in two. As I watch him go, a part of me wonders if I've just made the biggest mistake of my life by pushing him away, but then, he didn't fight much to stay either.

Chapter 24
JASPER

Three days. Seventy-two hours since I last spoke to Jane, and every minute feels like a weight on my chest. I keep telling myself it's for the best, that it's what *she* wanted, but damn if it doesn't feel like I'm the one breaking apart. I did call her first thing the next morning to tell her about the Freida incident in the park. I meant to tell her the night before, but as soon as I saw how sick she was about Londyn, I just couldn't. Freida posted it in the early hours of that morning, and I let Jane know that my PR team is in full damage control mode.

I explained to Jane our strategy, a sincere public statement that would show regret for any misunderstanding but also highlight my professionalism. We're clear about not admitting fault.

Freida's video on IG is currently dragging Jane and her business into this.

But now, I'm pacing my apartment, caught in a loop of rehashing our last conversation in the hospital room.

There's things going on with me that I just need to think about. What did she mean?

The elevator ride down to the lobby is more turmoil.

Reaching the lobby, I try to distract myself by checking for packages. The girl at the desk hands me a parcel, her smile polite. As I turn, package in hand, ready to go back to my apartment, the last person I expect to see walks through the door.

Rae-Anne.

"What are you doing here?" I ask, the words sharper than I intend.

"I wanted to see you," Rae-Anne replies, a desperate note in her tone. "Please, can we talk?"

I scan the lobby, filled with curious glances from the staff. The idea of taking her up to my place, letting her into my home, tightens something in my chest.

"Over here is fine." I nod toward the plush conversation area.

"How did you find me?" The tension in my shoulders rises as we sit across from each other.

She fidgets, avoiding my gaze. "Garrett, my son, he's good with the internet. He found this apartment complex on Reddit. We found a few wrong addresses before this one." Her hands twist in her lap, betraying her nerves.

"You've been stalking me?"

"It wasn't like that. You never called me back," she says with a wave of her hands, attempting to justify her actions.

I roll my neck. "You showing up, it's a lot to take in. First it was the training center and now here. It's my private life."

Rae-Anne's eyes lock with mine. "I've just missed you, and I wasn't sure you'd ever call me back."

"I don't know what you want from me. We can't just pick up and have a relationship. Those things take time. You can't keep following me around, or I'll get a restraining order." I can't look at her when I say it because I hate to be mean to her, but . . .

"I want to make amends," she insists as she leans in closer. "I made mistakes. I was scared, young, and lost. I thought it was the best thing for you."

It probably was.

She pulls out her phone. "Garrett's actually here. He didn't want to come in without getting your permission. Do you want to meet him?"

My stomach flip-flops. Not really. But . . .

Without waiting for my answer, she sends a text, and moments later, a tall teenager with dark hair walks in. He's so young looking, kind of awkward and gangly. My half brother.

He shuffles over and blushes as he shakes my hand and tells me how great it is to meet me. He sits down in a chair next to his mom. I take them in, looking for a similarity between us, but there's not much. He must look like his father.

"So, do you have a girlfriend, Jasper?" Her attempt to shift to lighter conversation feels forced.

"It's complicated."

She chews on her lips for a moment, then, "We're actually in a bit of a bind. I didn't want to mention it, but . . ."

I lean back, my arms crossing as unease hits. "Huh. A bind?"

She nods, launching into a list that seems rehearsed. "Well, first, there's my husband. You would really like him. Anyway, his boss is selling the construction company where he works, and we'd like to buy it. It's not very big, but it's a solid investment for the future, and we almost have enough for a down payment. And Garrett"—she glances toward her son—"his private school has raised their tuition, and I'm really worried about coming up with it."

"Oh."

She stares down at her hands. "Plus, we have medical bills, the mortgage on our house, and well, daily expenses. I took a lot of our savings to come here this summer and track you down."

I feel winded. "I see."

"And, not to sound presumptuous, but I heard about your new contract," she adds, her eyes locking on to mine with an intensity that feels calculated. "Forty-five million, wasn't it? Congratulations. That's really amazing. We can't even imagine that much money."

Garrett looks away from us and stares out the window, as if he might be embarrassed.

I keep my face impassive. "What exactly are you asking for?"

"Well, I hate to ask, I really do, but you have so much that I was hoping you might consider helping us out. We're family, after all, and we should stick together and make time for each other, like a fresh start. Holidays, weekends, things like that. We're just a train ride away."

Her mention of "family" stings.

How can she ask for money when all we share together is biology? And she talks of holidays and weekends as if her absence can be mended with a few meals.

Does she truly not understand the depth of her betrayal? The years she chose to be away from me as she built another family?

Sure, the note she left felt sincere, but my gut is telling me this was her plan all along. Good moms, like Jane and my adoptive mom and sisters, they love unconditionally. They don't abandon people only to come back when it benefits them.

"I'll think about it," I reply, though my decision is made.

I won't be a bank to someone who couldn't be a mother.

I stand, my movements stiff. "Goodbye, Rae-Anne. Garrett."

She's calling out to me, but I ignore her and turn away. My pace quickens as I head for the elevator, each step an attempt to put distance between us.

The elevator doors can't close fast enough, and when they finally do, I allow myself a moment to just breathe. I lean against the cool metal of the wall, closing my eyes.

Back in the apartment, I reach for my phone. I need to talk to someone. I dial Dalton's number, but there's no answer. Frustration wells up inside me.

I try calling Jane next, when I swore to myself I wouldn't, but I'm desperate for her calm. She doesn't reply, and fuck if it doesn't feel like a rejection. And I hate it. I hate it so much.

It feels like the walls are closing in, and isolation washes over me.

Unable to stay in one place, I decide to take a long, hot shower. The warm water cascades over me, but it does little to fix my thoughts.

After the shower, as I dry off, I decide. I need to get away, even if it's just for a little while. I begin packing a bag, tossing in some clothes and essentials. I need a chance to sort through the mess my life has become this summer.

Chapter 25

JASPER

The plane's touchdown jolts me awake. I look out the window at the rugged beauty of the Utah landscape beneath me. I smile. There's nothing like the sight of those mountains to remind me where I belong.

Navigating through the airport feels automatic, my feet carrying me swiftly toward the exit. Outside, Utah's crisp air is immediate. I slide into the driver's seat of the rental car and take off.

It's only been a few months since my last visit, but the pull of home never fades. As I roll into the driveway, anticipation tightens my chest.

The familiar turn off the main road leads up to my parents' house and land. As I drive up, the Tudor-style home I grew up in from age five looms into view. Its timber framing and steep roof have changed over the years, mostly expanding, thanks to additions funded largely by me. I don't mind it one bit. I'd buy them a brand-new house with every single amenity if they'd let me, but they love this place.

Behind them sit about two hundred acres of rolling hills and wildflowers. In the distance are the mountains. Close to the house is a barn with horses, more for the enjoyment of the grandkids. Someone comes and takes care of them.

A nurse visits three days a week to check in and bring groceries, giving me and my sisters peace of mind on days when they can't pop by for a visit.

Stopping the car, I take a moment to appreciate the peace.

This is where I'm from. These are my parents.

Before I can even shut off the engine, the front door swings open. Dad, still steady in his early eighties, offers an arm to Mom.

"Jasper!" Mom says warmly, reminding me of all the times she's waited for me to come home. First it was elementary school, then middle and high school, the late football practices, the weekends home from college. She's always waiting for me.

She's in her seventies, a pretty lady with short white hair and a big smile.

"I'm home!" I say, grabbing my duffel and stepping out of the car.

Dad wags his finger at me. "Thought you'd surprise us, did you? Does this mean you've gotten into some trouble with the coach?"

"Nah. He loves me. And it isn't a surprise if I texted you from the airport!"

Mom waits for her hug, and when I wrap my arms around her, her scent, a mix of lavender and home, washes over me.

"I missed you, Mom." I pull back and gaze down at her features, then press a kiss to her cheek.

She pats my back three times. One for me, one for dad, and one for her. It's her thing with her kids.

Inside, the familiarity of the house feels good. I take in the stone fireplace and comfy couches, all the senior pictures of me and my sisters, plus all the grandchildren.

Dad grabs my duffel, even when I tell him not to, and puts it in the hall near my old room. Mom takes a seat in her armchair. "We've invited the girls too. The twins are coming, but the rest of the grands are scattered around. How does a beef tenderloin sound for dinner?" she asks.

It sounds perfect.

Later, the kitchen buzzes with energy as my sisters Rayna, Callie, and Demy make their entrance. They are all local, but my sister Zoe, who lives two hours away, called earlier and said she'd be here in time for dessert.

Dad slices the tenderloin he had on the grill earlier, while me and Mom make the side dishes. She manages just fine to make a Caesar salad. Rayna gives me a kiss on the cheek when she sees me, while Callie starts a story about her latest work trip in Paris. Demy, the eldest, is the calm sister, and she listens with a small smile as she hugs me tight. I love each one of them in a different way, I guess. They've spoiled me my entire life. I've always been their little prince.

The house vibrates with the sound of Macy and Lacy racing down the stairs at Rayna's dinner call. Callie starts pouring sangria for the adults, and it's a regular Jannich dinner.

Dad, with that look in his eye that means he's about to dive into a story, leans in over the table. "Hey, remember the camping trip with Jasper and the raccoon?"

A collective laugh starts to bubble up, and I brace myself.

Macy leans in. "I don't think I know this story, but I need more Jasper-being-crazy stories to hold over him. What happened?"

I grunt, finding it hard to believe she's never heard this story. Dad loves to embellish it with each retelling.

Rayna takes the lead as she points at me. "It was on a camping trip. Jasper here decided to check out a trash can at our campsite. Didn't expect an ambush by three raccoons, though, did you? Anyway, he got surprised and sprinted away, screaming and waving his little arms all the way down to the creek."

"Those raccoons were monstrous," I retort. I look at the twins. "Your mom thought it would be super funny if she told me I had rabies. I was eleven and believed everything she said. I learned not to trust her that day."

Rayna rolls her eyes at me.

I flick a piece of lettuce at her.

Macy's and Lacy's eyes widen. "Did one bite you?"

"No bites, just a lot of hurt pride," Callie says dryly.

Demy laughs. "He ran so fast he fell into the creek, and I had to pull him out. Poor baby."

"We haven't gone camping in a while. We should do that again," Mom says.

I pretend to sulk, but inside, I'm basking in the love. "Because of that story, I can't even look at racoons on TV. They aren't cute. They're freaky. Their hands? The weird face mask. Holy cow."

Rayna reaches over and gives me a noogie. "You're a giant man who's afraid of racoons."

I huff. "They were skinny, hungry, vicious, evil racoons."

Dad grunts. "Actually they might have been kittens."

Mom nods. "I do recall a mama cat and her kittens that summer."

I toss my napkin up in the air in pretend exasperation. "Stop. They were bear-size raccoons."

And on it goes . . .

Later, me and my sisters lounge in the screened-in back porch, and the sounds of *Jeopardy!* float from inside where Mom, Dad, and the twins are engrossed in the TV. Zoe has arrived and sits next to me with her head on my shoulder in the swing. A soft wind blows, moving the string lights above us. With a glass of whiskey in hand, I savor the calm.

Rayna breaks the silence. "So, bro. Are you seeing anyone brave enough to join our family yet?"

"Yeah. We're ready for a sister-in-law who can handle us," Callie adds as she sips a glass of wine.

I deflect. "I've been swamped. Summer is a tough time."

"Lie detected. It's training. Heard you've been trying out some dates," Callie says with a sly grin.

Ah, the twins must have told her all the details about the matchmaking.

I think about Jane and how we parted. "There is someone, but I don't know what's going on right now."

Zoe nudges me gently. "I get that. Is she nice?"

"Very."

"Pretty?" Zoe asks.

I nod.

"At least give us a name," Callie begs.

I take a deep breath. "Jane."

Their interest is immediate, their collective lean-in almost comical.

"Ohhh, tell us more. Please," Zoe says.

"She's a single mom. She's six years younger than me and has a little girl named Londyn."

Rayna smiles. "And what makes her so special?"

"She's kind of naive in a way that's refreshing. But she's savvy too. She's used to taking care of herself, and she's a good mom." I pause, a frown forming on my forehead. "But there's something else. Rayna already knows, but my biological mom reached out." I hadn't planned on diving into this tonight, but I don't want to talk about Jane.

Rayna nods. "I figured there was more to your sudden visit. What's going on?"

I explain about Rae-Anne's reemergence and her ask for money. "I don't know her. She's like a stranger to me."

Rayna refills my glass, a silent show of support. "You haven't seen her in over twenty-five years. She is a stranger. This family is about more than just blood. We chose you. We love you. We will always be here."

Demy places a reassuring hand on my shoulder. "You're never alone in this."

Zoe nods her agreement.

"Let's make a toast," Callie says. "To our family."

"To family," I say as we clink glasses.

Later, I retreat to the quiet of my bedroom, the walls adorned with high school and college sports photos. I take out my phone, my thumb hovering over Jane's contact. Seeing Rae-Anne today weighs on me, and I want to hear Jane's voice.

I hesitate again, not ready to hit the Call button. She did ask for space, but here I am, calling.

Finally, I press Call and wait for her to pick up.

"Hey, angel, it's me," I say, trying to sound casual.

"Hi."

"Everything okay?"

"Yeah. Great."

"You sound off." I flip over and lie on my back on my bed and stare up at the ceiling.

"I'm fine, just tired. We're just getting back to normal. Londyn is seeing a specialist tomorrow, and I'm anxious to get started trying to figure it all out."

"I've been thinking about her. How is she?"

"We're fine, Jasper."

Are they?

I want to understand.

There's things going on with me that I just need to think about.

"Listen, if there's anything you need, or if you just want to talk, I'm here. I'm, uh, actually in Utah right now, but . . ."

There's a pause. "Oh, seeing the family?"

"Yeah. I was going a little nuts in the city, and I'm staying here for a while. Macy and Lacy have their dance competition in a week, and I don't want to miss it," I say, my gaze drifting to the window, to the miles between us. "After that, I'm due in Atlanta for training."

In other words, I won't be seeing you.

Is it enough time for her?

Another side of me wonders if I should have stayed, if I should have gone to her apartment and told her how I'm feeling.

I hear her breathing, and I picture her in my head, sitting on her couch, gazing out the window, with Londyn curled up next to her.

"I've been thinking about those tarot cards."

I sit up in surprise. "Yeah? Which one?"

"The Lovers, how it doesn't have to be about romantic love, but about making a decision that's true to yourself."

I don't know how to reply. If feels as if she's trying to tell me something, but . . .

"What do you mean?"

"We both have a lot going on," she says softly. "Let's talk later. I have a lot of cupid stuff, and it's Londyn's bedtime, so I'll go. Bye."

"Jane, wait—" I start, fighting back the frustration.

She hangs up, and I groan.

My unease just won't go away.

I'm here, she's there, and in between us are unsaid words.

But just hearing her voice . . .

I fucking miss her.

I wish she were here with me.

I thump my pillow hard.

I wish I hadn't left her.

I wish I had stayed and delved deeper.

Something's off, and it's not just the fatigue in Jane's voice, and I can't shake the feeling that I'm missing something.

I send a text. What is going on?

After fifteen minutes there's still no reply.

Me: Please call me.

Jane: I'm sorry.

I stare at it, anger bubbling up. For what? Rejecting me? Dumping me, because that's what it feels like. I toss the phone away.

◆ ◆ ◆

Several days later Rayna drives me to the airport.

"I could fly to New York and see Jane," I say aloud, more to myself than to Rayna. The idea has been playing on repeat in my mind.

Rayna glances at me, her expression thoughtful. "You have camp."

I sigh heavily, watching the buildings and trees zip by. "Something is off. Everything is clouded."

She nods. "Sometimes it's easier to keep walking a familiar path rather than a new one."

Her words hit home. The familiar path is training in Atlanta, the routine. Jane is uncharted territory.

"I just don't want to make the wrong move, you know?" I say, my gaze fixed on the horizon. "I don't want to pull away, but what if I'm not what *she* wants?"

She reaches over and gives my hand a reassuring squeeze. "Giving yourself to someone is always a risk."

"Thanks, Rayna. For everything," I say, pulling her into a quick hug as she stops at the drop-off zone. "But I'm never babysitting for you again."

She laughs. "Lie detected."

I watch her drive away, then head into the airport. Atlanta awaits, but my heart is tangled up in New York with a woman and a little girl.

I'm choosing the familiar path, the one with the least resistance, but with each mile that takes me farther from New York, I can't shake the feeling that I might be making the biggest mistake of my life.

Chapter 26
JASPER

As the plane climbs, I settle back into the plush seat of first class. The flight attendant offers me a drink, and I choose a whiskey, hoping it'll make the flight to Atlanta pass quicker. The clink of ice in my glass is the last thing I remember.

I dream I'm on a camping trip, but it's not just any trip—it's a family outing, and not just with any family.

There's a baby, with Jane's smile and my hair. Jane holds him as he sleeps, and I gape at them in my dream. I'm obviously the dad in the dream, but it's the me on the plane, and I've never seen that baby.

I look around at the forest we're in, at the creek with our tents next to it. My parents are there, along with my sisters and their kids. Rayna burns marshmallows, while Callie's trying to convince everyone to try guacamole on their s'mores. Demy and Zoe are wearing bathrobes and are going around and asking for the expensive shampoo.

A raccoon appears, and I scream like a little girl. It's the same one with little human-looking hands and a sly expression. Londyn rushes to it with bits of burnt marshmallow.

The raccoon puts on a cape made from a diaper and declares itself the protector of our camp. He holds up a stick as a sword. Londyn appoints herself as the raccoon's sidekick, and they run off into the forest.

I try to stop her, but I catch Jane's eye, and everything else fades. She tells me it's okay, that it's just a dream, that the racoon isn't really there, and she promises he doesn't have rabies and Londyn will be fine. "The Lovers," she says as she hands over the baby and—

I jerk away to reality and look around, hoping I didn't yell out during the dream and embarrass myself.

I collect myself as the plane begins its descent to Atlanta, with the lingering image of that baby.

Staring out the window, I rub my jaw, trying to decipher what is going on inside me.

The plane shudders as wind hits us, and the pilot's voice announces a severe thunderstorm warning and how our landing will be delayed as he circles around again.

The storm outside mirrors my thoughts. As lightning splits the sky, my mind only thinks of Jane and the dream.

Of possibilities.

Of surprises.

I recall going into the pharmacy to get the Plan B with Jane.

I recall the last time we talked when she brought up the Lovers, about a decision that reflected her true self . . .

I think about the baby in my dream.

What is my brain trying to tell me?

The plane's wheels hit the runway an hour later. I stride to the nearest ticket desk. "Need a flight to New York, the next one you got," I tell the agent.

Her fingers fly over her keyboard. She pauses, eyes meeting mine. "Got a seat on a flight in an hour."

I nod. Camp can wait. I'll text Coach and pay the fine.

Waiting for the flight, my mind's on fire. This move's gutsy, sure, but deep down, it feels right. Jane's pulling away, and I'm in the dark about what's waiting for me back in New York. But the urge to see her and close this growing distance between us is driving me mad.

The flight's a haze of nerves. My leg can't stop shaking. My head's spinning.

What if Jane's door's shut for good?

What if I never should have left her in the first place?

Yet, as New York's skyline draws near, peace takes over. This is it. I've got to lay everything out with Jane and spill my guts.

New York's lights blink below. She's down there. I can feel the bond from her.

Time to step up and grab hold of the future.

I'm coming for you, angel.

Chapter 27
JANE

Several days ago . . .

I'm behind the counter at the bookstore, ringing up a teenage boy who's buying the hardcover of the Kama Sutra. It's not the guy back in June who I caught using it as he made out with his girlfriend, but still, I press my lips together, trying not to smirk as I hand it over.

"Enjoy," I say.

He nods, and I chuckle once he's out the door.

I've lost ten female clients because of the video Freida posted, but I've let it go. Jasper said his PR team is handling it, and I'm leaving it alone. She was angry because she obviously saw me with Jasper. I chew my lips, recalling that magical day in the park with him and Londyn. I'm sure she saw how I looked at him. Maybe she saw how I adore him.

How I love him. With everything inside me.

I glance down at the pregnancy test peeking out from my dress pocket. Ugh. It's time to figure this thing out. I've put it off long enough.

I head for the bathroom, determined to face whatever result awaits.

Babs catches me just as I'm about to duck into the hallway. "Where you off to in such a hurry?"

"I have to pee."

"You just went."

"Are you watching my bathroom breaks?"

She cocks her head. "Should I? Are you feeling okay? You're pale. Just like yesterday."

"You're nosy."

She narrows her eyes at me, raking them over me like a mom checking if her kid is faking being sick. "Seriously, did I hear you throwing up earlier?"

Yes.

"No."

She wags a finger at me. "Something is off with you ever since Londyn was in the hospital."

I move to walk past her, and the pregnancy test somehow falls out of my dress pocket.

"Is that what I think it is?" she says with a gasp. She pounces on it before I can make a move. "Jane, is this a—"

I snatch it back, stuffing it into my pocket. "It's a thermometer! Yeah, checking if I have a fever."

"A thermometer that requires urine? Science has really advanced, hasn't it?"

"It's nothing." I try to sidestep her, but she's like a detective.

"Lord have mercy. Jane, are you—"

I cut her off, backing away. "I gotta go, Babs. I have to pee! We'll talk later." I turn and sprint for the bathroom.

I lock myself in the employee bathroom, my heart thudding in my chest. Alone, finally. I tear open the pregnancy test package with shaky hands.

A knock at the door nearly makes me jump out of my skin. "Jane? You know I can't let this go. I saw what I saw. Jasper? Does he know? Is that why you haven't been seeing him? Are you crazy? What are you going to do?"

"Just give me a minute, Babs!" I call out through the door. "And keep quiet. Someone might hear you!"

There's a pause; then Babs sighs. "Just let me in. Do you really want to do this alone?"

I've been doing the hard things alone for a long time.

This is just one more to add to the list.

But maybe that's been part of my problem.

Deep down I know what my inner flaws are.

I'm overly independent.

I'm cautious.

I struggle to accept help.

It's sculpted by trauma, by deep-seated fears of being a burden to someone.

My mom walked away without ever saying goodbye. She left her life behind and moved away. Tomas—well, I'm not sure he ever loved me at all. He left for his career.

And me? I've armored myself in independence—it's why I keep the possibility of help at bay.

Jasper has his own set of walls. We're two people shaped by our pasts who've learned to protect not just our hearts but also our very selves.

The intercom comes on. "Store alert, all employees, the Chicken Lady is about to walk in the door. Please come to the front and help."

I groan. The Chicken Lady is an older, wealthy socialite from the Upper West Side who dresses in the most divine clothes as she walks Lucy, her pet chicken, on a diamond-studded leash. She has been a member of many book clubs through the years. She's also donated several first editions on display that aren't for sale but are meant to draw people into the store.

The chicken is her emotional-support animal. Allegedly.

I've yet to see Lucy in a vest that declares it to be true.

Still, the woman is a former acquaintance of my gran's and loves to come in. Usually she sits in the café area and orders scones for herself and Lucy. Inevitably, the chicken makes a poo. Other customers freak out. And Magic, our bookstore cat who is currently on vacation with Emmy, once chased Lucy all over the store and nearly ended her.

The first time I spotted the Chicken Lady, I was with Gran as we strolled through Central Park. She was a vision in a full-length mink coat that looked like it had walked straight out of a 1940s Hollywood film. Next to her was a white chicken on a leash.

Gran told me the story of how Mildred had lost her husband and was never quite the same. She had all the money she could ever want, but she was lonely.

"I'm in the bathroom, so this one is all you," I tell Babs through the door.

She groans. "I refuse. She should clean up the poo!"

"She claims it isn't Lucy's. Always does. It's your turn. Go manage it."

"I really don't like you right now!" I hear her huff. "I just want to know who cleans the poo at her apartment." Babs's voice filters through the door again, her tone an octave higher in distress. "Jane! You owe me big time for this. I'm not kidding!"

I open the door just a crack. Babs glares at me, her face scrunched in disgust as she hisses, "Chickens belong on a farm or in a backyard. Not in a bookstore. You are too nice to her!"

"Go on," I say. "Take care of the customer."

She tightens her lips, whips around with a huff, and stomps down the hall.

I peek through the door, now wide enough to catch the full scene. I mean, come on, I can't miss this. I took care of Lucy last time anyway.

Babs is in full negotiation mode with the Chicken Lady, who's dressed extravagantly in pink Chanel with a pearl necklace. Lucy struts around as if she owns the place, her feathers reminding me of my cupid wings. Amazement hits when I see that this time Lucy is decked out in some kind of diaper with sequins on it.

Maybe she took to heart the last conversation Babs had with her about cleaning up after Lucy.

Lucy pecks at the scone the Chicken Lady holds out to her, sending a few more giggles my way.

Babs nods enthusiastically. "Oh wow, she looks beautiful, Mildred."

The Chicken Lady huffs. "Yes, she's wearing one now when we go out, although my girl has never pooped in here."

Babs smiles widely, clearly happy. "Still, she's setting trends. Imagine the attention she'll get on your walks in Central Park,"

Lucy pecks a little too close to Babs, and I laugh under my breath as Babs hops back to get away from her.

I shut the door and pull out the pregnancy test package, my fingers clumsy with nerves.

Then the unmistakable sound of Lucy clucking reaches me, a strange comfort in the bathroom. It's followed by Babs's exasperated voice, "Lucy, darling, let's try to keep the scones on the plate, okay?"

Here I am about to possibly change my life with a single test while Babs negotiates with a chicken.

I set the timer on my phone.

The timer goes off, and I take a deep breath and pick up the test and brace myself for whatever comes next. "All right, Jane. You've got this," I say, echoing the pep talks Babs usually gives me.

No matter what happens, I'll remember it along with a story about the Chicken Lady.

Chapter 28
JANE

I'm halfway through a cracker as I finish ringing up a customer. Glancing at the clock, I decide it's time. "Babs, I'm heading out to Carson's. Got to drum up some business," I say, wiping my hands on a napkin. "Can you lock up?"

She rolls her eyes. "Not the outfit again."

I chuckle, heading toward my office. "You know it's brought us clients. And those clients brought more clients."

"Don't remind me," she grumbles, but I can tell she's fighting a smile.

In my office, I change into the long white toga, securing the angel wings and adjusting the quiver on my back. I add a swipe of red lipstick.

Stepping into Carson's, I scan the room, getting a few curious glances, but the regulars have gotten used to me. I've been here several times, and it's gotten me at least five clients. The bartender even sends up a wave and a smile as he calls my name. I wave back.

Then I see him—a young man in a suit. Maybe around my age, he's alone at the bar with a stark-white napkin tied around his neck like a makeshift bib, but it's the cheese smeared on his shirt cuffs that really catches my attention.

In a way, he reminds me of Londyn, who always gets food everywhere but her mouth. I head over, my wings fluttering slightly with each step.

I slide onto the stool beside him. "The bib is a good move, but your cuffs didn't get the memo," I say, pointing out the cheese stains with a grin.

He looks down, then groans. "Ugh. Dining solo has its pitfalls."

"I'm Jane," I say as I extend my hand, not missing the firm grip of his handshake. "I run a matchmaking service, hence the outfit. Watching you with those cheese fries reminds me of my daughter. Couldn't help but say hi."

"Alexi. And this," he gestures to his bib, "isn't my usual charm. It's been a long-ass day."

I glance at the line of empty beer bottles crowding his space.

"Looks like you're having a rough time?"

He sighs, picking at the remains of his cheese fries. "Is it that obvious? Yeah, just ended things with someone at work."

I tsk. "Work and personal life—tricky."

"Especially when you're gay and trying to navigate a corporate maze." Ahhh.

"Our service is inclusive. My friend Brody helps with our LGBTQ+ clients."

Alexi's gaze softens. "That's good, but I'm not sure I'm ready to date. How about joining me for a drink? You seem interesting, and I need a distraction."

I laugh. "Sure. Sprite for me," I say.

He nods to the bartender, and we settle into an easy conversation.

Suddenly, the door to Carson's swings open with a bit of a flourish, drawing the attention of everyone in the bar. My breath catches in my throat as Jasper walks in. He's just as stunning as I remember—tall, with that effortlessly confident stride, his hair mussed as if he's just rolled out of bed, but somehow it looks gorgeous. He's wearing a fitted T-shirt that accentuates his broad shoulders and jeans that cling to the muscles in his thighs. His gaze sweeps the room, and it feels like time slows down.

My heart skips a beat, then another, as if it's forgotten how to keep a steady rhythm. It's only been ten days since I saw him—days of trying to convince myself that I'm okay.

But seeing him now, all those carefully constructed walls crumble.

I've missed him—his smile, his laugh, the way "angel" sounds when he says it.

He hasn't spotted me yet, his eyes scanning the crowd. I'm suddenly acutely aware that I should have washed my hair this morning and put on a full face of makeup. A part of me wants to hide, but another part is rooted to the spot, unable to look away.

When his gaze finally lands on me, there's a flicker of surprise, then a warmth that spreads across his face, lighting up his eyes in a way that sends a familiar jolt through me.

It's a look that says he's genuinely happy, and my heart feels like it's about to burst.

I gasp, a sound lost in the bar. It's ridiculous, really, how just seeing him can make me feel like this.

For a moment, there's no one else in the room but Jasper and me. The noise of the bar fades, and all I feel is this yearning that I've bottled up since he left the hospital.

And then he starts to walk toward me.

"Is that Jasper Jannich?" Alexi asks, his tone hushed.

"Yes. But please pretend you don't know him. His ego is so big already . . . ," I say, and Alexi smirks.

"He deserves to have an ego. He's hot."

"And straight."

Alexi chuckles. "He's yours, I guess. Lucky girl."

I chew on my bottom lip, watching every move Jasper makes as he walks closer to us. The way his blue eyes won't leave my face.

I glance away and look at Alexi. "Not so lucky. I think he knows something is up."

Alexi takes a sip of beer. "Knows what? Wait. He isn't coming to kick my ass, is he?"

"Maybe." My thoughts are scattered. "He's supposed to be at football camp, but he's here. Which means something has brought him here, which means . . ."

"Hey, tell him we aren't together, yeah? I don't want to die in this bar. It stinks. The fries aren't even that great. I only stopped here on a whim."

He shifts uncomfortably, eyeing Jasper's towering frame.

But Jasper doesn't spare him a glance. His eyes are stormy, yes, but not with anger. He looks vulnerable. Maybe a little scared.

I turn on my stool to face him as he gets to me, but before I can speak, he reaches for me, his hands gentle as he pulls me closer, then leans down and kisses me, a touch filled with tenderness.

When he finally pulls back, his gaze searches mine. "Jane Darling," he starts, then swallows. "This might sound crazy, but I had this dream about us, camping, with my family and Londyn . . . and a baby." He pauses, his thumb brushing my lip lightly. "I know it sounds insane, but it felt like a glimpse into the future. With you."

His hands frame my face as if I'm something precious. "I saw what could be, and it's everything."

My heart skips a beat. "What are you—" I start, but he silences me with a soft kiss.

"I know we've both been scared," he says, pulling back to look into my eyes. "But after that dream, I can't pretend. I don't want to. I need you, Jane. More than I've ever needed anything."

His voice is thick. "Seeing my bio mom again, it brought everything back. The feeling of being unwanted and left behind." He leans in, his forehead resting against mine, sharing his vulnerability. "I hesitated at the hospital when you needed space. I didn't stay and fight for us. I'm so sorry."

No, he shouldn't be sorry for that. I pushed him away.

His hands slide down to my shoulders. "I'm a mess, Jane. I've spent my life hesitating and not saying what I should when it comes to getting serious with women." His fingers gently squeeze, a silent plea for understanding.

I glance at Alexi. His mouth is open as he listens in rapt attention. I think his eyes shine a little.

I notice that even the bartender and a few patrons are silent as they listen.

Jasper takes a deep breath, and I focus back on him.

"After my mom left me at the truck stop, I ended up in foster care for six months. Like I told you before, I didn't speak for three months. I had no words. Nothing," he tells me. "I was in this limbo, hoping she'd come back for me. But she never did."

He pauses, swallowing hard, his gaze locked on me. "Then, my adoptive parents found me. They were everything I'd ever dreamed of, loving, caring, stable. But I was always afraid it would all just disappear. I used to get up in the early hours of the morning and wander around the house to make sure they hadn't left me."

My throat tightens with emotion.

"I used to hold my mom's hand all the time, up until I was nearly fourteen. I guess I thought if I held on tight enough, I could make safety last."

His lashes flutter, then open again. "On my tenth birthday, I secretly hoped my real mom would show up. It had been five years, and it felt like a milestone, you know, like she might come and tell me she made a mistake. When she didn't, something inside me just died. She was my real mom, my blood, but she didn't want me. Some holes can't be filled, no matter how much love you get from other people, and I know you get that, you do."

His voice softens. "You and Londyn are what I've been missing. That dream . . . it wasn't just a dream." He pauses. "I love you, Jane."

I suck in a sharp breath.

He gives me a smirk as he laughs sheepishly. "I know it's sudden, and I've been an idiot, but I'm here now. I'm back because I can't be without you. I want to love you forever, be everything you and Londyn need."

"Jasper," I say, my own voice trembling. "I need to tell you something—"

"You never took that Plan B," he says.

I shake my head, amazed that he knows. "No."

"Oh, shit, it's getting good now," Alexi says under his breath, but neither of us seems to care.

"Do you have something to tell me?" Jasper asks.

"I'm pregnant," I say, tears forming in my eyes. "From the first time we were together."

His eyes widen, a myriad of emotions flickering across his face.

"Pregnant?" he says in a low voice full of amazement. "Were you ever going to tell me?"

"Of course I would. It's yours. I just needed to think about it."

Silence, thick and heavy, stretches between us. I steal a glance at him, trying to gauge his reaction.

His throat moves as he swallows. "Wow. That's why you were sick at the hospital. It all makes sense now. I won't pretend I'm not shocked. But I care about you, more than I've ever cared about anyone. And this child, it's part of you. Of us."

"It's a lot to take on," I say, giving him an out.

He takes a step back and runs a hand through his hair. "Okay, don't move. Just give me a second."

And just like that, he's walking away and leaving me sitting there on the barstool.

There's silence in the bar as everyone watches him leave.

He paces outside the bar. Through the window, I see that his movements are erratic. He's talking to himself, his hands gesturing in the air. He just poured his heart out, confessed his love . . .

What is he doing now?

I consider following him, but something holds me back. This is his moment to process. The revelation of the pregnancy is huge, and even though his declaration of love was everything, I think he's grappling with the reality.

He stops pacing for a moment, looks up at the night sky as if he's seeking answers from the stars.

Then, he's on the move again, pacing.

I tap my fingers on the bar, anxiety building.

This waiting is torture, but I understand the need for a moment to breathe and think. I've been there, trying to find my footing when life throws a surprise my way.

Alexi places a comforting hand on my shoulder. "He'll come back," he says. "He just needs a minute. Also, if you have a card, I'll take it now. Find me somebody like Jasper, yeah?"

I nod, not really listening.

Jasper's reaction is understandable, but it doesn't make it any easier to watch.

Finally, he stops pacing. He stands still, takes a deep breath, and then turns back toward the bar. His steps are more decisive now, as if he's come to some sort of conclusion.

As he reenters the bar, his eyes find mine immediately. He walks up to me, takes my hands in his, and kneels down in front of me, right there in the middle of the bar.

"Jasper!"

"Jane," he says, his voice steady, "I won't pretend I'm not scared. This is huge. But I meant what I said. I love you, and I never want to be away from you again like I have been. I want to be a part of your life every single day. I never want to see you walk away from me. I never want to walk away from you. I need you and Londyn and this baby. I need it more than anything. I'm crazy about you."

Tears well up in my eyes as I listen to him. This is all I've ever wanted to hear from a man who loves me.

"Yes," I say, squeezing his hands. "I want that too."

"Is this a marriage proposal?" Alexi asks.

Jasper looks around the room, seeming to become aware of the others' rapt attention. "Yes."

He stands up and pulls me into a tight embrace. I feel my feet lift off the floor as he spins me around. The bar erupts in cheers and claps from the people who've been watching the drama unfold.

I lean into Jasper, feeling his heart beat in time with mine. I realize that no matter what challenges or surprises lie ahead, we'll face them together. Because that's what families do.

"Tell me you love me, Jane. I need to hear it," he says in my ear. "I'm a needy guy. I'm always going to need the words, and you haven't said them."

I lean back and gaze up at him.

I get why I've fallen for Jasper. It probably happened slowly, little interactions since the moment we met at the bookstore.

His way of being gentle without losing his masculinity. He listens, really listens, making me feel like I'm the only person in the world. He picks up on the little stuff, the things I throw out without thinking, and remembers them. His sunshiny charm.

He calls me "angel." He likes my scowl. He thinks I'm funny.

Just now when he opened up to me in front of all these people, some who probably recorded it, he wasn't afraid to show people who he is.

And the spark between us, it's been there from the start, growing stronger every day.

What I love most about Jasper is that he's *Jasper*. I love his ego, his sunshine, his charming grin, even his smirky grin. I love his depth underneath that. His soul.

I gaze into his blue eyes. "I love you. Because you are you. Because we're meant to be. You are a surprise I never saw coming, and it's the best one yet."

He gives me a blinding smile, one that could light up a room. "We're a match, angel. I knew it from the moment I asked you out in this very bar and you told me no. I'm never letting you go."

We stand there, hands clasped, and everything feels absolutely right.

Chapter 29
JANE

We pick up Londyn from preschool, then make the short walk back to my apartment. Londyn skips ahead, while Jasper and I follow, our steps in sync. He keeps glancing over at me, still a little freaked out, still happy. And each way, there's a rhythm between us.

Once we're home, the routine kicks in. We order Chinese and have dinner at the table.

Then it's time for Londyn to go to bed, but not without a bedtime story. She's adamant about Jasper being the one to read to her. I watch from the doorway, leaning against the frame, as he settles beside her on the bed, book in hand. His voice fills the room as he dives in, with Londyn hanging on every word.

As he reads the final words, he catches my eye and smiles. Quietly, he stands, making his way over to me, careful not to disturb Londyn as she curls up next to one of her stuffed animals.

"We make a good team," he says quietly, his hand finding mine.

"Yeah, we do," I murmur.

The glow of the TV screen casts a soft light in the darkened room, where we've decided to unwind with an episode of *The Vampire Diaries*.

Jasper sits close to me on the couch, his arm draped over the back.

"I've been thinking," he says, his voice thoughtful. "About us, about everything that's happened. Why didn't you . . . I mean, after that night, you could have made a different choice."

I've asked myself the same question a thousand times. "I believe in fate. Sometimes, life throws you a surprise and you lean into it and see where it takes you. I thought about the tarot cards and how my life was going to have good things." I smile. "Are you scared?"

"Terrified," he replies with a grin. "I can't believe we're going to have a baby."

"I have a doctor's appointment next week."

"I'm here for it. When do you want to get married? Also, you need to meet my family. You and Londyn need to move in with me too. It's bigger at my place."

His words hang in the air between us.

I draw a slow breath. The thought of weaving our lives together sends a thrill of excitement through me, but I worry about Londyn.

"I'm going too fast, aren't I?" he says with a smirk.

"Maybe just a little." I smile.

His thumb strokes the back of my hand, a gentle gesture. "Okay. I respect that. I get it. We'll do this slow. For Londyn and us." He tips my chin toward him. "We're scared, but we're happy. Am I right?"

I smile. "Definitely."

"We're going to be a family."

The word "family" fills me with peace. With Jasper by my side, and Londyn and the baby, I feel ready to face whatever comes. "I really, really missed you."

He kisses me on the lips. "Same, angel."

A while later, as we watch his show, an intense scene unfolds between Stefan, Damon, and Elena.

He squeezes my hand gently. "You have to like this show if we're ever going to make it."

I roll my eyes as he flashes a grin.

"Seriously, I'd take on a whole vampire clan for you."

I lob a pillow at him. He catches it, mock snarls, and pretends to pounce, showing off fake fangs. I fight back, forming a cross with my fingers, and we both end up laughing. Then, he pulls me closer, his hand finding its way to my stomach.

I place my hand over his. This touch feels like a silent vow.

"Hi there, kiddo," he murmurs, voice filled with a warmth that melts me. "Can't wait to see you."

Tears prick my eyes, full of joy. Resting against him, I say, "They'll have the world's best dad."

"And the most amazing mom," he adds.

Calm washes over me. With Jasper there's a rightness I hadn't known was missing. And here we are, ready for whatever comes our way.

Chapter 30
JANE

When the doorbell rings at 11:30 in the morning, I'm not expecting it.

I was hoping I would be able to catch a few hours of sleep before dealing with clients this morning. My list has grown, especially since my dating service is now publicly endorsed by a superstar quarterback. The media knows we're together. Freida's video didn't quite have the effect she wanted, though. It was more of a football-player-falls-for-his-matchmaker story and went viral.

I roll out of bed and pat my stomach and trudge to the door. Thankfully, at five months, the morning sickness has vanished, and I feel much better. Just tired. It was a crazy weekend at a football game, but fun. Rayna, Macy, and Lacy, along with Jasper's parents, met me there, and we sat in our box seats and cheered our team on to . . . well, not victory.

The Pythons lost, 13–27.

It doesn't matter, though.

Because if you looked on the field, at the smile on the face of the man who led his team, you'd have thought he won. The man can't seem to keep the grin off his face.

In fact, that's what Jasper tells me, before every game. "Doesn't matter what happens. I've already won."

That didn't mean I wasn't going to yell for them, hoping they'd pull out a win. It was a good game. I've never been so happy to be on a losing team.

But my content heart skips a beat when I peep through the hole and find him standing on my front stoop, dressed in the suit he wore to the game. The team must have come back this morning.

He looks like he's been up for hours, which means he barely slept.

I'm still dressed in my sweats. As I zip my hoodie over my tight camisole and pull open the door, scratching my head, he smiles, his eyes lighting up at the sight of me.

"What are you doing?" I ask. "I thought you'd go home and rest."

"I have something to say." He seems nervous, like he's had one too many coffees this morning.

"I haven't even had a chance to take a shower."

He leans in for a kiss, which is the quickest one ever since I haven't brushed my teeth.

He's nervous, fidgeting from foot to foot. The man with all the moves on the field looks like he has no idea what to do. It's cute.

"Is everything okay?" I ask. Gone are the days when I'd worry he'd bolt. He's a constant, never once showing signs of retreating or hesitating. He's there to pick up Londyn from preschool when I can't. He's at every doctor's appointment. He's here with us almost every night in my small apartment.

"I thought today was for resting. Londyn's set on watching *Mulan* with you tonight." She's over at Emmy's right now for the weekend since I went out of town.

"Good pick. But, sorry, couldn't wait," he says.

He's buzzing with energy, which is odd because he should be dead on his feet. Then he goes and—pulls out a ring box. "Got something for you."

My brain short-circuits. It's a diamond the size of a small planet.

A long exhale comes from him as he watches my face expectantly. It's stunning. I'm blinded by its sparkle. "This is . . . wow."

"I talked to Londyn about it," he says, words tumbling out in a rush. "She basically said get on with it already. Kid's got opinions."

"You actually asked her?" I can't help the grin spreading across my face.

He throws me a look. "Was I supposed to do the whole one-knee thing?"

"You did that at the bar, so it counts." I cross my arms and pretend to pout. "I was expecting maybe a skywriter, a marching band, and at least a couple of doves."

He drops to one knee while I tell him not to, but he doesn't get up. He looks up at me like he's about to offer me the world. "Jane Darling, how 'bout it? Wanna make me the luckiest guy alive? For real."

I lean against the door, half expecting my knees to give out. "Wearing that rock means I'm stuck with you, huh?"

"Glued, screwed, and tattooed. You're mine," he says, a softness in his voice.

"Guess that makes me your problem now," I manage to say, slipping my hand forward.

He slides it on, and it fits like it's been mine all along. "Just try getting rid of me now," he warns as he pulls me close. The world narrows down to the two of us as he kisses me.

"Let's not keep the future waiting," he says, ushering me inside with a hand at my back. "After all, we've got forever to get started on. And Londyn isn't here, which means . . ."

I tug him down the hall. "We've got a bed!"

Chapter 31
JASPER

Here I am, in Jane's hospital suite, heart racing as I walk the floor.

Babs leans against the wall. "Jasper, you're pacing so much you're going to wear a hole in the floor."

Andrew flips through a magazine, seemingly at ease. "Dude, you need to chill. Babies come when they come. And screaming moms are totally normal," he says, not looking up.

I know he's trying to be helpful, but his words are like gasoline on my already blazing anxiety.

"I'm not screaming," Jane announces from her bed grumpily. "I want everyone out of here, except Jasper and Emmy."

The nurse chuckles under her breath as she tells me that it won't be much longer now and leaves the room.

I return to Jane's side, taking her hand in mine. Her grip is strong, and I wince.

"Hey," I say, trying to sound more confident than I feel. "You're doing amazing, you know that?"

Jane shoots me a look. "I feel like I'm trying to bench-press a truck."

I laugh, and she cracks a smile, which is all I'm aiming for.

"If anyone can bench-press a truck, it's you, angel. You're strong."

"Babs and Andrew leave, mumbling something about getting coffee. It's just me, Jane, and the faint beeping of monitors now. I pull up a chair closer to her bed, not wanting to let go of her hand.

Emmy hovers near the door, her phone in hand, probably texting updates to the family chat. "You got this, sis," she says, before stepping out to give us some space.

Jane's breathing changes, her focus inward, and I'm in awe. "Talk to me," she says between breaths. "Distract me."

"What do you want to hear?" I ask, ready to recite the dictionary if it'll help.

"Tell me why you love me," she says.

"Where do I start?" I squeeze her hand. "I love you because you're the bravest person I know. You face everything head-on, no matter how tough it is. I love how you make me laugh, how you argue with me. I love your fierce loyalty to those you care about, how you've welcomed me into your life and made me feel like I belong."

She listens, a smile tugging at the corners of her mouth.

"I love how you are with Londyn, how you're going to be with our baby. You're going to be an incredible mom to two or three or four or five, and I can't wait to see it."

Jane's grip tightens, another contraction rolling through her. "Keep talking," she breathes out.

"And I love that you're making me a father," I continue. "I can't imagine doing this with anyone else. You, me, Londyn, and this little one on the way, we're a team."

She relaxes slightly. "Thank you," she says, her eyes meeting mine with a love so deep it nearly knocks me off my feet.

The nurse returns, checking the monitors, then Jane. "It's almost time," she says, and everything in me tightens with anticipation.

Jane's brow furrows as another wave of contractions hits. "Jasper, I think . . . I think I want the epidural."

I chuckle nervously, remembering the pact we made. "Uh, babe, remember? You made me swear—on my first batch of lasagna—that I"

Babs and Andrew leave, mumbling something about getting coffee. It's just me, Jane, and the faint beeping of monitors now. I pull up a chair closer to her bed, not wanting to let go of her hand.

Emmy hovers near the door, her phone in hand, probably texting updates to the family chat. "You got this, sis," she says, before stepping out to give us some space.

Jane's breathing changes, her focus inward, and I'm in awe. "Talk to me," she says between breaths. "Distract me."

"What do you want to hear?" I ask, ready to recite the dictionary if it'll help.

"Tell me why you love me," she says.

"Where do I start?" I squeeze her hand. "I love you because you're the bravest person I know. You face everything head-on, no matter how tough it is. I love how you make me laugh, how you argue with me. I love your fierce loyalty to those you care about, how you've welcomed me into your life and made me feel like I belong."

She listens, a smile tugging at the corners of her mouth.

"I love how you are with Londyn, how you're going to be with our baby. You're going to be an incredible mom to two or three or four or five, and I can't wait to see it."

Jane's grip tightens, another contraction rolling through her. "Keep talking," she breathes out.

"And I love that you're making me a father," I continue. "I can't imagine doing this with anyone else. You, me, Londyn, and this little one on the way, we're a team."

She relaxes slightly. "Thank you," she says, her eyes meeting mine with a love so deep it nearly knocks me off my feet.

The nurse returns, checking the monitors, then Jane. "It's almost time," she says, and everything in me tightens with anticipation.

Jane's brow furrows as another wave of contractions hits. "Jasper, I think . . . I think I want the epidural."

I chuckle nervously, remembering the pact we made. "Uh, babe, remember? You made me swear—on my first batch of lasagna—that I wouldn't let you cave for the epidural. You were very specific: 'Even if I beg, plead, or threaten to name our child after a football player from a rival team.'"

She glares at me, her gaze enough to make a lesser man flee. "I was not in labor when I made that promise."

"But you said you wanted to go all natural. You compared yourself to a warrior queen."

Her grip on my hand tightens, her nails digging in just enough to remind me that she means business. "I'd happily trade my warrior-queen crown for a nice, big shot in the back."

"Come on, now. You're doing amazing. Remember the breathing techniques? Hee-hee-hoo, hee-hee-hoo?"

"Hee-hee-hoo yourself. If you don't get that anesthesiologist in here right now, I'm going to start thinking up some very creative names for our son."

"All right, all right. I'll get the nurse."

It was too late for the epidural, and now he's here. I stand, holding my son for the first time, the weight of this tiny life in my arms, emotions washing over me. He's so small, so fragile.

As I look down at his peaceful face, awe fills me. His fingers, his soft breaths—every detail about him is a marvel.

Memories of my own mother, the one who brought me into this world, flash through my mind. The abandonment I felt for so long, the questions that clouded my heart, they all seem to converge in this single moment.

As I gaze at my son, I realize something. The pain of my past, the absence of my biological mother—it's all led me to this. It's taught me what it means to truly love, to give unconditionally, to be the parent I never had.

I see a future filled with love, a promise to be there for him in all the ways I missed growing up. I silently vow to give him the security that every child deserves.

He will never question his worth. I will be there for every step, every fall, every triumph.

As I look up to see Jane watching me, gratitude hits. We've created a new beginning for us as a family.

The sun slips through the blinds, and I blink. We haven't slept a bit. But I'm not tired. Because I know this is the start of everything I want.

Most of all, I want her.

Completely. Forever.

With our son sleeping in the hospital bassinet next to the bed, I hold Jane's face in my hands and kiss her.

Her eyelids flutter as she says sleepily, "I love you."

And for the first time in my life, I'm too dumbstruck to think of a single punch line. The only thing I can think of is what I'm feeling with every cell of my body. "I love you, too, Jane. And Londyn. And Jace Andrew Jannich."

I stand in our apartment, battling a dirty diaper. At three months, our little guy is all gassy smiles, oblivious to the assault he's unleashed. It's July, over a year since we first got together. Just last month, we were married in a quiet ceremony with our family around us, but now, it's back to the real world.

"All right, champ, let's tackle this," I say as I open the diaper. The stench slams into me, and I gag. "Jane! This is a two-person job!"

Londyn struts in, eyeing the situation with disdain. "Mom, Jasper's being weird again!"

"I don't like the poop," I whine.

"You're such a drama queen," she says as she rolls her eyes and walks back out.

"This is biohazard-level stuff," I argue to no one, fumbling for wipes and a clean diaper, wishing I had paid more attention during those YouTube tutorials.

Jane floats in, ever the calm one. "Struggling?"

I give her my best help-me eyes.

She laughs, taking over with the skill of a seasoned pro. "You'll get the hang of it. It's all in the wrist."

I watch in awe as she wraps up the job with finesse. Her transition from bookstore manager to matchmaking CEO from our apartment has been seamless, leaving Babs to run the bookstore.

"Diaper crisis averted," she announces, washing up. "You owe me."

I pull her close and kiss her lips. "I owe you everything."

Just then, Londyn tugs at my sleeve, all business. "Park? You promised to take me on the lake."

I nod, energized. "Park it is."

I glance back at Jane, who's watching us with an all-encompassing love.

In the chaos of new fatherhood and the family I never knew I needed, I realize that life's surprises aren't just twists in the road—no, they're the stepping stones guiding us to where we're meant to be. Every unexpected turn has brought me to a destiny I couldn't have dreamed of. My family is my unexpected destiny, with love that binds us all together. And it's more beautiful than I ever could have hoped.

Epilogue

JASPER

Years later, we dive into what's now known as the Annual Family Camping Extravaganza. This time, the Smoky Mountains of Tennessee play host to our adventures. We've claimed a large chunk of the campground, with RVs and tents and a couple of rented cabins.

Graham and I are grilling. We're surrounded by the aroma of hot dogs and hamburgers. "We'll be kicked to the curb if we mess up dinner," he warns as he skillfully flips a burger.

I chuckle, passing him another hot dog. Last night was the girls' turn to cook, and they fried fish and hush puppies. My mom made her coleslaw, and everything was perfect. It put more pressure on the guys to do well on their turn to cook.

"As long as we avoid setting the place on fire, we should be fine," I say.

The air hums with the sound of our family. Jane sets up a picnic table, her focus slightly intimidating. Emmy and my sisters help put down tablecloths, then set out the side dishes.

Dad, with Mom next to him, shares embellished camping stories with the kids. "And then, the bear, massive as a mountain, decided to join our dinner," he declares, stretching his arms wide, drawing gasps from them.

Hazel and Jace don't look fazed, but little Jett, our youngest, is scared. He starts to tear up, and Jane sweeps in and picks him up and kisses him on the top of his head.

I'm still playing football, having racked up two more championships. Jane and I, we're a team. She's expanded her matchmaking empire, snapping up a storefront near our place with Mr. Darden's investment. I offered to give her money, but she wants to do this on her own.

As for my bio mom, she's been a ghost since that awkward apartment visit. But I did right by my half brother, setting up a college trust for him. It's the least I could do; he's innocent in all this. We're not exactly chatty, but we keep tabs on each other online.

Tomas and Londyn finally met officially as father and daughter after Jane and I tied the knot. She spends a week with him every summer, and he makes the trip to see her a few times a year. They're building their thing, step by step. He might be her father, but I'm her dad. She tells me all the time.

"All right, everyone, dinner's ready!" I call out, and the stampede begins.

They line up by the grill.

Londyn towers over the other kids. She's going through her awkward phase with grace, and likes to order the other kids around.

Jace is our little explorer, and always has a grin that spells trouble. He's got my gaze and Jane's fierce nature. Currently, he's locked in an intense argument with Hazel over who'll take the crown in our family sprint.

And then there's Jett, our baby at nine months, sporting curls and wide blue eyes that miss nothing.

How did fortune smile so broadly on us?

I glance down at the gold charms on my chain, small replicas of the cards she drew that night when I read her tarot cards. It's a gift Jane gave me on our wedding day. She wears one just like it. It's a reflection of us, of being true, of having familial blessings.

"Hey, Dad, can I have two hot dogs?" Londyn's voice pulls me back.

"Planning to grow another inch tonight?" I say, handing them over.

She smirks, an expression that looks a lot like mine. "I'm gonna be taller than Andrew."

Andrew hears her and pouts. "Whatever."

As Londyn dashes off, Jace tugs at my shirt. "I want burgers. With extra cheese, please." His eyes are wide, hopeful.

"Extra cheese, coming right up," I reply, flipping a burger onto his plate.

Rayna approaches. "Hey, Jasper, think you could grill some veggies for me? Trying to eat healthier."

"Grilled veggies it is," I agree, setting aside a portion of the grill for her request.

Next, Callie saunters over, phone in hand. "Jasper, I need a photo of you grilling. For the family album," she says, aiming her phone at me.

I pose with the spatula, and she snaps away.

Demy and Zoe wander over. "Any chance I could get a slightly burnt hot dog? I know it's weird, but I love the crunch," Demy says. Zoe gets the same.

Jett crawls close to me, and I get nervous with him close to the grill and scoop him up and put him on my hip.

Jane joins us, a smile on her face as she watches the kids.

Damn, she's beautiful.

This is my world—Jane, Londyn, Jace, Jett.

"What do you want to eat, angel?" I ask.

She smiles. "Surprise me."

I pull her close and kiss her on the lips. "I love our surprises."

"Dad, come on! We're starting the race!" Jace calls out after we've finished eating. He tugs at my hand.

"All right, all right, round up all the adults, except for Grandma and Grandpa. Everyone has to run, even the twins."

As we line up for the race, with laughter and cheers around us, I sigh happily. This is what life's all about—this family, this love.

The End

AUTHOR'S NOTE

Dear Reader,

Thank you for reading *My Darling Jane*. I hope you enjoyed reading it as much as I did writing it. Below is an added bonus.

Dear Ava is one of those powerful books that sticks with you and doesn't let go. It was called "one of the best romances of 2020" by *Southern Living*, and I'm happy to share a small excerpt with you after *My Darling Jane*. Please see my website for a list of content warnings.

With over eighteen thousand reviews, it has a rating of 4.5 on Amazon. If you enjoy enemies to lovers, he falls first, zany friends, and a strong female heroine, this might be your next read.

Best,
Ilsa Madden-Mills

Wall Street Journal bestselling author Ilsa Madden-Mills delivers a gripping enemies-to-lovers, secret-admirer romance.

The rich and popular Sharks rule at prestigious, ivy-covered Camden Prep. Once upon a time, I wanted to be part of their world—until they destroyed me.

The last thing I expected was an anonymous love letter from one of them.

Please. I hate every one of those rich jerks for what they did to me.

The question is, which Shark is my secret admirer?

Knox, the scarred quarterback. Dane, his twin brother. Or Chance, the ex who dumped me . . .

Dear Ava, Your eyes are the color of the Caribbean Sea. Wait. That's stupid.

What I really mean is, you look at me and I feel something REAL.

It's been ten months since you were here, but I can't forget you.

I've missed seeing you walk down the hall.

I've missed you cheering at my football games.

I've missed the smell of your hair.

And then everything fell apart the night of the kegger.

Don't hate me because I'm a Shark.

I just want to make you mine.

Still.

—Angie's Dreamy Reads

DEAR AVA

EXCERPT

Ilsa Madden-Mills
Copyright © 2020

The sun beats down on me as I get out of my older-model Jeep Wrangler, Louise, and give her a little pat. There's a dent on the driver's side—came that way—and the paint is rusted at the edges of the hood and over the wheels. I worked three summers waiting tables at a dingy all-night diner in downtown Nashville to buy her, and it's my sole possession in the world. I paid for it with carefully scraped-together money from every tip I got, and I got plenty because I was the best waitress there, pasting a broad, welcoming smile on my face for every truck driver, blue-collar worker, and late-night drunk person. Sometimes if the waitstaff was full, I cleaned the kitchen, took out trash, or mopped the floor. Lou would text me anytime one of his servers didn't show up or called in sick, and I'd drag myself up out of my bed at the group home and jog the two blocks to the diner, half-asleep but ready to put the time in for the dollars.

Louise isn't pretty, but she's mine.

Parked next to me is a sleek black Porsche, and on the other side is a red Maserati. I sigh. Almost a year that I've been a student here, yet nothing has changed.

I sweep my eyes over the grounds ahead of me. Welcome to Camden Prep, otherwise known as my own personal hell, a prestigious private school in the middle of Sugarwood, Tennessee, which happens to be one of the richest small towns in the United States, home to senators, country music stars, and professional athletes.

Bah. Whatever. I hate this place.

Slinging my backpack over my arm, I sprint through the parking lot, carefully evading the cars, recalling a freshman guy who accidentally scratched another car once, and belonging to one of the Sharks, no less. Later, they cornered him in the bathroom and made him lick their shoes. The best advice for anyone who isn't a Shark is to stay away from them. Don't look. Don't touch. Pretend they don't exist. Those guidelines got me through my freshman and sophomore years. Junior year—well, we won't even go there. But now that it's my last year, I'll be living by those rules again.

Tension and apprehension make my heart race more and more the closer I get to the double doors of that ivy-covered main entrance bookended by two castle-style gray turrets. The final bell for classes hasn't rung yet, and I have exactly five minutes to get to my locker and get to class. Arriving late was my plan because *a girl like me has to have a fucking plan.*

As I jog, I tug at my new school uniform, a midthigh red-and-gold plaid skirt, something the administration instituted to blur the lines between the haves and the have-nots. As if. Everyone already knows who the rich kids are and who are the ones like me. Just look in the freaking parking lot. "I love you, Louise," I mutter. "All these jerks have is something their parents bought them."

I stop at the door, inhaling a deep breath. You'd expect a regular glass door for a school, but this isn't an ordinary place. The door here is made from heavy beveled glass, the kind you see in old houses. Freshman year, I thought it was beautiful, with the red dragon carefully etched into the upper section, but now—ha. Dread, thick and ugly, sucks at me, sliding over me like mud even though I gave myself a hundred pep talks on the twenty-minute drive in from the Sisters of Charity in downtown Nashville.

"Steel yourself," I whisper. "Beyond these doors lie hellhounds and vampires." I smirk. If only they really were. I'd pull out a stake and end them like Buffy.

Sadly, they are only human, and I cannot stab them.

I pat down my newly dyed dark hair, shoulder length with the front sides longer than the back, a far cry from my long blond locks from last year. Cutting and dying my hair was therapy. I did it for me, to show these assholes I'm not going to be that nice little scholarship girl anymore. Screw that. I gather my mental strength, pulling from my past. I've sat in homeless shelters. I've watched Mama shoot needles in her arms, in between her toes, wherever she could to get that high. I've watched her suck down a bottle of vodka for breakfast.

These rich kids are toddlers compared to me.

So why am I shaking all over?

No fear, a small voice says.

I swing the doors open to a rush of cool air and brightly lit hallways. The outside may look as if you've been tossed back a few centuries, but the inside is plush and luxurious, decorated like a millionaire's mansion.

Smells like money, I think as I stand for a second and take it all in. It's still gorgeous—can't deny that. Warm taupe walls. White wainscoting. Crown molding. Leather chairs. And that's just the entrance area. I walk in farther, my steps hesitant. Majestic portraits hang on the wall, former headmasters alongside framed photos of alumni, small smiling faces captured in senior photos. The guys have suits on, and the girls are in black dresses. By the end of this year, my picture will be encased in a collage and placed with *my* classmates'. A small huff of laughter spills out of me, bordering on hysteria, and I push it back down.

Students milling around—girls in pleated skirts and white button-downs like mine, guys in khakis and white shirts with red-and-gold ties—swivel their heads to see who's coming in on the first day of classes.

Eyes flare at me.

Gasps are emitted.

Fighting nervousness, I inhale a cleansing breath, part of me already regretting this decision, urging me to turn around and run like hell, but I hang tough. I swallow down my emotions, carefully shuffling them away, locking them up in a chest. I picture a chain and padlock on those memories from last year. I take that horror and toss it into a stormy ocean. There, junior year. Go and die.

With a cold expression on my face, one I've been practicing for a week, my eyes rove over the students, not lingering too long on faces.

That's right, Ava Harris, the snitch/bitch who went to the police after the party, is back.

And I'm not going anywhere.

All I need is this final year, and I might be able to swing a full ride at a state school or even get a scholarship to Vanderbilt. *Vanderbilt.* My body quivers in yearning. Me at a prestigious university. Me going to class with people who don't know me. Me having something that is mine. Me making my own road, and it's shiny and flat and so damn smooth . . .

My legs work before my brain does, and as I start down the hall, the crowd parts, more students seeing me and pausing, eyes widening.

The air around me practically bristles with tension.

If I were a wicked witch, I'd cackle right now.

My fists clench, barely hanging on to my resolve.

Piper rushes up and throws her arms around me. "She's back! My main girl is back! OMG, I HAVE MISSED YOU SO MUCH!"

Seeing her exuberant, welcoming face is exactly what I needed. Pretty with long strawberry blond hair pulled back with two butterfly clips, she's been my friend since we had a chorus class together freshman year. She can't carry a tune, but I love to sing. I had a solo at every single concert at Camden BTN. Before That Night.

She smiles as she squeezes my hand. "I'm so glad to see you. Also, my parents are insisting you come to dinner soon. It's been a while."

Indeed.

Before I can answer, someone jostles into us, moving away quickly, but not before I hear "Snitch" from his lips.

My purse falls down with the force of his shoulder.

And so it begins.

Helping me get my bag, Piper turns her head and snaps at the retreating back of the person who bumped into me. "Watch it!" Then, "Jockass!"

Rising up, I crane my neck to see who it was. Red hair, football player: Brandon Wilkes. I barely know him.

She blows at the bangs in her face, schooling her features back into a sweet expression even though her eyes are darting around at everyone as if daring them to say one word against me. "Anyway, I'm glad you came back. We haven't gotten to talk much, and that is your fault, which is fine. I gave you space like you asked."

She never did pull punches.

I haven't called her like I should have, but I needed distance from this place and everyone here. I tried in the beginning, but when she'd bring up school and the football games and her classes and everyday things about the day-to-day at Camden, I felt that pit of emptiness tugging at me, a dark hole of memories and people I didn't want to think about. Her life went on—*as it should have*—while I was stuck wallowing in the past.

"But you're here now." She smiles, but there's a wobbly quality to it. She jumps when she hears her name over the intercom, talking fast as lightning. "Yikes! I need to run. My mom is here. Can you believe I forgot my laptop on the first day? I'm such a ditz! See you in class, 'kay? We have first period together, yes?" She gives me a quick hug. "You got this."

Do I?

Truly, I want to run and get back in my car and leave this place behind forever, but then I think about my little brother, Tyler. Goals . . . must stick to them.

Before I can get a word out—typical—she's gone and bouncing down the hall like Tigger from *Winnie the Pooh*.

I miss her immediately, feeling the heat of everyone's eyes on me.

It's funny how no one really noticed me during my freshman and sophomore years here. Nope. I was the girl who kept her head down and blended in as well as I could, trying to keep my upbringing off the radar . . . until the summer before junior year when I ran into Chance at a bookstore and he showed interest. Then when school started, I got it in my head to be a cheerleader. Mostly, I told myself it would look good on my college applications—plus I assumed it would take less time than soccer or tennis—but the truth is I did it for *him*. I wanted Chance and Friday-night football games and parties with the in crowd.

The lockers seem a million miles away as I push past all the onlookers, my hands clenched around the straps of my backpack. Whispers from the students rise and grow and spread like a wave in the ocean.

And of course . . .

The Grayson brothers are the first Sharks I see, holding court with several girls as they lean against the wall. Knox and Dane. Twins.

I flick my gaze in their direction, keeping my resting bitch face sharp and hard, taking in the two guys, their matching muscular builds, tall with broad shoulders. They may look almost identical, but they're like night and day. Knox is the cold one, never smiling, that scar slicing through his cheek and into his upper lip, disrupting the curve of his mouth and the perfection of his face. I swallow. Screw him.

I refuse to spend this year afraid.

His lips twitch as if he reads my mind, that slash on his mouth curling up in a twisted movement, and I glare at him.

"You don't scare me," my face says.

He smirks.

Thick mahogany hair curls around his collar, and his eyes are a piercing gray, like metal, sharp and intense, framed by a fringe of black lashes. His scrutiny doesn't miss much and makes me antsy—has since freshman year when I'd catch him looking at me, studying me as if I were a strange bug. When I'd get the guts to boldly look back—Like what you see?—he'd huff out a derisive laugh and keep walking. I'm beneath him. A speck. He as much as said so after our first game last year.

"What do you want?" he says with a sneer as I ease in the football locker room. Cold eyes flick over my cheer skirt, then move up and land on the hollow of my throat. It's not cool enough at night for our sweater uniform, so tonight my top is the red-and-white V-cut vest with CP embroidered on my chest.

"Where's Chance?"

He stiffens, then huffs out a laugh and whips off his sweat-covered jersey along with the pads underneath.

His shoulders are broad and wide, his chest lightly dusted with sparse golden hair, tan from the sun, rippling with powerful muscles, leading down to a tapered and trim waist. He has a visible six-pack, and my gaze lingers briefly on a small tattoo on his hip, but I can't tell what it is. He isn't brawny or beefy looking like one might expect from a guy blessed with his athletic prowess, but sculpted and molded and—

Dropping my gaze, I stare at the floor. I shouldn't be ogling him. Chance is my guy.

I hear male laughter from one of the rooms that branch off from the locker room, maybe the showers, and I deflate, guessing that's where Chance is.

Glancing up, I intend to ask him to tell Chance I came by to congratulate him on his two touchdowns, but my voice is frozen. Knox has unlaced his grass-stained pants and is shucking them off. His legs are heavily muscled and taut, unlike the leaner build of Chance. His slick underwear is black and tight, cupping his hard ass, the outline of his crotch—

"Like what you see, charity case? You can look, but you can't touch."

Anger soars, replacing my embarrassment. I know I'm just the scholarship girl at Camden, but why does he have to constantly remind me?

"Don't worry about me touching anything. I don't like ugly." The words tumble out before I can stop them. I meant his superior attitude, not his face, but I see the moment when he freezes and takes it the wrong way.

He touches his face, tracing his scar while his jaw pops. "Get out. Only players allowed in here."

"Asshole," I mutter as his laughter follows me.

Rumor is, Knox doesn't kiss girls on the lips, but no matter how bad that scar screws up his face, he's the head Shark nonetheless.

Today, he's wearing a fitted white button-up, his tie loose as if he's already annoyed with it. He spends a lot of time in the gym, I imagine, working on that muscular body, maintaining that quarterback status. He holds my gaze for several seconds before dropping his and looking down at his phone.

I hear him laugh under his breath.

Some things never change.

ABOUT THE AUTHOR

A #1 Amazon Charts, *Wall Street Journal, New York Times,* and *USA Today* bestselling author, Ilsa Madden-Mills pens angsty new adult and contemporary romances. A former high school English teacher and librarian, she adores all things *Pride and Prejudice,* and of course, Mr. Darcy is her ultimate hero. She's addicted to frothy coffee beverages, cheesy magnets, and any book featuring unicorns and sword-wielding females.

Feel free to stalk Ilsa online! Join her Facebook readers group, Unicorn Girls, to get the latest scoop and talk about books, wine, and Netflix at www.facebook.com/groups/ilsasunicorngirls. You can also find Madden-Mills on her website at www.ilsamaddenmills.com. And don't forget to subscribe to her newsletter at www.ilsamaddenmills.com/contact.